The ROSEWOOD CHRONICLES

PRINCESS at Heart

CONNIE GLYNN

PENGUIN BOOKS

PENGUIN BOOKS

UK | USA | Canada | Ireland | Australia
India | New Zealand | South Africa

Penguin Books is part of the Penguin Random House group of companies
whose addresses can be found at global.penguinrandomhouse.com.

www.penguin.co.uk
www.puffin.co.uk
www.ladybird.co.uk

Penguin
Random House
UK

First published 2021
This edition published 2021

001

Typeset by Jouve (UK), Milton Keynes
Printed and bound in Great Britain by Clays Ltd, Elcograf S.p.A.

The authorized representative in the EEA is Penguin Random House Ireland,
Morrison Chambers, 32 Nassau Street, Dublin D02 YH68

A CIP catalogue record for this book is available from the British Library

ISBN: 978–0–241–45837–2

All correspondence to:
Penguin Books
Penguin Random House Children's
One Embassy Gardens, 8 Viaduct Gardens, London SW11 7BW

MIX
Paper from
responsible sources
FSC® C018179

Penguin Random House is committed to a
sustainable future for our business, our readers
and our planet. This book is made from Forest
Stewardship Council® certified paper.

Dedicated to every single delivery driver who brought me food during the COVID-19 *lockdown*

Prologue

When you live by the sea, you can smell summer storms brewing. The tide sucks in the water, whispering out a salty sigh that churns up the scent of approaching rain.

When Ollie was young, he'd been scared of the storms. It was his best friend, Lottie, who'd taught him they were nothing to be afraid of. She'd recount the tale of the Little Mermaid and how her journey had begun with a wild and courageous storm, so ferocious it had sunk a ship.

What Lottie failed to mention was that the mermaid's destiny was to turn into a pile of sea foam. Once Ollie discovered that, the fear stuck with him like a scar. Even now that he was sixteen, the distant rumble of thunder sent a tremor of fright skittering across his skin. Lottie loved the storm because she said it was the start of something new – because no matter how violent the raging winds and rain, no matter how loud the thunder, a storm meant the tension would be released, that the earth would be fresh and cool once more.

But for Ollie a storm meant only trouble.

Summer had come and gone in the blink of an eye. It was time for Ollie to head back to school, and a storm was rolling over the horizon. The humid weather was building to breaking point. His shirts clung to his skin with sweat, and he could never get the sticky feeling off his fingers no matter how much he showered. His mother, Manuela Moreno, however, seemed unaffected, cooped up in her oven of a studio or cooking her spicy dishes in the stuffy kitchen. The idea of being back at school, away from this unbearable heat, actually felt good. More than anything, he needed a distraction.

'Ollie?' His mother's voice pierced his bedroom. 'Hurry up, or you won't have time for breakfast. I'm not letting you start back at school on an empty stomach.'

'Coming, Mamãe!'

Another white-hot flash lit up the blue walls of his bedroom, startling him as he reached for his backpack.

A lot had happened over the summer, most of which he'd had to be updated on by Binah. Ever since Lottie had started at her new school, the mysterious and prestigious Rosewood Hall, his comfortable little world had been turned completely upside down. Despite his disapproval, Lottie had taken a job as a Portman for the royal family of Maradova, pretending to be Princess Eleanor Wolfson. This allowed the real princess to live a 'normal' life. Having met the real princess, Ollie could see why she preferred to remain undercover. Ellie Wolf, the name she preferred to go by, was a thunderstorm in human form. Nothing about her screamed 'princess'. She was all dark eyes and moody stares. The confident way she moved, the lazy way she laughed. She was just like the storms he'd been afraid of as a child, the very same storms that Lottie adored.

And that was just the princess. Even worse was her Partizan, Jamie: a bodyguard who looked as though he'd never smiled in his entire life. Ollie still remembered him leaning against the door frame in the kitchen, as still and patient as death, and equally as foreboding.

Lottie had been thrust into their world of royal conspiracies and secret evil societies, and now Ollie had been dragged in too, everyone banding together to try to find the identity of the Master of Leviathan, a strange and menacing group whose only goal was to destroy the Maravish royal family.

Sitting at the kitchen table, Ollie drifted into a daze, shovelling pancakes into his mouth like an unthinking machine. He didn't even taste the maple syrup. He swallowed down a mouthful and it stuck in his throat, choking him. He rubbed his chest frantically.

'Chew your food, Ollie,' his mother scolded, placing a reusable water bottle in his backpack.

He nodded absent-mindedly, thoughts turning back to the summer and the terrible secrets that had been revealed.

He and a group of Rosewood students had sneaked into Rosewood Hall. They'd ventured beyond the walls into the sleeping school to steal an ancient diary that had belonged to the founder. Reading it, Ollie had discovered that the school's founder was Lottie's ancestor – a long-lost Ottoman princess, Liliana Mayfutt.

Of course, being related to lost royalty would never be enough for Lottie. There was more. The second layer of secrets they had discovered was a set of twin swords, one buried at Rosewood and one at its sister school in Japan, Takeshin. The swords had their own secret – that an age-old and powerful bond between the two school founders stretched back to when Liliana had hidden away in Japan after escaping from the palace in the seventeenth century. After that she'd ventured to England and founded the school there.

But the icing on the secret cake was the most terrifying news Ollie had ever received. With the help of some students at Takeshin, he and his friends had discovered that Leviathan, the mysterious group who'd targeted his best friend ever since she'd started her new life, was led by Claude Wolfson, Ellie's uncle. Wolfson had abandoned the throne, then he'd been exiled from Maradova and his younger brother Alexander forced to take on the role of king. None of them knew Claude's ultimate plan, but Ollie knew one thing with absolute certainty – Lottie was at the very heart of the intrigue, and there was nothing he could do to save her. Not yet.

He shook himself from his thoughts. 'I'll head off before it starts raining.' He kissed his mother on the cheek, grabbing his backpack and one last pancake before heading out of the front door.

A familiar red van pulled up. 'Good morning, Ollie. Glad I caught you,' said a voice.

Ollie smiled at the postman. 'Good morning, Mr Harris.'

'I've picked up a postcard for the Pumpkin household,' the postman said, his sunburnt cheeks turning round and friendly. 'No one's been there for a while, so I thought I'd bring it over to you. You were always good friends with that Lottie girl.'

A menacing rumble of thunder disrupted the air. It rolled over Ollie like a premonition of trouble arriving. Something Ollie had come to realize over the past year was that trouble always sought Lottie out – just like the thunderstorm. A myriad of awful possibilities exploded in his head: news reporters who'd figured out her Portman secret, a threat from Leviathan, news that her stepmother was coming home. The letter could be about any one of these.

Mr Harris pulled out a postcard with a picture of a white-sand beach. Lemon-yellow lettering read: *Havana*. Ollie could practically smell the rum and cheap aftershave wafting off it. There was only one person who'd send a postcard like this. It conjured an image that was far, far worse than any of the possibilities he'd already thought of.

He took the card, trying to be as calm as possible. 'Thank you. I'll be sure to pass it on to her.'

'Say hello to your mother for me, Ollie,' replied Mr Harris as he headed back to his van.

The world swirled. Ollie knew he shouldn't turn over the postcard, that he shouldn't read it. Whatever was on the other side could only be bad news. But Lottie had to know what was coming, surely? With a gulp, Ollie flipped it over. The writing was smudged, probably done in a hurry, but the words were clear, as was all the trouble they would bring.

To my little princess, Charlotte,

It's been far too long, and Beady tells me you're working your way into high society.

    She has also brought it to my attention that you have not been living in the old house, so I hope you will understand that it's become necessary to sell it.

Much love,
Your father

Ollie looked up to see Mr Harris's van disappear out of sight, and with it any chance of returning the cursed postcard. He could only hope Lottie would be able to handle the bad news.

PART ONE

The Nightmare

1781 painting by Henry Fuseli

1

Night had consumed Wolfson Palace. Ornaments and portraits that dazzled in the sunshine now lay dormant, waiting for life to be kissed back into them like a cursed princess.

Wiggling her toes, Lottie did her best to stave off some of the cold that was seeping through the palace floor. She was jet-lagged after returning from Japan and still feeling disorientated from everything that had happened over the past few days, not least her discovery about Leviathan. Lottie tried to hold herself upright, focusing on the wall of shiny diamond jewellery while the king's advisor went to work around her in the crimson room, side-stepping the purple-velvet ottoman in the centre.

'This won't do.' Simien narrowed his eyes at the reflection in the ornate mirror, his liver-spotted hands firmly placed over Lottie's shoulders, turning her from side to side to get a better view of the puffy-sleeved dress he'd had her put on, which made her look remarkably like a strawberry blancmange. 'Perhaps a high neckline and padded shoulders will balance out that *very* long neck that you've exposed.'

Dizzy with the dressing room's thick perfume clouds, and feeling more like a marionette than a human being, Lottie let

9

her imaginary strings go slack when Simien finally turned back to the dresses, searching through them to find something that would work with Lottie's new messy bob.

'Whatever you think is best,' Lottie called out, hoping to move the process along without giving away her impatience. She had somewhere she needed to be, and she couldn't have Simien knowing that; she couldn't add to his stress.

It wasn't simply Lottie's hair that had everyone on edge; the whole palace felt like it was on a tightrope, ready to topple over at any moment if someone so much as breathed too deeply. Five days had passed since the nightmare in the Rose Wood, and, while Lottie was desperate to figure out Leviathan's plan, first she had to contend with Ellie's family, and that meant she had to be as presentable as possible to soften the blow of the terrible discovery she'd made.

'I think it's best if we avoid a media scandal over your hair. It's the last thing we need,' Simien hissed, tutting to himself.

Lottie couldn't help sighing. She felt like the only person in the world who didn't look at her hair as if it was a disaster or even something to be concerned about. There was only one person who understood, and she was hundreds of miles away in Japan.

Thinking about Sayuri filled Lottie's head with motorbike fumes and sharp, intelligent glances from midnight-black eyes. It made her chest ache like part of her soul had been snipped away. The summer they'd just spent at Takeshin had changed everything. The friends she'd made in Banshee, the motorbike gang, Miko, Rio and Wei, and their notorious Pink Demon leader, the silken-haired Sayuri who'd become more like a sister, were on the other side of the world but felt close to

Lottie's heart. They were linked not o...
by the secrets their ancestors had truste...
swords – one of which had saved Lottie by
Lottie felt calm as she stared at herself i...
moving up to twiddle the ends of her fres...
But as soon as her skin met the curling ends o... ...
memory jolted through her like a static shock. Sh...
gripping the sword, flicking it up ... ...
through her hair, freeing herself from Ingrid's and Leviathan's
grasp, then running until her lungs burned.

Letting go, she tilted her chin up, marvelling at how much
older the trim made her look. Ellie had done an immaculate
job, the cut framing her apple-cheeked face, leaving her body
lighter and revealing a version of herself that felt more Lottie
than ever. The only problem was . . .

'You look too much like your real ancestors,' Simien
moaned behind her, mumbling a series of curses. 'We need a
Wolfson, not a Mayfutt.'

It was undeniable. Lottie looked the spitting image of her
ancestor Liliana Mayfutt's male alter ego, William Tufty,
right down to the splatter of freckles on the bridge of her
nose. Every time she spotted them she felt like the ghosts of
her family were watching her and expecting something.

'Don't slouch.' Simien reappeared behind her, holding a
butter-yellow dress up to her, its shoulders protruding like stiff
whipped cream. 'We need to make sure your princess image
is still intact to lessen some of the queen mother's distress
over this unfortunate discovery.' He didn't need to say the
name out loud. The whole palace could feel the severity of
the situation like a hard grip on their necks.

...ing briefly up at the clock, Lottie felt her patience ...ing thin and, just as she thought she'd have to make an excuse and plant a well-timed yawn, Simien, at last, relented.

'This will have to do, I suppose,' the king's advisor said, straight and tapping at the temple by his glass eye before ...ack on the hanger. 'Now make sure you go ...d night's sleep for the meeting tomorrow,' he said, attempting breeziness, but Lottie could hear the grave tone that he was doing his best to hide.

Lottie had one more stop before she retired for the evening. After changing into something more comfortable, she waited until she was sure the rest of the palace had gone to sleep and sneaked out of her bedroom door, listening carefully for any movement.

A floorboard on the stairs squeaked beneath her feet and she froze. Heart pounding, she strained her ears for any response.

Silence.

She crept into the long marble corridor, where the ghostly faces of the previous rulers of Maradova looked down at her from their gilded frames. Ignoring their eyes, she paused at the largest painting.

Alexis Wolfson, the man who'd seized the throne of Maradova hundreds of years ago, stared down at Lottie with piercing eyes, the same wild green as a forest at dusk. His long black hair fell thickly around his broad shoulders. Draped in protective pelts, he looked more warrior than king, but his smile was warm. Gazing up at him, Lottie wondered why *she'd never* paid this portrait more attention. It had taken

Ingrid's cryptic words for her to notice him, and now she could see why he'd been so adored.

Just like Alexis, Ingrid had said. It was one of two statements she'd shared that day in the woods. The other, and more confusing, was simply: *Why is Jamie your Partizan?* It was a question meant for the real princess, and Lottie was determined to find out what Ingrid had meant. Why was he Ellie's Partizan?

Pulling herself away, Lottie walked to the end of the corridor until she reached the black sheep of the family, and the very person to whom Ingrid devoted herself – Claude Wolfson, Ellie's uncle.

His painting hung in a black frame, a dark reminder of the fate that would befall any royal who turned away from their responsibilities. In his exile he'd waited, plotting, building an army. Now they knew that the mysterious goat-masked man who'd tormented Lottie and her friends for the past two years had been him. But why?

'Hello, Goat Man.' She found a strange satisfaction in using his nickname when he looked so proud. Perhaps this was how Ellie felt whenever she defied authority.

'You can say his name, you know.' Ellie's voice drifted down the corridor, dark and bitter like coffee. 'Everyone's acting like it's some terrible curse word.'

Turning slowly to face her princess, Lottie braced herself, remembering that it wasn't just her image that had changed. Even so, it made her mouth go dry.

In the glow of the moonlight Ellie was dressed in a long black robe fit for a funeral, her face floating in the dark. She looked utterly exhausted. A sheen on her pale skin made her complexion look like alabaster, and the darkness beneath her eyes looked stained with ink. Lottie wondered if she'd slept at all since they'd learned about her uncle being the Master of Leviathan.

Taking a sweeping step forward, there was something dangerous in her eyes.

'Claude Wolfson, Claude Wolfson, Claude Wolfson,' Ellie repeated as if she were calling on the bogeyman, looking around with her hands outstretched. 'See? Nothing happened.'

Lottie flinched at her tone. Ellie was obviously angry.

'You're late,' she said, ignoring Ellie's teasing. 'What's wrong?'

Ellie's face dropped, and Lottie felt guilty as she took in her smudged eyes and chewed lips. She had to believe she'd done the right thing in telling Ellie about her uncle, but seeing her like this it was hard to feel like she was helping anyone.

'I had to steal this from the post room; it could have got us in serious trouble.'

From an inside pocket, Ellie pulled out a postcard, passing it to Lottie so she could see the elegant painting of a bamboo forest on the front. She could smell it, like a scorching-hot summer and the fizzy tang in the air after fireworks.

Flipping it over, Lottie stared at the six lines of simple text.

Dear Princess,
Please keep an eye on Haru for us.
His sabbatical is still regrettably a mystery.
Stay safe, and remember our fates are linked by the sword.
                                    Sayuri, Miko, Rio and Wei

'She sent it here, to the palace,
to Ellie's voice that sounded like fear,
sound you expect from a cornered dog. 'It's
What if someone had seen it?' Ellie groaned,
in her hands. 'No one knows Haru is part of L
for us and Ani and Saskia.'

Trying to keep calm, Lottie pocketed the postcard. It felt warm nestled next to her heart, despite the terrible reminder that Haru was waiting for them when they returned.

'Is this why you wanted to meet me?' she asked, wishing she could do something to put Ellie's mind at ease.

'No.' Ellie shook her head. 'I need to ask you a favour.' Her gaze wandered once more to the painting of Claude.

'Anything.'

'I need you to promise you won't tell my parents about Haru being part of Leviathan tomorrow. Not unless I say so.'

'Wait, what?'

Ellie's eyes snapped back to Lottie's, her sleepy demeanour melting away. 'I'm serious, Lottie. After what you found out about my . . . about Claude, I feel like my parents are hiding things. Tomorrow I'm going to tell them I'm sick of it.' Ellie's hands curled into fists. 'I can't believe they're not letting Jamie attend. We can't let them keep things from us. We should be vigilant; we have to –'

'Jamie's not attending?' Lottie's mind felt muddled, sure she'd misheard, but Ellie shook her head *again*, *letting her know it was very real*.

'*It's weird, isn't it?*' Ellie looked vindicated for a moment, glad to see Lottie equally as perplexed. 'They won't say why, keeping it intimate, just me, you, Grandmother my parents.'

The news was like a *boulder,* knocking Lottie right back into the Rose Wood, Ingrid's voice snaking *into her thoughts* once more. *Why is Jamie your Partizan?*

Shaking it off, Lottie grabbed one of Ellie's clenched fists and squeezed. From the way her friend's hand trembled, Lottie could sense a long-growing resentment in her princess towards her secretive family. 'Let's see what your parents and grandmother have to say tomorrow. Then you can decide what you think is right for everyone.'

'But –'

'I'm on your side, Ellie, no matter what.' This was the truth – a fact she could always fall back on. Everything she did was for the good of her princess, the girl who made her feel whole. 'And if you decide that's what you want to do after we've spoken to them, then OK.' Lottie spoke steadily but her chest felt hollow at the idea of keeping Haru a secret any longer. 'Can we do that?'

Seconds felt like decades while she waited for a reply, and all the while Claude stared down at them, watching, waiting.

'OK, yeah,' Ellie said at last, her fists uncurling. 'I'll try to keep my cool tomorrow, for you.' A semblance of Ellie's old charm crept back into her smile, but it faded quickly. 'We should probably go to sleep. I'm not thinking straight. I'm tired and it feels weird being back here, and . . . yeah.'

'Don't worry, I understand.' Lottie linked her fingers with Ellie's.

Ellie lay her chin on Lottie's head, wrapping her arms round her neck until they were slotted together. Lottie could feel the flicker of Ellie's pulse where her cheek rested against her neck. She was so warm; it made her want to melt into her, visions of their kiss from so long ago fluttering through her mind as soft as butterfly wings, but then Ellie pulled away.

'I'm sorry,' she said softly, and Lottie couldn't tell what Ellie was apologizing for. 'Let's head upstairs.'

Silently they made their way back to their quarters. They said goodnight at Lottie's door, hands drifting apart. And, as Lottie climbed into bed, her head filled with images of Alexis and Claude, Haru and Jamie, and Ellie, Ellie, Ellie.

But when she thought of Ellie's tired eyes, the way she'd crumbled when they'd discovered that Leviathan's tricks all led back to her family, and the secrets and lies . . . she wondered was any of this really what was best for Ellie?

Was Lottie helping anyone at all?

2

A fire had been lit in the great hall. Amber flames flickered in the depths of the black-stone hearth, trying and failing to warm the cold, echoing room. Above, out of reach of the flames, was a family portrait of King Alexander Wolfson, his wife, Matilde Wolfson, the queen mother, Willemena Wolfson – all stony-faced and unsmiling – and at the centre, still just a young girl, Princess Eleanor Prudence Wolfson, next in line for the throne of Maradova.

Ellie remembered the day they'd posed for the painting. She'd sneaked outside to play with Jamie and tripped in the mud, dirt clumping in her hair and on her face and hands. Her grandmother had been furious with her and Jamie. As punishment, the old woman had forced Jamie to sit quietly and watch the whole time, and told Ellie that the longer she fussed, the longer Jamie would have to sit still. Ellie wished the fire would burn the whole canvas to ash.

It had been six days. Six measly days since Lottie had uncovered who the Master of Leviathan was, the person who'd been hounding them and their friends, searching for cracks and weaknesses to exploit. Part of Ellie had always known that everything was her fault. She tore her gaze away from the painting to stare at her real stony-faced family, all lined up and looking small in the grand surroundings.

In spite of the delicate cherubs painted on the ceiling and the apricot-velvet drapes that lined the barred window behind the throne, the throne room had always felt more like the inner workings of a factory. She could practically hear the engines of the palace whirring. Something stunk about this whole meeting. Not only was Jamie missing but so was Sir Olav, her father's Partizan. Her family must be hiding something, had probably *always* been hiding something, and she wasn't going to let their secrets hurt anyone else.

If it wasn't for her promise to Lottie, she would have stormed in and demanded they all cut the lies immediately. But she wouldn't. She owed her this much.

'First we must remove Claude's painting from the entry hall,' announced the queen mother.

Willemena's voice creaked like an old rocking chair, and Ellie had to bite her tongue not to scream. Instead she glanced over at Lottie. It still gave her pause to see Lottie's hair so short after what Ingrid had done to her in the woods. Whenever she looked at the girl she adored, she was reminded of everything she'd caused by letting her get close. And here was her family, choosing, as usual, to try to cover it up with a pretty yellow dress and a diamond hair clip.

Don't lose your temper, don't lose your temper.

'I can understand the desire to remove all traces of your son Claude from the palace, ma'am,' Lottie began, her voice calmer and more patient than the royal family deserved. 'And, while I think that is an excellent idea for your peace of mind, more urgently I believe we need to figure out Claude's ultimate plan. We need a way to stop him and Leviathan. If you have any information, perhaps –'

'Yes, yes, all traces of him,' Willemena continued as if Lottie had never spoken, banging her wolf's-head cane on the floor so hard it sent vibrations through the oak. 'Whatever was left of him, take it away and have it burned.'

There was no need to look at Lottie this time. It was clear that Ellie's grandmother was avoiding something. All the paranoia Ellie had been feeling sparked inside her again like a city coming to life after a blackout. Her family were lying. She didn't know about what, or why, but she couldn't let them get away with this.

'With respect,' Lottie said, 'removing Claude is one step, but we must also look at –'

'We must make sure there is not a speck of him in evidence by the time the decennial Golden Flower Festival comes round.'

What? Ellie could hardly hold herself together.

Lottie tried again. Only the faintest hint that she shared Ellie's shock came across in the way her eyelids fluttered. 'Pardon me, ma'am. I fear I've misheard you. Are you really planning to host another Flower Festival? I thought you'd decided to halt them indefinitely after what happened last summer.'

The Flower Festival, Ellie thought, grinding her teeth at the awful memory of the night Lottie had nearly been kidnapped a year ago.

'Not just a Flower Festival.' Willemena banged her cane again as if it were Lottie who was being preposterous. 'This is the *Golden* Flower Festival. We have it every ten years and allow the citizens of Maradova to explore the grounds. If we don't stick to our traditions, people will suspect something is wrong, and after the disaster with the media this summer no one can know there are any cracks in the Wolfson family. *No one.*' She banged her cane once more for good measure, causing Lottie's eyelids to flutter even faster.

'Ma'am, I'm not sure if –'

Ellie stepped in front of Lottie before she could finish. 'I think what Lottie is trying to say, is that, with all due respect –' *of which there is none* – 'removing Claude's painting achieves nothing. Neither did exiling him in the first place. You can't all keep pretending that nothing is wrong. It will blow up in our faces.' Ellie's voice came out weary and ragged, not her usual angry, sarcastic tone.

Her father glared at her. 'Eleanor, we are trying to have a civil discussion.'

Anger burned on her tongue as she met his eyes. 'And you. We know what you did. Lottie's been polite enough not to tell you how she found out all this mess led back to our family but we know you've been hiding things from us.'

'What on earth are you talking about?' Her father's tone was still harsh but she saw his mask slipping, worry giving itself away in the furrowing of his brow.

'We know what you threw away and covered up for the sake of the Wolfson name. We know about your letters to Kana, your first love.' She took a moment to relish the shock this would cause her father, but his face remained inscrutable. Only her mother reacted, looking so hurt that Ellie recoiled.

The letters proving her father's secret relationship with another student he'd met while studying abroad had originally been Claude's weapon, a way to discredit the crown – except that Ellie had taken it for herself. She'd expected the impact to be a sharp and sleek stab, something to draw out the poisonous blood of her family and all the harm they caused everyone they met for the sake of the throne, only there was nothing satisfying about their reaction at all.

'I think there is a lot of confusion right now.' Her mother spoke in her usual sighing melody, only this time it was tinged with pain. 'Perhaps we need –'

'Why isn't Jamie here?' Ellie interrupted, determined not to let her mother's hurt stop her from asking the questions she needed answered.

On speaking his name, Ellie could immediately picture Jamie, the bandages on his upper arm from the shallow knife wound he'd taken from Ingrid, the stony look on his face, suffering through everything, always for her and her family. It made her sick.

'Jamie isn't part of the immediate family, Eleanor.' This time her grandmother answered.

Ellie stared pointedly at the painting above the fireplace again, wanting to make sure they all knew what she was talking about when she spoke her next words. 'That's never been a problem before.'

The silence that followed was music to her ears; her family couldn't hide anything from her any more.

'Excuse me, ma'am, if I may?' Lottie's clear, calm voice brought an embarrassed flush to Ellie's face. She hadn't meant to lose her temper. 'Could we possibly take a moment's recess while I talk to Ellie privately?'

Without waiting for permission, Lottie grabbed Ellie's arm and led her out, their footsteps echoing in the silence of the great hall.

After the heavy doors had banged shut behind them, Lottie turned to her, her serene mask dropping to reveal a flood of worry. 'Why did you do that?'

Ellie paused, taken aback. 'Didn't you see the looks on their faces? I want them to know they can't hide anything from me.'

'This isn't a game, Ellie! We're trying to get to the bottom of this before something terrible happens.' Lottie's voice was only a raised whisper but it made her feel guilty.

Ellie shook her head in frustration, running her fingers through her hair like she was trying to pull out all her awful feelings. 'You shouldn't have to worry about any of this. They're the ones who are impossible to talk to. They don't seem to want to *solve* anything, and now they're going ahead with the Flower Festival next year. They're completely unreasonable.'

'Yes, you're right. But that doesn't mean we shouldn't keep trying. I'm sure if I keep talking to them, eventually they'll see they need to be open and honest.'

Ellie found herself once again in awe of how Lottie could always soothe her, always say the right thing, until she said exactly what Ellie absolutely didn't want to hear.

'Why don't we tell them about Haru? I bet if we tell them we can all put our knowledge together to figure out what they want and why they keep targeting Jamie.'

Ellie froze, all her paranoia and frustration rushing back. 'No, we're not telling them about Haru,' she said calmly, remembering the look on her grandmother's face when she'd mentioned Jamie. 'That's our secret.'

'Ellie, I just don't see how this is going to help anyone,' Lottie pleaded.

'It helps me, Lottie, because it's one thing in all this chaos that I have control over. And if they're keeping secrets from me, then I can keep secrets from them.'

'This is mad. You're acting like –'

'Like what?'

'It doesn't matter,' Lottie replied, her defeated look making Ellie feel sick with shame. 'Let's just go back in and I'll try to salvage what I can.'

She didn't look at Ellie as they made their way back through the creaking door into the frigid room. Ellie's guilt was quickly replaced by anger when she saw her family whispering together. They turned, looking like a pack of wolves caught unexpectedly, feasting over what Ellie could only assume were more secrets.

'Are you ready to have a civil discussion now?' her father asked.

Ellie just caught the hint of a quiver in his eyebrow and she glanced at Lottie, whose face was once again a mask of calm, and nodded.

'We have some information we want to share,' Lottie said, and Ellie froze. She wouldn't tell them about Haru, would she?

No, she'd never betray her. Lottie was the one person she could trust. But Ellie's hands trembled, sweat building on her palms.

Please, Lottie. Please not you too.

'In the woods Ingrid said a few cryptic things,' Lottie began. The relief that washed over Ellie's body was so intense she thought she might collapse. 'The first was that Claude would be welcomed back "just like Alexis". She seemed to be suggesting that –' Lottie hesitated – 'that you, King Alexander and Queen Matilde, would be disposed of. We can't rule out the possibility that this may well be the reason they needed the mind-controlling capabilities of the Hamelin Formula.'

Ellie couldn't help sucking her teeth in shock, but her parents hardly reacted.

'And the second and slightly weirder one . . .' Lottie glanced at Ellie but quickly continued. 'She asked me why Jamie was my Partizan.'

'Wait, what?' Ellie spluttered. 'You never told me any of this.'

'I'm telling you now. I thought it would be best if your whole family heard it together.' The hint of regret in Lottie's voice made Ellie angry all over again, this time because Lottie had had to shoulder the burden of this terrible information. 'Of course, Ingrid meant the princess of Maradova, but I just thought it was odd, and perhaps you would know why she would . . .' Lottie trailed off, her eyes widening as she stared at the hearth.

Ellie followed her gaze. At the far end of the hall, the fire danced, caught in a powerful wind that had howled down the chimney. Flames contorted like a misshapen body until suddenly the fire blew out completely. A dark cloud of ash spluttered out like the whole palace were coughing up dirt, as if the very building itself was sick. The ash settled in a long black line right up to the steps of the throne platform, like a filthy shadow.

No one said a word. With the one source of warmth in the room gone, the breath in Ellie's lungs turned icy. Above, looking down at them in judgement, the painting of the Wolfson family had darkened, all the soft light upon it extinguished completely.

It was Ellie's mother who spoke first.

'Wasn't that strange?' Queen Matilde laughed, an odd sound that was more like a panicked bird. 'Thank you, Lottie, that's very useful; we will discuss it privately.' She rubbed her forehead, causing a tendril of hair to fall out of its carefully arranged chignon. On either side of her, King Alexander and Willemena were staring at the empty fireplace like they'd seen a ghost. Ellie had never seen her family behave like this; it was as if the Wolfsons were crumbling in front of her. 'I'm afraid there's nothing we can share with you right now but hopefully we will be able to build on it soon. Now I think it's time you were getting ready to head back to Rosewood.'

They were being dismissed.

Lottie nodded, and Ellie found she did not want to stay in the cold dark room with her family behaving so oddly. In fact, she wanted to get herself and Lottie as far away from them as possible.

3

The purpose of a Partizan was to protect. They didn't ask questions or get upset about orders. The only thing they concerned themselves with was keeping their master safe – whether their master liked it or not. Jamie had repeated this to himself over and over again while trying to read in his room. Usually he could rely on Louisa May Alcott for an easy distraction, and yet he'd not been able to absorb a single word. Instead he'd spent the last hour trying to understand what possible reason there was for him to be excluded from this meeting. And not just him, but Nikolay and Simien also. Surely if he was to protect Ellie and Lottie, he should know about any danger?

Something had disturbed Lottie and Ellie during the meeting, that much was obvious. Lottie had appeared outside his bedroom door earlier than he'd expected, and he knew her well enough to spot the cloud of gloom looming over her, although there was something else too. She looked as though she were chewing over whatever had happened, trying to pick out some vital piece of information, and, strangest of all, she'd stared at him like he was part of the puzzle.

A thoughtful quiet followed them on the journey back to Rosewood after the two girls filled him in on Ingrid's cryptic words, Ellie's parents and their state of denial, and the news about the Flower Festival.

But the truth was there was more to Jamie's desire for knowledge than the simple need to protect Ellie and Lottie. He wanted revenge.

Ever since he'd let Ingrid go, he'd been overcome by a bloodthirsty longing to find his real enemy: the person who'd caused so much trouble for Lottie. Thinking about how he'd found her in the woods, cut up and so changed from the sweet naive girl he'd met two years ago, his muscles rippled like vipers beneath his skin, eager to be used. He didn't want petty little fights with pawns like Ingrid and Julius any more; he wanted to find the person who was really responsible, and make them pay.

'Well.' Ellie threw her hands in the air, disturbing the quiet they'd established on the final part of their journey to Rosewood.

'Well what?' he asked in a low voice, sneaking a peek in the rear-view mirror at Lottie, who was curled up half asleep on the back seat like a house cat. She looked so peaceful and small, a little ray of light in the dwindling evening sun.

'Aren't you curious about what Ingrid asked Lottie?' Ellie tried to match his tone. 'The one about why you're a Partizan? Doesn't that strike you as weird?'

Lottie stirred, her eyes opening so suddenly it was as if she'd been tuned in, waiting for this exact conversation to spring up, like some kind of Leviathan information radio tower. 'Yeah, it's strange, right?' she said, no hint of sleepiness in her voice.

Part of him found it funny how she sat up so quickly, but mostly it made him sad to see her so consumed by the conversation, her moment of peace quickly over.

'No, I don't think it's weird,' he replied frankly. 'Should I?' His lips curved slightly and he was surprised how easy it was to make jokes with Lottie again, only she didn't smile back. Her brow furrowed. 'It's the same question I've always heard,' he added quickly. 'People want to make me question whether I want to be a Partizan, and I can assure you both it's not going to work.'

Lottie didn't seem convinced, and she watched him, eyes, clear as a blue sky, searching his face like there was a secret there even he didn't know. It was just a flicker, but he saw it, her eyes drifting to his chest where his wolf pendant was still absent, and he tensed at the thought of fastening the clasp round his neck again.

Feeling uncomfortable, he turned instead to his real princess. Ellie was the exact opposite of Lottie. Her pale skin was purple in the blue light outside, violet bags under her dark, crescent eyes. She'd become subdued since the news about Claude – that he was the man behind Leviathan – and she'd been more comfortable staying in the shadows. She'd become even more of a closed book than usual, like everything was on her shoulders and she was refusing to share the burden.

Ellie didn't bother to respond to his loyal declaration. They all knew how she felt about him being a Partizan.

And, right on cue, Lottie sensed the drop in mood and put on a smile that cracked through the gloom. 'Well, it will be nice to be back at school at least, back home.' She turned, dreamy-eyed, to the car window, pushing her forehead up against it, and Jamie waited for that look of untainted wonder she always got when she saw the school approaching, only it didn't come. Before he had a chance to catch it, two figures walked out in front of the vehicle, causing Jamie to make an abrupt stop.

Falling back into their seats with a thud, Jamie looked out at the two men in black jackets who'd gestured for them to slow down. On instinct his brain searched the car, making a note of every escape and the easiest way to neutralize attackers.

'What's going on?' Ellie asked, her eyes going wide.

'They have Rosewood emblems on their jackets,' Lottie announced, trying to calm herself, yet she still moved into the middle seat away from the approaching men.

They were close to the school, near the drop-off zone. In the distance, like a beacon, the golden gates of Rosewood shone amber in the late afternoon, calling them to safety, but now that he had stopped Jamie saw something else: dark shapes moving around like bugs. Squinting, he saw that they were more men in black, pacing the entrance to Rosewood like an armed guard.

One of the men tapped on the window, signalling for him to roll it down, which he did, but only by an inch.

The man on the other side looked more tired than threatening, his thin moustache retaining a stream of sweat.

'Are you students?' he asked, a formal note to his voice putting Jamie at ease.

'Yes, sir – is something wrong?'

'Can we have your names, please?'

Ellie reached into the glove compartment to pull out their documents and passed them to Jamie.

The moustached man surveyed the paperwork through the window before nodding. 'OK, go on ahead. Have a good evening.'

Jamie rolled the window back up and started the engine again.

'What the hell was that?' Ellie asked, and Jamie could see she'd been preparing for a fight.

'I'm not sure, but look.' Jamie pointed in front of them.

Both Lottie and Ellie looked to where they were usually greeted by a clear cobblestone path and dewy roses in full bloom – there were more men in black jackets, right up to the gate.

'I don't like this,' Lottie said, and something flickered across her face, as if she knew something but didn't want to say it out loud.

At the gate, Jamie climbed out first. 'Wait here,' he told the girls, leaving them in the car while he went to see what was happening.

Trapped behind the gilded bars, Rosewood Hall, usually standing so tall and proud at the end of the path, looked humbled. The setting sun behind the aged stone towers sent long crawling shadows across the grassy banks on either side where the roses blossomed, while dark areas bloomed like bruises across the old building. It looked misshapen and twisted in the odd light.

Jamie flipped an internal switch, putting on his most commanding and persuasive voice. 'Can someone please explain what's going on here?'

The man in front of him let out a long sigh, clearly tired of answering the same question all day. 'There was an incident last night so we're handling security checks for everyone entering the school. We'll need to take your car keys in order to give your vehicle clearance, but you'll be able to find it in the car park later.'

It wasn't a clear answer, but Jamie figured their best option was to get inside and then find out what had happened. He waved the girls out of the vehicle, making sure to stand between them and the men.

'Did you find anything out?' Lottie whispered, and he shook his head as they followed the man to the entrance. The heavy gates moaned on their hinges. To Jamie it sounded like they were angry, each squeak a scream at being handled by the rough hands of the security guards.

Once in the school grounds they were left alone, the men in black shutting the gate behind them again with a metallic clang, only it didn't feel like something was being locked out; it felt like they were being locked in.

An eerie silence followed them to reception, and it became more peculiar when they opened the door to find the hall empty. There was no one, no receptionist at the desk, no admin staff jostling about with books and documents, no students waiting in a line by the office door, and as they walked through into the courtyard there was nothing but dust floating in the strings of light through the caged cherry tree in the middle.

Jamie opened his mouth to say something when he heard commotion beyond the courtyard, hundreds of footsteps and the low hum of chattering, and beyond the archway, like a vision into some strange other world, they could make out students heading across the lavender-lined paths towards the field like a migration of birds.

Ellie scratched her head, and the three of them watched as students from all houses pushed past them to cross the bridge. 'This is really weird.'

A few students stopped to stare at them, pointing and whispering, as if whatever was happening was somehow their fault, and Jamie was ready to pull a girl from Conch House over to the side for questioning when a familiar bird-like voice caught their attention.

'There you are.' Binah shot up from a bench by the bridge where she appeared to have been waiting for them, her tiny frame allowing her to squeeze through the hordes of students with ease. 'You're just in time for the emergency assembly.'

Up close, Jamie could smell sun cream on her skin and see the summer glow that still clung to her, only her face was pulled taut, no hint of a relaxing holiday left in the serious look she gave them.

'The what?'

'Hey, watch it.' A girl from Ivy House pushed past Lottie, muttering something about her hair while giving her a venomous stare that made Jamie grind his teeth.

'Something happened last night while you guys were away,' Binah relayed, pulling Jamie's attention back from the girl and already marching them in the same direction as the other students. 'Someone broke into the school . . .' She trailed off and Jamie knew there was something she wasn't saying.

'What happened, Binah?' Jamie asked, keeping his voice low.

Fiddling with her yellow Stratus prefect sash, Binah glanced sideways at Lottie from behind her round glasses. Her already large eyes seemed to double in size, heavy lashes making her look like a wise owl. 'The person who broke in –' she shuddered, clearly not wanting to repeat it – 'they were a reporter; they grabbed one of the boys from Year Eight, Dom Nguyen, and they threatened him. It was really traumatic.'

'That explains the security,' Lottie replied, her eyebrows knitting together with worry.

They were just outside the sports hall, a smell of lemon-scented cleaning products washing over them as students filtered in to find a seat on the tiered benches.

'What aren't you saying?' It was Ellie who asked the question, grabbing Binah's arm to get her to look at them face on.

Binah let out a long sigh, ushering them over to the side of the doorway and out of earshot. They regrouped by one of the water fountains, away from the other students who were gossiping among themselves.

'The guy who broke in,' Binah began, pushing up her glasses, and Jamie noted how her lips pursed, like she was trying to hold back the story. 'He was deranged. Dom said he was like a zombie, that he could hardly communicate with him.' She paused, letting the information sink in, all of them thinking the same thing, that the symptoms sounded dangerously like the effect of the Hamelin Formula. 'And he kept saying the same thing over and over again.' Binah gulped, looking at each of them in turn. 'He kept saying he wanted a picture of the princess's pretty new hair.'

4

They'd been gone for two days, just two days, and in that time the safety of the school Lottie loved so much had been destroyed, and, worst of all, she was sure she knew who the culprit was.

The hall was buzzing with feverish energy, every inch of the tiered benches occupied, with everyone grouped by their house colours: purple, yellow and red. None of them wanted to be there, and they kept staring at Lottie.

Trying her best to ignore it, she focused on the lines on the basketball court, following them like a maze, anything to stop her from looking at the crowd, or, even worse, at the furious faces of Ellie and Jamie beside her.

'Good evening, students.' Headmaster Croak took his place in the centre of the court, right hand resting against a simple wooden walking stick. He'd always looked old, spongy and mottled like a dried-up baked bean, but since the summer he seemed to have aged about a hundred years. Yet it didn't make him appear any more frail. Instead he looked more like an ancient wizard, and his long patchwork cloak and what could only be described as an emerald Santa Claus hat that further served to cement that image.

'Thank you all for your quick and orderly response to this emergency assembly,' he began, looking around with gloomy intensity. 'We have a few points of discussion and we'd like you all to please remain calm and understanding while we go through them.'

'Nothing like telling people to stay calm to encourage them not to freak out,' Ellie whispered to Lottie.

With everyone's attention on the headmaster, Lottie allowed herself to glance around, searching for the rest of their friends. Anastacia, Saskia and Raphael were the easiest to spot, the three of them standing out like supermodels at the top of the Conch House bleachers, and yet even their immaculate appearance couldn't disguise the dread on their faces. Next she searched the yellow Stratus benches to find Lola, Micky and Binah, only there was something off about the twins. Their usually pale skin was tinged with a sickly green hue and they looked like ghosts of their former selves.

Finally she looked along the purple Ivy rows to find Percy. He generally blended into the shadows, but she found him nonetheless on the bottom bench next to the school councillor who translated for him in sign language. He stared ahead in horror, his sunken eyes watching the scene play out like it was bringing up some awful memory.

'We shall start with the good news,' the headmaster bellowed, clearly expecting this to be worthy of applause. No one responded, and he coughed before continuing. 'Despite everyone's concerns with regard to the changing school rules and schedules, we will still be going ahead with our Presentation of the Pillars in the spring term, or, as some of you students prefer to call it, the PoP.' Again he waited for applause and was met with silence. 'Our school is founded on three pillars, righteousness, resolution and resourcefulness, and you are all in the house for whose pillar you have the closest affinity. The Presentation of the Pillars takes place every three years and gives you each the chance to use your creativity, charm and wit to create something in honour of your house's namesake: Florence Ivy, Balthazar Conch and Shray and Sana Stratus, respectively.' The headmaster paused, looking up through his caterpillar eyebrows to make sure all the students were paying attention before he dealt his last card. 'Participation is mandatory and will go towards your university applications. We look forward to seeing what you all have to offer. Now –' he quickly swept his hand to the side, welcoming the Conch House mother up to hit them with the bad news – 'we will be breaking down the new school rules we have decided to put in place for safety reasons. Dame Bolter, if you would, please.'

Nervous chatter began to erupt through the students, everyone anxious to hear about the incident from the night before, but they were quickly stunned into silence by a sharp look from Dame Bolter. She stood nearly six feet tall, her long, athletic body and shaved head matching her fierce warrior glare. They all knew Mercy Bolter used to compete in the Olympics, but seeing her command a room so easily made her seem more like a god than an athlete, and exactly what one would expect of the Conch House mother.

Lottie searched the hall again, secretly hoping she wouldn't spot who she was looking for.

'I'm sure everyone is very concerned about Rosewood's plans following the unfortunate incident involving a break-in last night,' Dame Bolter began, her voice booming through the hall like a foghorn. 'To put the rumours to rest, the trespasser was a reporter from an online website, and they were looking for a particular student who we shall not name.'

Everyone immediately glanced at Lottie, and she felt Ellie and Jamie tense at her side, the former's hands clenching into tight fists.

'They appeared unable to behave or think rationally, and threatened a student,' continued Dame Bolter.

Lottie felt sick to her stomach, thinking of Dom having to go through something so scary – she could only imagine what he was feeling right now – and all because . . . She paused in her train of thought, turning to Ellie, and she nearly bit her tongue.

Her princess was shaking, her tired eyes blazing with a simmering storm, and upon her lips, barely audible, she whispered like a curse, 'This is my fault.'

Lottie wanted to tell her that wasn't true, but before she could Dame Bolter carried on.

'It has been decided that, due to the high volume of students here from important families, we need to reconsider our security within the school, starting with a strict eight-thirty curfew for all students, which we will be implementing via a registry system,' she announced, and immediately whispers and chatter broke out while Dame Bolter went on with the list of limitations. 'We will also be blocking off the Rose Wood completely with a high fence, and we will be placing security around the premises; no one will be allowed to enter or leave the school without permission, and, yes, that includes those of you in the sixth form.' The whispers among the students grew in volume, a low moan coming up through the crowd like the sound of a creaking ship. 'I know some of you in higher years were looking forward to the privilege of leaving the campus during lunchtime and on weekends, but for the foreseeable future we will be retracting that privilege. These measures have been suggested by a trusted member of faculty, and we hope you can understand their importance and help keep our school a safe and secure environment.'

Lottie felt her heart race, but not because of anything that Dame Bolter had said or the outcry from the students, but because of a scent in the air, warm and disarming, like a summer breeze. She knew who it was, and when she turned her head she saw him walking down the steps beside her to join the other teachers and assistants.

Haru.

His hair was just as fluffy as she remembered, with a splatter of freckles across his nose like constellations, and big brown eyes with heavy lashes behind a pair of thick brown glasses. The moment he caught her eye his mouth split open in a smile so soft it felt like lying down in freshly cut grass. She could almost have believed that he was simply a sweet and kind Partizan on sabbatical, but she knew better. She knew he was part of Leviathan, a spy with an unknown plan, and that somehow this was his doing.

It took all her strength not to scream when he turned his smile on Jamie, leaving her to watch, helpless, as Ellie's Partizan returned him a nod of respect, oblivious to the true identity of the young man he called his friend.

'With you all here, we would also like to take this opportunity to introduce you to a new member of staff.' Dame

Bolter held out her arm, gesturing for Haru to join her, which he did to more whispers from students who were already falling for his charms. 'Haru Hinamori will be joining us as a teaching assistant for the year, all the way from Rosewood's sister school in Japan. We hope you will give him a warm welcome.'

A slow applause started up among the student body that gradually became more enthusiastic when the Partizan waved bashfully out at the crowd, sharing one of his tooth-achingly sweet smiles, instantly winning everyone over with his perfect performance of a charming and innocent heart-throb. It was just as the applause was dying down that she caught the moment – so fast she nearly missed it – when Haru latched on to her, the flicker of a shadow falling over his face. The mask dropped, revealing his true self for a split second.

A thought sliced through her mind like a blade. *He knows you know.*

The sickly fear that accompanied it made the hall feel like it was spinning, and all she wanted to do was get out of there, to the safety of her dorm as fast as possible.

They had to tell Jamie about Haru, she decided. Despite her promise to Sayuri and Ellie's stubborn determination to deal with their problems by herself, they couldn't keep Jamie in the dark, not when there was a fox hiding in their coop. She had to persuade Ellie this was the right thing to do.

Dame Bolter clapped her hands twice, making a boom like a thunder crack. 'You're all dismissed.'

5

It was still summer and the air was warm and gentle, blowing in through the open windows in the breakfast hall with the thick scent of freshly cut grass and roses. It would have been easier to enjoy the blooming flowers and gardens were it not for the men in black jackets marring the landscape. There were two outside the Ivy Wood gate, and the noise of the new fence being installed felt like a drill through Lottie's skull.

I just have to make it through the day, she reminded herself. *Then we can form a real plan.*

Everyone agreed they needed to meet in the secret study after class the next day to recap and discuss the meeting with Ellie's parents. In the meantime it was Lottie's job to persuade Ellie they needed to tell the others about Haru.

Lottie should have noticed something was wrong when they'd entered the Ivy breakfast hall to find their usual place by the window had been taken. It wasn't until she had carried her porridge and jam over to where Ellie, Jamie and Percy were sitting that she noticed the hundreds of eyes pointing at her like daggers. Hands covered whispers and giggles that made her feel self-conscious. When the rumour had spread that she was the undercover princess of Maradova – the rumour that had led to her becoming a Portman – she'd become used to people staring. But this was different. It felt angry and cruel.

She was just about to take her seat when it happened. Marcy something-or-other, a girl from her year with short red hair who'd always seemed perfectly nice, approached. Lottie could smell a sweet scent like baby powder.

'Thanks for ruining everything, Your Highness,' she hissed, and with no chance for Lottie to react she kicked her chair out of the way, causing Lottie to fall backwards, porridge spilling down the front of her purple tartan pinafore.

Ellie and Jamie were at her side in seconds, standing between Marcy and Lottie.

'What's your problem?' Ellie growled, getting right up in the girl's face, and Jamie put a hand on her shoulder.

'I think it's pretty obvious who the problem is.' Marcy jutted her chin out at Lottie, still sprawled on the floor in shock. 'This whole school would be better off if you'd just leave.'

For a second it looked like Ellie was getting ready to throw a punch, until Jamie yanked her back, and he towered above Marcy, looming over her in clear warning. 'Go back to your table or I'll drag you there by your ankles.'

Lottie could only watch, bewildered, as the Jamie she thought she knew transformed into someone angrier, someone threatening.

Marcy slowly blinked and then skittered away like a scared animal.

Ellie's hand stretched out and Lottie took it without looking, focused on Marcy who was now rubbing her forehead, her gaze glossy and unfocused. It was then she noticed Percy, his sunken eyes wide, calculating everything he'd witnessed. She knew they were both thinking the same thing. That this was more than a simple case of angry hormones. This smelled sickly sweet and dangerous, just like the Hamelin Formula.

In one swift movement Ellie had pulled her up, bringing her into the safety of her arms.

'Are you OK?' the princess and her Partizan asked in unison.

Opening her lips to reply an automatic yes, Lottie found herself staring out at the dining hall instead. The long tables were lined with faces all staring at her, all waiting to see what she'd do next.

With as much dignity as she could muster, Lottie let go of Ellie's hand and marched over to serve herself another bowl. 'I think I'm going to go and change and eat my breakfast upstairs,' Lottie replied, using every ounce of her princess training to save face, the edges of her smile ready to crack.

A princess would not waver in the face of adversity, she told herself; one hint of weakness and they'd pounce on it. At her side she sensed Jamie and Ellie daring anyone to say anything. Safely behind the dining-hall doors, they waved Percy off and he signed to Jamie that he'd see him soon.

'You're not going to finish your breakfast?' Lottie asked, and Jamie shook his head.

'I don't think it would be a good idea for me to hang around in there. I don't want to cause any more of a scene.'

Ellie nodded in agreement, but the words made Lottie shiver. It was unlike him to be so volatile, and it transported her back to the day she'd cut her hair away, sitting on the bench in the sun, the way his hand had brushed her cheek. The first time she'd seen that fire in his eyes.

Internally she shivered at the memory, a part of her desperate to know what he'd been thinking, or if he thought of the moment at all, but she pushed the feeling down, waving Jamie goodbye with a lingering look, and followed Ellie to their dorm with her sad-looking bowl of plain porridge and banana.

The moment the door shut, Ellie's face curled into a furious snarl. 'I cannot believe she did that to you,' she growled, pacing the wooden floor like an animal prowling the corners of her cage. 'I won't have anyone talk to you like that, Lottie. No one.'

Ellie was practically blowing steam out of her ears, but Lottie wasn't worried about Marcy. She was worried about what had made Marcy behave like that, and she had to admit she was also starting to worry about Jamie.

Ellie turned, giving Lottie some privacy to change while she stared daggers out of the window. Halfway through zipping up the pinafore over her fresh shirt, Lottie felt the words bubble out of her.

'Do you think Jamie has been behaving oddly?' she asked without really thinking it over; it sounded childish and irrelevant in light of the matter at hand. 'I mean,' she said, correcting herself quickly, 'I think we need to make sure we're paying attention to him as much as we are everything else, especially after everything he went through in Tokyo. I just want to know he's OK.'

Framed by the wispy curtains on either side of the balcony, Ellie turned, looking dramatic and ghoulish in her half-buttoned shirt with her inky-black hair. If Lottie hadn't been so nervous, she would have wanted to paint her.

'Do you have to worry about everyone else all the time?' There was a bitterness to Ellie's words, something festering beneath them that had nothing to do with what had just taken place.

Lottie was about to relent, but she shook her head, knowing what Ellie was really upset about. 'I'm going to get us some coffee so you can calm down.' She paused at the door and turned back to her princess, who was still riled. 'It's not your fault, Ellie,' Lottie said sternly, and she could see from the way Ellie flinched that she'd touched a nerve.

Grabbing two reusable coffee cups, Lottie headed to the kitchen, thankful to find it quiet, and filled both mugs, one with a black coffee and three sugars, and her own with a caramel latte. She smiled to herself as she put the lids on, thinking fondly on what an unlikely pair she and Ellie were, only the feeling quickly turned into something else when she thought of the tired inky stains under her princess's eyes.

Lottie had to believe she was doing the right thing, that Ellie would be OK and that they'd get through this together, like they always did. Nothing had knocked them down before.

Unstoppable, she thought, her fingers reaching for her newly cut hair, which reminded her of her ancestor. Already feeling better, she made her way back to their room.

As she was turning into the stairwell and past the post nook, she stopped short.

There was something in her cubbyhole. Above the label for her name, peel-thin and almost unnoticeable, there was a letter. Placing both cups down on the hallway dresser, she peeked inside to find a skinny manila envelope with no address, only a name. Her heart skipped a beat – the letter was addressed simply to *The Princess of Maradova*.

At first she expected something mean, another student angry about the security changes, but she could sense something more sinister. The words were written with deliberate and painstaking elegance.

Breath ragged with anticipation, she flipped open the envelope, and could smell it as sweet as a warm summer's day. It made her nauseous – there was only one person who carried that scent around with them.

Slowly, like it might bite her, she removed the letter, bile at the back of her throat, because she already knew who it was from, and it couldn't be anything good.

It was brief and to the point, and made all the blood in Lottie's body turn to ice.

To the princess,
Now you have witnessed what we can do, I'm sure you are
eager to avoid any more unpleasantness.
Meet me outside the Conch pool at lunch.
Do not tell anyone. I'll know if you do, and you certainly
won't want to be the cause of any more problems for your
friends.

Any good feeling she'd managed to cling to crumbled to dust inside her. Invisible fingers clasped her throat, choking all the air out of her, and they wouldn't let go, even when she forced herself to take a deep breath in.

This was Haru's work, it had to be – and the threat was clear, stealing any plan she had to tell the rest of the group about him. What would he do to anyone if she told them? What was he capable of?

She thought of Dom, the boy who'd been subject to the reporter's attack, and Marcy, her face cruel and unflinching as she stared at Lottie. She couldn't let that happen to any more people; their safety came first.

With a bubble of panic building in her chest, Lottie squeezed her eyes shut, visualizing her tiara on top of her head, the delicate weight of it, the cool silver against her skin, and she conjured the words that would calm her: *Be kind, be brave, be unstoppable.* But even her mantra couldn't cover up the truth, because this was the most alone she'd ever been in her life.

Vampy greeted Jamie outside the boys' dorm, yellow eyes materializing out of the shadows as the cat weaved between his legs, still angry with him and mewling at the indignation of being abandoned for two whole days.

'Hello, you big spoiled brute.' Jamie picked up the great lump of a cat, letting Vampy rub against his face possessively.

The room he shared with Percy was back to the way they liked it, everything for school kept in painstaking order, while their shared collection of books flowed over every surface. Laid dog-eared on Percy's bed was the copy of *Frankenstein* Jamie had lent him next to a notebook filled with annotations. It was a relief of sorts to be back at Rosewood, to hear Percy's gentle breathing at night like a lullaby. He sat on his bed, muscles slowly untensing after what had happened in the breakfast hall. Absent-mindedly rubbing Vampy's tummy while the cat continued to purr aggressively, he closed his eyes, pretending for just a moment that everything was normal, that there was no Leviathan, no Claude, no Marcys or reporters, nothing in the world for Ellie or Lottie to be afraid of.

When he finally got up, the cat let out an outraged hiss.

'Don't you judge me,' Jamie growled back, before opening his wardrobe. Double-checking he couldn't hear anything from the corridor outside, Jamie pushed at the back, the wooden panelling coming loose with a click. Curving his fingers round carefully, Jamie pulled the false panel away to reveal a hidden back. All along the dark oak was a spiderweb of information linked with a net of string to connect the pieces. Over the past week Jamie had been weaving together every clue and item they had, from the symbol Leviathan used to their obsession with his princess's family. Now he was going to add everything he had learned the night before. He wrote the words out carefully on bits of paper.

Why did Ingrid bring up Alexis Wolfson?
What do they want with the king and queen?

He was going to leave it at that when he remembered Lottie's face, the small pout she'd made when they'd interrogated him about how he was feeling in the car, and he added one more bit of paper.

Why am I Ellie's Partizan?

He began sticking these new clues to the spiderweb, and in the very centre was what he hoped it all might lead him to. Carved into the wood with a penknife were four simple words that made his blood pump with the promise of vengeance, for Lottie, for Ellie, and for everyone close to him that Leviathan had tormented.

Where is my enemy?

6

Getting through the first half of the day was a living nightmare. Lottie watched the bright purple clock on the wall ticking away, edging closer to the end of English, and she begged it to slow down, knowing that she'd soon have to face Haru. Usually she loved Ms Kuma's classes. The English department was airy and decorated with wondrous murals featuring images and quotes from famous novels, but right now it felt claustrophobic; all the colours and words were closing in around her like she was trapped in a book.

She hadn't told Ellie, or anyone, about the letter she'd received. Haru's threat meant that it was impossible for her to get the words out.

'*Thrice he assay'd, and, thrice in spite of scorn, tears, such as angels weep, burst forth!*' Ms Kuma intoned, her elegant face peering over the top of her copy of Milton's *Paradise Lost*. 'Can you tell me what that means? That he *assay'd*?'

Lottie raised her hand to speak but was cut off by another girl in what felt like a calculated interjection. 'It means he tried to speak, ma'am, but each time he opened his mouth he'd start crying,' said Billy Levine, a Stratus girl who Lottie knew from her habit of nabbing a number of leading roles in the school musicals. Looking very pleased with herself, Billy gave Lottie a wicked smile, her short, curly bobbed hair bouncing beneath a yellow beret like it was taunting her.

Even Lottie's favourite class wasn't safe from Haru's poison.

'It's not just regular crying, though, is it?' Ms Kuma continued. 'These are angels' tears, suggesting that there is still some goodness left in him at this point. That he still has regrets. Or perhaps it is his greatest deceit.'

Interrupting with a high-pitched trill, the bell went. The second she heard it, Lottie leaped to her feet like she'd been given a military command, packing up her bag with a sickly unease, each item taking her one step closer to Haru.

'Now wait a moment!' Ms Kuma gestured for everyone to sit back down, making Lottie wince. 'With the Presentation of the Pillars coming up in the spring, I want you all to start thinking about how you'll pay respect to your house namesakes. If any of you Ivy students want to discuss powerful women in poetry or literature for a Florence Ivy tribute, please do not hesitate to see me. Same goes to Conch students, although I'm not sure I will be much help there. And my fellow Stratus students –' she beamed out at the room, her gaze falling naturally on Billy, who was clearly a favourite – 'you know you can always come and chat to me any time. You're dismissed.'

Lottie went to stand up, and Ms Kuma stopped her again. 'Lottie, could I borrow you for a chat, please?'

'Of course!' Lottie smiled, putting to work all her princess training. She watched the rest of the class filter out, yellow, purple and red blending together as each of them stared at her. It wasn't the usual nods and goodbyes she was used to. It was cold and alienating, and it reminded her of the damage Haru had caused.

'Now, Lottie,' Ms Kuma began, standing up and straightening her bright fuchsia trouser suit that made her look a bit like a maraschino cherry, with a sugary sweet perfume to match. 'Every year that we do the PoP we pick one student who will perform a tribute to William Tufty.'

Lottie squeezed her lips together to stop a stunned laugh escaping, wondering what Ms Kuma would think if she knew Lottie had William Tufty's heirloom in her bag right now, or that she'd found his secret study in a Stratus basement.

'The other house mothers and I have been discussing it, and we would be delighted if you would do the honour this year. The headmaster informs us you've expressed an interest in our founder before and you clearly have the same passion for folklore and fairy tales.' Ms Kuma stopped short, looking Lottie up and down, cleaning her glasses as if that might somehow change what she was looking at. 'And I must say –' she blinked a few more times – 'since you've cut your hair short, the resemblance is rather uncanny. If I didn't know you were next in line for the throne of Maradova, I'd almost think you two were related.'

Lottie put on a show of touching her hand to her chest in humble surprise, fingers meeting her wolf pendant. 'Wouldn't that be funny?' she jested. 'I'd be delighted to pay tribute to our founder, despite not being related to –' Her throat closed up. 'Excuse me,' she said. 'Yes, I'd be happy to.' This new task weighed down, heavy and uncomfortable, upon Lottie; it was an unwanted distraction.

'Excellent, thank you.' Ms Kuma extended her hand for Lottie to shake. 'We look forward to seeing what you prepare.'

The walk towards the old Conch pool was painful. Lottie felt like the Little Mermaid after she'd traded away her tail, each step one hundred stabs into the soles of her feet. She was counting herself lucky for not having bumped into Ellie or Jamie, but she was also ignoring how creepily empty this area of the school was. Bramble bushes arched over the mud path, with stinging nettles jutting out around the mulberry trees. This was the only area of the school that felt truly wild, like the Rose Wood had reached in and reclaimed the space.

Approaching the cast-iron gate, she wondered how she'd get in, and if Haru really expected her to climb over.

This is a terrible idea and you are a fool and anything bad that happens to you from here on out is your own fault.

The Jiminy Cricket on her shoulder was relentless. She wished she'd brought something to protect herself, perhaps sneaked out the ancestral sword that was still lying under her bed or grabbed a particularly heavy book, anything. As it was, all she had were her own two legs that were still sore from running away from Ingrid only a week ago. Despite how good she'd become at running, she couldn't kid herself; she'd only got away from Ingrid because she'd surprised her, and she wasn't sure she'd be able to do the same with Haru.

Pushing open the gate, she winced at the furious shriek it made. Her body was on high alert, waiting for the inevitable ambush that she'd walked into.

The last time she'd seen the outdoor pool was two years ago when they'd foolishly broken in during New Year's. Back then, water still filled the green tiles up to the lip of the pool, reflecting the black sky until Jamie had fallen into it, shattering the stars. Now, the water had been drained, the stones cracked where the weeds broke through, and there was an empty hole in the ground waiting to swallow her up.

'Hello, Princess.' Haru's voice was as soft as butter, his freckled face appearing to her from the gazebo like a trickster spirit of the woods, a Puck or Pan. 'I hope you were not too alarmed by my letter; it was simply important you took it seriously.'

He sauntered down the steps and along the side of the empty pool, the light through the trees casting shadows over his skin, his features constantly warping, impossible to pin down.

'Thank you for being on time.'

The way he spoke always had a formal quality to it, one that was both delicate and detached, at odds with his fluffy hair and doe eyes. He smiled at her from the other side of the pool. Only this wasn't his usual summer-breeze smile that left you forgetting you should be afraid; this one made her feel small, like she was a dog who'd pleased her master.

Lottie was torn, not sure if she should continue to pretend she didn't know who Haru *truly* was, or dive right in and get it out of the way. Haru watched her the whole time, a laugh teasing the corners of his mouth, as if he knew exactly what she was thinking.

'Please don't patronize me with this fake charm,' Lottie said at last, using all her willpower to keep her voice steady. 'Why are you here? What do you want?'

Lottie noted that Haru didn't approach any further; he stayed at the other side of the pool with his hands out in the open, almost as if he was doing it on purpose, to put her at ease.

'I only want to avoid any unnecessary trouble,' he replied coyly, tilting his head with a pout that made him look almost cute. If Lottie hadn't seen what was beneath that mask, she could easily have fallen for it. 'It's come to my attention that you are aware of my alignment, and we can't have you hurting anyone with your misguided attempts to interfere.'

Lottie baulked. 'Me? I'm not the one hurting people.'

Something flashed across Haru's face, sharp and deadly, and it made Lottie take an involuntary step back. She was glad it was her here and not Ellie. She could get through this if it meant keeping her and everyone else safe.

'You have no idea what you do,' Haru said, his smile quickly blooming again, leaving Lottie with little time to process what he meant. 'Who else knows?' he asked, the two of them facing each other head on across the empty pool.

She kept her mouth firmly shut, refusing to throw Anastacia, Saskia and Ellie under the bus, which only made him laugh – and, worst of all, it was a honeyed laugh, the kind that made her feel like they were both in on the joke.

'Never mind.' He shook his head. 'I'm pretty certain I know already, and I think it's wise that none of you told Jamie. Very courteous of you.'

Lottie bit her tongue, furious that she hadn't persuaded Ellie and Sayuri to tell him, but now it was too late.

'It's your responsibility to make sure they don't interfere, and your reward will be their health and safety. Now . . .' Haru said, taking a seat at the edge of the pool and gesturing for Lottie to do the same until their feet were dangling over the ledge. The bottom smelled like wet dirt and there were old leaves and debris beneath her black pumps. 'While you were away, I found something in the woods, something that had been entrusted to me. It didn't take long for me to piece together where it had come from and what it meant.'

Claude's wolf pendant, Lottie thought, feeling the weight of her own round her neck. It was the one thing all the Wolfsons shared, proof that she'd been welcomed into the pack. She'd had to leave Claude's broken pendant in the woods when she'd run away from Ingrid.

'Your uncle sends his regards, Princess. In fact, he wants to keep in touch,' Haru declared, snapping Lottie out of her thoughts.

'What?' She was still trying to come to terms with what Haru knew, and now he was telling her that Claude, the Goat Man, the Master of Leviathan himself, wanted to keep in touch with her? The very thought made her shudder.

'Here is what's going to happen.' In a flash Haru removed something from his jacket. 'I will act as your delivery boy.' He held out a small manila envelope, similar to the one she'd received earlier. 'I'll pass these on to you, and I expect you to give your replies to me. And don't worry,' he added, gifting her a fox-like grin, 'I promise I won't read them.'

Lottie felt hot and yet she was shaking as if it were the dead of winter. She could still remember finding Jamie, feverish and afraid, begging her to get as far away from the Goat Man as possible. He was the looming shadow that followed them, always just out of reach, but now he was close enough that she could practically feel him under her skin.

'Why on earth would I agree to that, after everything he's done to my friends and family?' She tried not to let the fear seep into her voice.

'I am not finished yet,' Haru said sharply, reminding her she didn't have a choice. 'We want to give you a chance to put things right, and I am here to keep an eye on you, to make sure you and your little friends stop interfering in business that you do not understand.'

Lottie recoiled, feeling like Haru really was a teacher at the school and that she was being reprimanded.

'These are not requests. These are rules.' His eyes locked on hers like a vice, forcing her to hold his gaze. 'You have seen what we can do, but we would much rather avoid any serious unpleasantness.'

It was another threat, and Lottie could only gulp it down, thinking of Dom, Marcy and Ellie and all her friends.

'Do you understand?'

Lottie nodded.

'I want to hear you say it.'

Any ounce of pride Lottie had was shattered, and she looked up through her furrowed brows, not hiding any of her anger when she replied: 'Yes, I understand.'

Even though Haru was on the other side of the pool, she could still smell the toasted marshmallow scent that followed him around, like he was right there, hand at her neck.

'Good.' His summery smile spread back over his lips like frosting, covering up his harshness, and it made her feel crazy, like she'd imagined the whole thing. 'Now, are you ready to hear the rest of our rules?'

Lottie went to nod again, but Haru's eyes narrowed.

'Yes, I'm ready,' she said, gritting her teeth, and wishing she could kick him into the bottom of the empty pool.

'Along with giving me your replies to Claude once a week, I will spend one hour alone with Jamie, completely undisturbed. If you fail to allow this, we will take your Partizan by force.'

'No.' Lottie said it without thinking, and in that split second she really felt like she could take Haru on, a trained Partizan, if it meant keeping Jamie safe. Haru didn't look angry. On the contrary he seemed pleased with her response.

'You have my word that no harm will come to your Partizan, as long as you keep everything secret from him. I only want to get to know him.' He spoke earnestly, and in spite of everything she felt a strange connection to Haru, as if they'd both just discovered they were fighting the same war. But she must not have looked convinced because he put his hand on his heart with not an inch of irony, and continued, 'If any harm comes to your Partizan under my watch, I will turn myself in and leave you alone forever – that is, so long as you keep to your side of the bargain. If Jamie so much as suspects me, I cannot be held responsible.'

Lottie nearly choked. 'What do you want with Jamie anyway?' She could feel dandelions in the cracked tiles by her palms.

Haru smiled again, as if her question was endearing. 'We only want to put things right.'

Lottie felt like she was back in the Rose Wood again, Ingrid whispering in her ear. And, despite herself, her fingers twitched, as she wondered what might be in the letter Haru held.

'So how does that sound?' he said, interrupting her train of thought and flicking the envelope in his hand around, taunting her. 'You follow my rules, behave yourself and keep your friends in check, and I promise nothing bad will happen to any student at Rosewood Hall.'

It was a tempting proposition. Lottie thought of Ellie and the purple marks under her eyes that wouldn't go away. The idea that all she had to do was say yes and Leviathan would give them a semblance of normal school life, that only Lottie would have to carry this burden and everyone else would be free, left her feeling like there was no other choice.

'You promise that everyone will be left alone? That we can just go about school as normal?' Lottie asked, feeling guilty.

'That's what we want,' he said.

Letting out a long breath, she hardly needed to reply. It was clear from the way her body went slack that he'd won. 'OK.'

All of a sudden Haru jumped down into the empty pool, taking long steps towards her, his feet crunching against the leaves. She was too frazzled to consider moving, but he didn't reach up to touch her; he only bowed slightly, holding up the letter like a gift.

'For you,' he said, and Lottie noticed that his head was at perfect kicking distance from her foot.

Fighting this urge, Lottie took in a big breath and grabbed the envelope, realizing as she laid her eyes on the elegant script that they'd never had any power at all.

7

Nothing was going right. In fact, Ellie was pretty sure the whole world was currently conspiring against her and all she wanted to do was run to the bridge and scream into the abyss below.

Pulling at the hem of her damned tartan pinafore, she tried to cover up some of her exposed skin as she pushed the Stratus Side door open with her shoulder. It was club hours, and Stratus students tended to be in the library. Despite this, she checked and double-checked to make sure the coast was clear before she approached the stone statue of the falcon Elwin, the Stratus mascot, and the door to Rosewood's greatest secret.

Twisting the 'W' until it turned into an 'M', she waited for the cogs to turn, the sound always making her jump even if she was ready for it, until the bird slowly lifted, revealing the staircase below. It was a shame none of the Stratus students could use this secret room that was hidden in their house quarters as inspiration for their Presentation of the Pillars tribute, but this place was Lottie's secret, so Ellie and her friends would protect it with their lives.

Rubbing her arms at the cold that sighed out from the hidden door, she began her descent into the secret study that had belonged to the school founder, the lost princess Liliana Mayfutt under her cover identity of William Tufty – the very study that had revealed Lottie's true heritage. Ellie hadn't ever given much thought to the secrets and resemblances that Lottie had inherited – the underground study, the tiara heirloom, and her matching wild honey hair. So why did it now leave a hard lump in the pit of her stomach? One that was shaped unmistakably like guilt.

She could be so much more without you, a voice sneered in her mind.

She could hear them talking as she lingered at the end of the winding stairwell, peeking into the room without giving herself away as Raphael's distinctive hybrid Los Angeles and Oxford English accent echoed through the door.

'So the fire just blew out completely?' Raphael sucked his teeth, turning to Jamie for an answer and receiving only a shrug in response.

The twins were being strangely quiet in the corner, absorbing the information like two creepy ornamental dolls while they nibbled anxiously on nearly gone lollipops. The look on Micky's face was vague, the kind of half-there stare adopted by people who weren't comfortable with what they were hearing.

Part of Ellie wondered if his expression was something to be concerned about, but she was also selfishly relieved she'd missed having to listen to Lottie recount their meeting with her family. She wasn't sure she could keep a level head if she had to live through it again.

'Perhaps it was a freak weather event?' Binah offered, snapping Ellie out of her thoughts. 'Sometimes rain-cooled air can produce descending columns of wind with destructive damage comparable to the high-velocity gales of a tornado.' Although the two are not to be mistaken for the same thing.'

Ellie was sure she'd be the last one there after her accident at lunch, and she was itching to explain to Lottie why she hadn't been able to find her in the dining hall, so she was more than a little surprised to find Saskia and Anastacia were nowhere to be seen.

'Is that going to be on the chemistry exam?' Raphael asked, jotting it down in his notebook that was supposed to be for Leviathan information.

'Yes, it's on page fifty-six. I read ahead.' Binah turned to the side, her canary-yellow prefect cloak fanning out around her shoulders. 'You can borrow my notes if you like.' She signed to Percy and he nodded, then the two of them huddled together to copy Binah's meticulous notes.

Ellie watched the scene like she was peering into a snow globe. Surrounded by twinkling fairy lights and the delicate star ornaments that hung from the ceiling above, everyone on the other side of the glass looked like they were floating in a dream.

They could just be normal students. They would be happier without you, that same voice sneered again, and before she could stop herself she let out a grunt of frustration.

'Ellie, thank God.' Lottie almost jumped on her, and the deep indent of worry on her brow made Ellie want to curl up and die. She hated that she was the cause. 'Where were you? Why are you wearing a pinafore?'

They all stared at her as if hell had frozen over.

'*Bad day?*' Percy signed, and she hated how obvious it was.

'Sorry I'm late – I had to drop my regular uniform in the laundry room.' She scratched at the back of her head. 'Someone spilled coffee all over me just as lunch started.'

Jamie lifted an eyebrow, but she shook her head, letting him know she was fine.

Ellie coughed, trying to hide how she was feeling and move the conversation along. 'Have you made any progress?'

Binah sighed, tapping her jaw in thought where she stood by the blackboard. 'I'm afraid the information is unsatisfactory. Nothing the royal family said during the meeting takes us any closer to understanding Claude's motivation, nor his ultimate goal.'

Binah, along with Anastacia and Saskia, were their only friends at Rosewood that knew Ellie was the real princess, meaning she was always careful with her choice of words.

What was more worrying was the look Lottie gave her, still focused on the pinafore that hung awkwardly over Ellie's body, eyes flickering a mile a minute. Puzzle pieces were slotting together, making her apple-blossom lips set into a hard pout. But Lottie didn't have time to question her as footsteps echoed towards them, like the sound of an angry giant.

'I swear when I find out whose idea this was I'm going to –'

'*Arrêtes*, Saskia!'

From the dark of the stairwell appeared Saskia and Anastacia, twenty-five minutes late and both holding their Rosewood Library reusable coffee cups.

Anastacia noticed Lottie glancing at the cup in her hand and scowled. 'No, we are not late because we got coffee.' She strode into the room in a cloud of perfume, her blow-dried mahogany hair flowing behind her.

'We're late because of this!' Saskia gave a powerful kick with her left leg, and Ellie stared at the metal band fastened round her ankle.

Only Jamie reacted, sucking in a breath.

'I've been *leashed!*' Saskia screeched indignantly, slamming her foot down.

'What is that?' Raphael asked, shuddering like it was some ugly accessory she'd actually *chosen* to wear.

'It's a tracking band,' Jamie said. 'Some people request them from the Partizan council so they can track their Partizan in case they're compromised, but most people consider it a violation of privacy.'

Ellie winced, unable to think of anything someone as carefree as Saskia would hate more, and she noticed how Lottie's lips quivered, as if she was trying to hold something in.

'Apparently one of the new school security found out about the little, um –' Saskia coughed awkwardly, giving a sideways glance to Lottie – 'kidnapping attempt when I was under Leviathan's influence and requested that I only be allowed to attend classes again if they can track me and make sure I never leave the grounds.'

Anastacia put a comforting hand on her girlfriend's shoulder, their Partizan and master bond melting away into something even more powerful. Then she sighed, pulling a mirror out of her bag to check her make-up, and her eyes flickered up to Lottie and Ellie for just a second, like they were being frisked. 'It's truly been the day from hell. I've got a detention tomorrow,' she said, and everyone turned to her.

Anastacia Alcroft getting a detention was unheard of. It would be like the queen of England going to a warehouse rave. It was unfathomable. 'Yep,' she continued, distracting herself with the mirror so she didn't have to make eye contact. 'My book went missing before Mr Trigwell's calculus class and he thought I was making excuses for not doing my homework.' Lottie winced, knowing just how difficult the notorious maths teacher could be. 'The strange thing is, though, I know I put it in my bag. It was almost as if someone stole it, specifically to get me in trouble.' Once again her sapphire eyes shot up, and this time they stayed on Lottie, honing in like a missile. 'Perhaps any number of the students are angry about who I choose to be friends with.' Her voice was shards of glass grating against Ellie's skin.

'Don't be rude,' Ellie immediately growled, knowing exactly what Anastacia was suggesting.

'I'm not being rude, Ellie; I'm being realistic.' Anastacia snapped her mirror shut, and the rest of the room went quiet. 'People are really angry with Lottie for what they assume is somehow her fault, and *we* have to assume, with everything we know about how the Hamelin Formula works, that the reporter who broke in and attacked Dom was under its influence, and that, therefore, this is part of a Leviathan plot.' She gave Saskia, Ellie and Lottie a hard look each, a warning. 'I think it's time we told everyone about –'

Ellie could almost hear the words on the tip of Anastacia's tongue; she was about to tell the others about Haru, and Ellie knew that if she did Jamie would lose it. He'd never forgive her for keeping this secret. A part of her couldn't help feeling that maybe she deserved his outrage.

From the corner of the room came a sound somewhere between a whimper and a plea that rattled Ellie's bones. When they turned, they only caught a glimpse of Micky's crumbling face before he rushed out.

'Micky!' Lola called after him. 'I'll go and calm him down.' She was looking directly at Percy, the two of them sharing the same concern. Percy's head dipped to the side, a question, and Lola appeared to answer a wordless yes before vanishing herself.

The rest of them turned to Percy in unison, knowing he'd be their best bet at understanding what had just happened since he was dating one half of the twins. He was against the wall by the blackboard, looking like a ghost, a thick gloom that was different to the regular shadows he dragged around with him, his black hair resting over his eyes, cutting up his features with thick lines.

'*We were waiting to speak to you about that,*' he signed, his weary gaze cast downwards. '*Lola and Micky . . . their dad has taken a turn for the worst; we're not sure he has very long left, so for the moment –*' he shrugged, hesitating over his next words – '*I don't want either of them coming to these meetings. I warned Micky it would upset him too much and, well, you can see for yourself.*'

Everyone's faces dropped, a reminder that there was more going on; there was always more. This was what they should all be able to focus on, exams, clubs and their friends and families, not this stupid Leviathan stuff – this should be Ellie's problem only, but she'd infected everyone with it.

Ellie turned to Lottie, whose eyes were glossy with tears, probably already taking on this burden too, then slowly she looked at her Partizan.

Jamie was as unreadable as ever, but as soon as he locked on to Ellie she knew they were sharing the same thought, a wordless agreement that came out in a long sigh.

'This meeting is over,' Jamie announced. 'Let's reconvene next week. There's clearly a lot on people's minds with the PoP, exams and family matters, and we don't have any new information, meaning there's no point in keeping you all here.'

Lottie opened her mouth to say something, but her focus was on Ellie, and slowly it closed again, locking away whatever thought had almost spilled out of her throat.

'Is that really OK?' Raphael asked, looking like a guilty dog. 'We'll stay if you need us.'

'No, it's fine,' Ellie said, clearly shocking Lottie with how controlled she was. 'Everyone, go. Go and live your lives.' And then she did something she'd never done before; she gave the room that fake smile she had learned from Lottie, praying that she could hold it long enough to convince them.

There was only a moment's hesitation, with Percy the first to make a move, unashamed that he'd rather be comforting his boyfriend than be deep in the bowels of Rosewood, dishing up old and awful memories. Raphael was next, giving Jamie a wave at the stairwell, followed by Binah, then Anastacia and Saskia.

Ellie spotted a look of panic on Lottie's face, like her mind was trying to scrape something together.

'How about we meet up next weekend after we've had some time to think?' Lottie offered, her fist meeting her palm and a determined look that was completely at odds with what Ellie had witnessed a second ago. Because this one was fake.

Anastacia seemed to pick up on something, pausing at the lip of the stairwell. 'How about a self-care day in my room?' she replied. 'To take our mind off things, just us girls?'

'Yes, great idea, Ani,' Lottie said, beaming, her eyes a little too intense. 'I have so much I need to get off my chest.'

Both of them nodded, hoping Jamie wouldn't clock anything suspicious. Ellie scrutinized them; it was no coincidence Lottie was trying to form a meeting with Anastacia and Saskia, the only other people who knew about Haru's and Ellie's real identities.

The other girls nodded, instantly understanding that Lottie had something to tell them. Ellie just hoped it wasn't more terrible news.

It wasn't until they'd gone that Lottie turned to Ellie, hands balled up at her sides, her face looking like her heart was about to shatter into a million pieces. 'Why did you do that?'

Neither of them responded, but Ellie could feel in the way Jamie's breathing turned deep with regret, shadows growing long over his face like he was hiding away, that they were both thinking the same thing. She was the first to say it aloud.

'Just leave it, Lottie.' She spoke calmly, as though this was the most important realization she'd ever had. 'You need a break from all this as well.'

8

When Ingrid was a little girl growing up in Peć, before she'd signed up to be a Partizan, one of the nuns at the children's home used to tell her: *There is always someone worse off than yourself. At least you are not a monkey with an allergy to nuts.* And despite how miserable the last month had been, despite her crumbling plans, she found herself remembering that phrase, and turned her attention to Julius.

It had been a long time since she'd thought of the children's home at all. The ugly brown rug in the dining room, the one squeaky floorboard that would always tell on her when she tried to sneak to the kitchen at night, and the stench of boiled cabbage that clung to every room in the house. The other children had been happy there, but Ingrid was always being told that she was spoiled, naughty, which just made her go around with a furious pout, determined to make sure she got just as much, or more, than the other children. A man from the Partizan council had visited not three days after she'd turned twelve – and one week later she'd met Julius at the training camp. He was easy-going and generous in all the ways Ingrid was not. At first she'd thought him a fool, continually patient with her, even when she bit back, but he persisted, taking her under his wing, showing her the ropes, laughing her off whenever she snapped or hissed – and they were still a team today.

'You'd think I was dying with how you hover around me,' Julius groaned, his Southern twang making everything sound like a joke.

Ingrid scowled. 'I just like your room.'

'Liar.'

Julius had broken his arm during his chase of Saskia and the princess in Tokyo, ending up in a hospital near Shinjuku. It had taken a lot of money to persuade the authorities to sweep the incident under the rug and get Julius back to the compound in Yakushima. Worst of all, they'd both failed. Jamie had got away from her and they hadn't got even a lick of revenge on Saskia for what she'd done to Julius's eye.

'We're leaving,' Ingrid confessed, knowing Julius hated being uprooted – that, like her, he craved a place to make his own. 'The Master says it's time to leave Japan.'

After a long sigh, Julius winced, using his good hand to rub at his broad stubbly chin. 'Where are we going?'

'He has another sympathizer in Germany, a friend from his time at university to whom he's promised favours once our plan is complete.'

'Closer to Maradova?'

'Closer to England.'

'Ah, of course.' Julius whistled. 'One thing at a time.'

His remaining good eye started to close, his pain meds making him lethargic. It didn't help that the room stank of sandalwood incense. Ingrid decided now was a good time to get him some food so he'd have something to eat when he woke up.

Stepping out into the ugly windowless corridor, Ingrid's ears pricked, a telltale pitter-patter coming from round the corner. Clasping the spider knives sheathed at her side, Ingrid continued down the corridor, her kitten heels echoing a metallic click-clack against the walls. Her wrists only hurt a little now, the dull ache a ghostly memory of the injury Jamie had given her in Tokyo.

As Ingrid approached the corner, a black-clad figure darted out, skidding on the floor and aiming a knife at Ingrid's face. With lightning speed, Ingrid lunged out of the way, the knife whizzing past her nose, and with a quick flick of her spider blade she sent her attacker's knife flying into the wall with a clang. In one more swift movement, she grabbed the figure and spun them round until they were on their knees.

'Oopsie!' The person laughed, before biting down hard on Ingrid's wrist, forcing her to let go.

'Stella, you brat,' Ingrid hissed. 'Where's your brother?'

Stella grinned, her freckled face contorting to reveal a set of teeth obscured by pink braces. 'Behind you.'

Ingrid turned like a tornado, preparing for the inevitable attack, only there was no one there. Behind her, two voices joined in hysterical laughter.

'Made you look!' they chorused.

'I remember when you were both quiet and bearable,' Ingrid growled, turning to face them.

Stella and Sam were their youngest and latest Leviathan recruits, hand-picked by Claude for a specific project that he was planning. When they'd first arrived, Sam had been a quiet boy, keen to be useful. His older sister was similarly dedicated to pleasing people. As it turned out, the behaviour had been unreliable; they'd been playing an ambitious game – to become the Master's favourites. If Ingrid didn't watch her step, they'd succeed. She used to think they were little mice, not worth paying any attention to, but now she realized they were rats.

Sam tutted, his hazel eyes locking on to Ingrid's. 'Useless Julius and insignificant Ingrid.'

Stella chimed in. 'It's true because it rhymes.'

Ingrid could kill them both; she knew she could. They'd never finished their Partizan training. In fact, they'd most likely have never been allowed to graduate – they were too sloppy. This perhaps explained why they'd joined Leviathan, knowing it was their best and only option to rise to the top.

'It doesn't rhyme, you little idiot,' Ingrid spat, turning to the kitchen.

'Doesn't mean it's not true!' Stella called after, the two of them falling into pace just behind her. 'Can't you take a joke?'

Ingrid didn't reply.

'Where did you go the other day?' Sam asked, his nose twitching like he'd picked up a curious scent. 'You were missing for nearly five days.'

Ingrid froze for just a second at the kitchen doorway. She'd been careful to cover her tracks when she'd gone to Rosewood Hall to seek her revenge on the princess and her Partizan. She'd burned the letters they were going to use to expose the Maravish royal family, along with any evidence of her flights or travel. The only mistakes she'd made were the injury she'd accidentally inflicted on Jamie, not to mention the fact that she'd nearly got herself caught. All because that stupid spoiled princess had evaded her, again. If they found out any of this and told the Master, especially after she'd been given strict orders not to go anywhere near Jamie, he would never forgive her.

'I needed some time away.' She kept her answer vague as she made her way into the cold kitchen. 'To repent.'

'Probably for the best.' To Ingrid's irritation, the siblings were still following. 'After how you disappointed the Master in Tokyo.'

Ignoring them as best she could, Ingrid began fixing two plates of food.

'Good thing the Master finally realized you shouldn't be allowed near the Partizan he wants.'

'Did no one tell you they don't allow rats in the kitchen?' Ingrid said with a scowl, grabbing some fruit and two caramel pudding cups from the storeroom.

'Haru is so much better for the job, don't you agree?' Stella's voice was like acid on her skin. 'Apparently he's already got the little princess in tow, and Jamie adores him.'

Perfect Haru. When Ingrid thought of him, every hair on her body stood on end. Everything about him was fake. 'Shut up,' she growled in warning.

'Are you disagreeing with the Master's choice?'

'Don't you two have something you should be doing?'

'Nope.' Stella shrugged, checking her fingernails. 'We're getting ready for school.'

'What?'

'We're going to school,' Sam replied.

'St Agnus's in Maradova. We start next week.' They both turned to watch her reaction now. 'Didn't the Master tell you?'

Ingrid picked up the tray of food and started back to Julius's room, her neck bristling at the sound of Stella and Sam bursting into laughter again behind her.

'Oh, Crow!' Sam called after her, rushing to the doorway. 'Completely forgot, the Master wanted us to tell you something.'

Ingrid froze, itching to hear from Claude, despite what felt like an eternity of being in his bad graces. She needed to know she could still be useful to him, that he still trusted her.

'He says, if Haru continues as he is, the Maravish Partizan will definitely see our side, with no need to use the Hamelin Formula on him . . . yet.' Stella and Sam looked at each other. 'He wants you to – how did he phrase it? – stay away from Jamie should he choose to join us.'

Ingrid's fingers curled round the cold metal tray, a million furious thoughts racing through her head. 'Thank you.' Then she marched off.

By the time she reached Julius's room and shut the door behind her, her whole body was shaking. *You just have to wait,* she told herself. Everything was messy right now because they were getting close to the final stages of their plan. Once it was executed, she'd get what she'd been promised. Everything would finally be right in the world and she would be part of that.

'What's wrong?' Julius asked, his eyes fluttering open slowly.

Ingrid turned to him, her train of thought coming abruptly to an end. It was like being thrown off a horse, landing her

76

back in Rose Wood, the choking scent of roses and lavender filling her nose while thorns scratched her ankles and tree roots tripped her. She was back by the giant oak tree, her fingers tightening over golden curls, when the princess of Maradova had escaped her grasp by slicing through her own hair. Why did that image keep coming back to her? Why couldn't she escape it?

'The Maravish royal family,' Ingrid growled. 'That's what's wrong.'

9

Summer had woven a garland round Rosewood, the blooming flowers filling the air with heady scent. Walking alone to the library, Lottie watched as the shadows of lone clouds glided over the path.

She paused outside the library, marvelling at the curved white building, cream and yellow flowers like lace spiralling up its bones. She put on her best smile, finding it came easier to her here, her favourite place in the school. No one could suspect she was here to do anything other than study. This was something she had to handle on her own, especially given how everyone had been at the meeting.

People stared at her as she stepped inside, but she was starting to get used to the irritable whispering that followed her everywhere. The midday sun shone through the stained-glass rose at the top of the library, which drowned the books in a coral glow. House emblems hung above the office alcove and it was underneath them, in a booth, away from any snooping eyes, that Lottie chose to do what she'd been dreading the most.

With Ellie at fencing and Jamie on a run with Raphael, Lottie was alone, and neither of them would have to know the extent of how much she *wasn't* taking a break. It was her job as a Portman to shoulder such burdens; it wasn't something she could put away at a moment's notice.

Carefully she pulled out two history books and a textbook, laying them on the table. Nestled in the history book was the envelope – the cursed object Haru had given her that she still hadn't opened. She wished more than anything she could contact Sayuri, that they could do this together, but she had to do this on her own. It was the only way to protect everyone.

Slipping her finger under the glued-down surface of the envelope, she imagined Claude's tongue sliding along the paper, and all she could see was the forked tongue of a snake. As soon as it ripped open, she could smell it: spiced wine, rich and intoxicating, wafted up like perfume from the scented paper inside.

She shook the contents out on to the table: an A5 oblong of thick black card coated with a glossy finish. In the centre of the card elegant gilt lettering shimmered when she moved it in the light.

To my charming young niece

Lottie paused immediately at the condescending language; Ellie would have torn it up right then and there.

Although I have delighted in our little games these past two years, there comes a time when those in charge must decide when too much fun has been had, and, though it delights me to see my own niece play along and solve each puzzle, our next game is one of a far more serious nature.

It is my understanding that you are, like me, a lover of folklore, so, while I give you a chance to put right what has been wronged, I gift you these clues to set you on the right path.

Sometimes stories wield power greater than we know.

This is your first clue.

The whole letter made Lottie feel . . . icky, the kind of childish disgust usually reserved for bad smells and gross pranks. With shaking hands, Lottie turned the card to find a carefully drawn illustration depicting a golden stag wearing a crown. The image melted in the light, the ink disappearing and reappearing. And then it vanished completely, a shadow falling over the paper.

'A curious alternative to invisible ink,' a bird-like voice chirped from behind her.

Shoving everything inside the textbook, Lottie slammed it shut, turning so fast she nearly fell off her chair. 'Binah!' she gasped, clutching her chest as if her heart might jump out of it. 'How many times have I told you not to sneak up like that?'

Binah wasn't much taller than her, even with Lottie sitting down, but her black ringlets were carefully arranged in a topknot that gave the illusion of height.

'My apologies,' she said, removing her glasses to wipe them on the edge of her tank top. 'You just seemed so engrossed; I was curious.' A wry smile twitched at the corner of her mouth, and Lottie knew she'd seen more than she was supposed to.

Lottie let out a short breath and grabbed Binah's arm, pulling her into the booth. 'You can't tell anyone, Binah. This is serious.'

'My lips are sealed; this is just between me and the royal trio.'

Lottie squirmed awkwardly, an embarrassed blush creeping over her, giving her away.

'Oh!' Binah held her finger up, eyes going wide, and Lottie could practically see the light bulb turning on above her head. 'They don't know, and that's why you were acting so strange during the meeting, because you *do* have more info.'

'I'm not keeping it from them . . . I can't – I-I have to keep it secret to protect everyone or –' Before Lottie could stop herself, tears were pricking her eyes, threatening to spill over. If Binah knew then she'd be in danger, and she couldn't put anyone else at risk.

'Whoa, whoa, it's OK!' Binah's voice was soothing like warm milk and honey, and she carefully placed a hand over Lottie's. 'Whatever this is, you shouldn't be shouldering it on your own. Let me help.'

'You don't understand – he said if I told anyone about this, the school would be in danger, all of you would be in danger.'

'Who said this?'

Lottie could feel Haru and Claude right behind her, their hands holding her back.

'Lottie,' Binah prompted, and when she looked up those dark brown eyes reminded her of the great oak tree in the Rose Wood, firm and sure, offering comfort to all who sought it. 'I promise I'll keep the secret safe. We can face this together.'

And, just like that, the curse was lifted.

'Haru.' She whispered his name, looking around to make sure no one was listening. 'He's part of Leviathan, and –'

The noise Binah made was halfway between a squeak and a splutter. 'Of course,' she breathed. 'That's why everything started happening when he arrived . . . And the way he looks at Jamie . . . Oh dear, oh dear.'

Lottie nodded, shuddering at the thought that Haru was looking at Jamie in any sort of way. 'He blackmailed me on Monday.' She swallowed hard, shaking off the last traces of the treacherous phantom hands on her shoulders. 'He gave me a list of rules I have to follow if I want to keep everyone safe, and by telling you I've already broken one.'

Binah was perfectly still, and Lottie thought of an old grandfather clock, the cogs all working away under her calm demeanour, putting everything into place.

'He gave me this letter, it's, uh . . .' Lottie hesitated again, still feeling gross. 'It's from Claude.'

'Oh me, oh my,' Binah said simply, her eyes somehow even wider.

'Yeah. I have to write a response. It seems like some kind of riddle or puzzle.'

Binah lifted her head, glasses glinting, and for a second it looked as if she were drooling. She licked her lips. 'A puzzle, you say?'

It was such a completely ridiculous and yet entirely normal response for Binah that Lottie couldn't stop the bubble of laughter that spilled out of her mouth, and once it started it wouldn't stop, each hiccup making her feel lighter.

'Hey, it's not my fault I'm an enigmaholic.' Binah's voice cracked with laughter.

'Is that even a word?'

'No, but it should be.'

Lottie wiped her eyes, trying to hold back more giggles, until she finally let out a long sigh, opening up the book again to find the cursed 'gift' from Claude.

'We're having a secret meeting tomorrow – Ellie, Saskia, Anastacia and me – but they have no idea of this terrible bomb I'm going to have to drop on them. You should come. I could use some help figuring out how to tell them about Haru's rules.'

'Hmm,' Binah mused, not hiding any of her doubt. 'You need to tell them about this letter from Claude eventually too, especially Ellie. You know that, right?'

Waving off the question, Lottie located the card. 'What I *need* to do is write a reply.'

'We'll do it together,' Binah said.

When Lottie looked down at the black card, she saw it had got scuffed from being roughly hidden away, leaving it looking less regal and more feeble. It looked defeatable.

'Yeah, OK,' she said. 'Just us two.'

10

To the Goat Man,

Thank you so much for your very generous clue, and for humouring your silly little niece. Nothing says 'I care' quite like blackmail.

While I am indeed familiar with folklore and fairy tales (how kind of you to notice), the crowned stag seems out of place; my upbringing tells me it should be a wolf instead.

Now, with all things considered, I think it would be acceptable for me to ask a question myself, and I'm sure, oh great and wise uncle, that you will be happy to answer.

So I must ask, with morbid curiosity, why do you want my Partizan?

Regards,
Your ever-charming young niece

The glue tasted bitter against Lottie's tongue where she dragged it over the envelope, sealing away the letter with begrudging acceptance. Writing each word had felt like she was making a deal with the devil. It sickened her to think that it was meant to be Ellie in her place.

Shoving the letter in her bedside table, Lottie locked the drawer, dreading having to take it out again and give it to Haru, like a dog bringing their master the daily newspaper.

The bathroom door opened, and from a cloud of steam and the mellow scent of the men's body spray she used Ellie emerged in a black hoodie and ripped jeans, rubbing her hair with a small towel. It still made Lottie's stomach lurch in a distinctly pleasant way to see Ellie out of her armour, no dark eyeliner or lipstick, just her bare skin. It was so soft and pale it looked almost transparent.

'You ready to go?' she asked, not quite meeting Lottie's eyes.

'Yep,' Lottie said with a tight-lipped smile, thinking *no*.

Anastacia and Saskia were waiting for them in the Conch dorms for their meeting of the people-who-know-Ellie-is-the-real-princess-and-Haru-is-a-member-of-Leviathan gang, or 'the inner circle' as Lottie was calling them in her head. But her mind was a tangle of anxiety, all of which she couldn't let Ellie see, because today was also the day Haru had requested his first hour alone with Jamie, something she absolutely did not want to think about.

Anastacia's room was like something out of a luxury interior design catalogue, combined with a fluffy pink teenage fantasy. Indeed, it had featured in *Toffy* magazine when they'd run a piece on the 'Best Rooms in British Boarding Schools'. Lottie had the very page pinned up in her old bedroom.

The room had been titled *The Catwalk Queen of Conch House* and had an equally over-the-top copy to accompany it.

Classic Parisian-style decor with a plush twist. Note the mix of plum reds and rich pinks to complement the delectable walnut furniture, each piece selected carefully, from the antique canopy bed frame to the mirrored armoire, all blending effortlessly with the personal touches. Chanel memorabilia, designer make-up over the dressing table and gold-framed photos above the headboard, all telling of the edgy but innocent pizazz of the elite youth. Even the view of the sports field from the twin alcove windows, with the athletic students in their matching uniforms, looks more like a scene from a renaissance painting. This room is everything you'd expect from the elusive and exclusive Rosewood Hall.

The picture had been added to since then, with Anastacia's Rosewood Lancers fencing gear and jacket proudly displayed by the door for all to marvel at.

Standing by the bay window that looked out over the field, Saskia peered out through the curtains, eyes glazed.

Anastacia turned to them from her dressing table, hairbrush still in hand. 'Good, you're here,' she said. 'We have a problem.'

'Don't we always?' Ellie moaned, throwing her open backpack haphazardly to the floor, contents spilling out. The action was a little too aggressive, like a wolf letting out a warning growl.

Saskia finally turned to them, gesturing with her chin for them to look at something.

Lottie went over and could smell Anastacia's Chanel perfume on Saskia – and a completely unwarranted thought came over her: how would it feel to have Ellie's scent lingering on her in the same way? She quickly shook the thought off, embarrassed.

She saw what Saskia had been gesturing towards. Like a bronze statue in the afternoon light, Jamie stood on the field, stretching and looking more like he was preparing for a battle of the gods than a friendly race. Next to him, also getting ready, were Raphael and Haru.

Ellie let out a curse in Maravish, sucking in a breath so hard it sounded like a snake's hiss. Lottie's words dried up in her mouth. She'd allowed this.

'They've been out there for about twenty minutes so far just . . . playing.' Saskia shrugged. Through the window, they saw Haru lean back, guffawing, while Jamie rubbed his forehead, the silent laugh on his lips obvious. 'I guess we can safely assume Raphael has made a terrible joke – again.'

It was such a strange sight because it wasn't strange at all. Three young men laughing and joking in the hot sun, sweaty and content. Haru had promised Lottie that Jamie would come to no harm if she followed his rules, and, whether she liked it or not, it seemed the most relaxed Jamie had been in a long time.

She turned to Ellie, and by the way her fingers had curled into fists she could tell she was thinking the same thing.

'I was going to go out and intervene, but, and I hate to say it,' Saskia said, running her hand through her thick blonde curls, 'my Partizan instincts are telling me there's no threat. I think they're just having fun.'

Ellie said nothing. The only indication she'd even heard her was a small twitch in her jaw.

'We can keep watch over them from here at least,' Lottie offered, knowing if any of them intervened it would get them in trouble anyway.

'If Haru isn't presently trying to kidnap anyone, shall we get on with talking about what we're going to do with him please?' Anastacia demanded from her throne at the dressing table. 'I have to get started on my Balthazar Conch tribute and I have absolutely no idea where to begin, not to mention Saskia's being watched like a hawk by those miserable security guards. All this is causing me more anxiety than I care for and, if I'm not careful, it's going to make my skin break out.'

Lottie and Ellie's eyes met, and like opposing ends of a magnet they quickly flickered away again. There was a tight feeling in the air, everyone waiting to see how Ellie would react, but she was hardly moving, still staring daggers out of the window.

'We need to make sure Haru and Jamie aren't ever alone,' Ellie said at last, and Lottie's self-preservation burned up in a panicked blaze.

'Maybe it's a good thing,' she spluttered, words tumbling out of her.

A voice in Lottie's head immediately demanded to know what on earth she was even saying, which the looks on everyone's faces seemed to mirror.

'I mean,' she continued, grappling for some sense, 'maybe if we can control a small amount of time for Haru to interact with Jamie, we can ask Jamie what they talked about and try to gain some new information – maybe even figure out why they want him?'

Lottie felt like a complete traitor, each word burning her throat like poison, while her brain tried to reason with her that this was for everyone's good – and might even save Jamie's life.

'Wouldn't that be easier if Jamie was in on it too?' Saskia countered, with Anastacia nodding along in agreement, and Lottie's face went hot in a way that had nothing to do with the temperature.

'Sayuri is counting on us,' Ellie said. 'Haru is her Partizan, and she wants to keep his involvement with Leviathan under wraps.'

The room was starting to feel very small, and Lottie squirmed with guilt.

'I believe that was only because they were using him as an unwitting source to farm information,' Anastacia said, and every word made the room shrink another inch. 'That doesn't apply now.'

'Not to mention these are completely different circumstances. People are in danger,' Saskia added.

Lottie agreed. They should have revealed Haru's duplicity the moment they'd arrived in Maradova. But Lottie had made the one mistake the king had warned her about all that time ago – she'd put Ellie's desires before Ellie's safety and now they were trapped.

'Lottie, are you OK?'

It wasn't until Saskia's words hit her that Lottie realized how rapid her breathing had become. The air felt too thin; just when she was sure she was going to burst into a million pieces, a soft tap came from the door.

'Hello! Sorry I'm late.' Binah's cheery face peeped through the door and it took Lottie a second to remember she was the one who'd invited her. 'I forgot to get the time we were meeting from Lottie, and I had to deliver a gift to Lola and Micky.' Binah came in, pulling off her canary-yellow beret and hanging it by the door, completely oblivious to the tension in the room. 'Actually, after we're done discussing Haru, perhaps we could think about something we could do for them in this difficult time, maybe bake them a cake; you know they love –'

'You told Binah about Haru?' Ellie's voice was a spark, turning the whole room electric, a storm flashing in her eyes. Upon instinct, Saskia stepped protectively in front of her girlfriend.

'I had to.' Swallowing her anxiety, Lottie fumbled for the best way to de-escalate the situation. 'She can help.'

'Help?'

'Yes, I –'

Ellie turned on Binah like a storm at sea. 'Help with what? Help solve all the problems my stupid family caused?'

Lottie knew that she had to speak up. 'Ellie, you don't understand. None of you do.' She looked to Anastacia and Saskia now apologetically. 'I . . . I . . .' Binah gave her a soft nod, signalling for her to go on. 'Haru knows we know.'

The whites of Ellie's eyes flashed, and she took in a choked breath like she'd been winded.

Lottie continued. 'He's put rules in place and, as long as we stick to them, everyone at Rosewood, including us and Jamie, will be safe.'

No one moved, and the only sound in the room was a mumbled expletive from Saskia.

'What happened to Dom, the extra security stopping anyone from leaving, all the little problems that have been cropping up, I think that was all him. It was a warning. He said we have to just go about our normal school life, and he wants one hour a week with Jamie,' Lottie relayed, filling the silence; yet the one thing she couldn't mention was Claude's letter. It was as if Claude's hold on her was too strong. She felt like her skin was covered in slime, and it was catching in her airways, stopping her from saying more.

'How long have you known this?' Ellie's voice was distorted, grating against Lottie's ears like sandpaper. 'When did you agree to this?'

There was electricity in her words that jolted an answer out of Lottie. 'Since Monday, but Binah only found out the other day.'

'OK, what I think we all need to do is –' Anastacia stepped forward, but, before she could continue, Ellie pushed her aside, coming right up to Lottie where she blocked the light completely.

'Hey, don't –' Saskia snarled, but Ellie wasn't listening.

'You told Binah about this? Before *me*?'

'No, I . . . It wasn't like that. I couldn't. It was an accident – those were the rules. I –'

For a second Lottie thought Ellie was going to shout at her, but instead she pulled back, her hands clawing at her face.

'This is all my fault,' she gasped, eyes darting from side to side. 'I did this. If I'd just let you tell my parents about Haru . . . If I hadn't been so stubborn and thought that I could fix everything myself . . . And now . . .'

She burst out into a string of expletives in Maravish that made Lottie wince. The way Ellie looked, coiled in on herself in anguish, felt wrong.

91

Lottie stepped forward. 'Ellie, it's not your fault. I just want to help you. I'm sorry –'

Ellie held up her hand. '*Briktah*, Lottie, I know,' she snapped, but it felt more like a scared dog than an angry bark. 'Please just stop apologizing. *I'm* the one who should be apologizing. We always do this to you.' She righted herself, glancing around the room, a twisted hint of a grin spreading over her lips, as if she'd finally understood some terrible joke, and, just like that, she pushed back her hair and the mask was on again. 'I'm gonna go and cool down,' she said with a great sigh. 'I'll see you back at the dorm tonight. Everyone just forget this stupid meeting, forget Haru and Leviathan, and go back to your lives. I'll deal with this.'

'Ellie –' said Lottie.

She was stopped by a roguish half-smile, an echo of the one her princess used to wear with such ease.

'It's fine, Lottie. I said I'd deal with it. See you later.'

The door thudded shut behind her, hardly a slam, yet Lottie felt it reverberate through her like an earthquake.

'What about Jamie?' Saskia's voice was gentle, a fragile plea for a fellow Partizan.

'All I know is that we have to keep him in the dark about Haru,' Lottie admitted, clutching the wolf pendant at her chest. Some unspoken decision had been made by Ellie just now, and she could tell by the way her heart thudded painfully that this was different from her usual outbursts.

11

'Where do you disappear to?'

'Excuse me?'

Jamie watched Haru, fascinated by how much strength he was able to cover up by simply slipping on a shirt. They were cooling down in the locker room after training on the field, although Jamie was quite sure Haru had only called it training to trick him into some frivolous racing games.

'Your princess and her friends. Sometimes at lunch and during free periods I cannot find you anywhere.' Haru glanced over from where he was pulling his tie into position, his heavily lashed brown eyes as comforting as hot chocolate. 'It's like you vanish into thin air.'

His gaze was soft, his tone sweet, and, despite what Jamie had seen he was capable of, he didn't seem like a Partizan at all.

'We've all been through a lot. We like to keep to ourselves,' Jamie replied, avoiding any mention of Lottie's hidden study.

'Do you talk about Leviathan?'

Jamie's head caught in his T-shirt, leaving him stuck in the fabric until Haru's hands carefully pulled it into position. It made him feel like a child, and angry heat bloomed in his cheeks at the intrusive question and the patronizing gesture, yet he didn't leave.

'Why are you worrying about something that doesn't concern you?' he asked instead, the words coming out harshly in his embarrassment. 'And why have you come to Rosewood?'

'I worry about anything that causes you or your master trouble, Jamie-kun,' Haru said, calling him by the pet name he'd used in Japan. 'Your well-being is important too.'

When Haru smiled up at him from tying his shoes, Jamie's boundaries instantly dissolved. It felt like Haru could melt away any misgivings he ever had like butter in the sun. It worked every time and soon he found himself following Haru through the corridors, away from the gym, to Dame Bolter's office, alone with him again.

When they had learned that Haru was taking a sabbatical at Rosewood, Jamie had been filled with confusion. Partizans were allowed them once they reached the age of twenty, and subsequently every five years after, but all the Partizans he knew of turned them down. It simply wasn't the done thing. He kept thinking of Haru's master, Sayuri. Perhaps they weren't close; perhaps Haru was planning to quit being a Partizan altogether. It was as if he treated his position as nothing more than a job that he was free to leave at any moment. Jamie couldn't imagine being so casual about his own vocation to protect Ellie. It was Haru's apathy that fascinated him so much. But was it apathy or something else – something more dangerous?

Jamie blocked out the thought. He hated that he could never trust anyone. He hated that he was so cold to this person who only seemed to want to be friends. Why couldn't he just let himself believe in someone else for once? Why did he always have to make it so hard?

'Just a second; I have something for you,' Haru called behind him.

The Conch House mother's office was filled with trophies and cultural artefacts from her travels during her time as an Olympic athlete, all of them glittering proudly on the mahogany shelving behind her desk. The room was also immaculate, with virtually no sign of human disturbance except for a small wastepaper basket in the corner that was filled almost exclusively with orange peels.

From the doorway Jamie looked at his companion, who was now searching through the house mother's top desk drawer. 'Should you be rifling through that?' he asked, lifting an eyebrow.

Haru chuckled. 'Don't worry – this is my drawer. I do a lot of errands for her in this office so she let me have this for my things.'

Curiosity getting the better of him, Jamie followed into the office, leaning over the desk to take a peek into Haru's drawer of 'things'.

The inside was a mess, entirely at odds with Dame Bolter's perfectly ordered room, and it was no wonder he couldn't seem to find what he was looking for. Jamie was about to take a step back when his attention snagged on something that seemed out of place, a tattered old locked box.

'What's that? he asked, pointing to it.

Haru pulled it out gently, as if it were a sacred item made of gold and not a simple wooden box with a withered lock. 'This?'

Jamie nodded.

'Would you believe me if I said it's where I keep my secret diary?' he replied, grinning as he gazed at it.

Jamie regarded Haru. If Jamie tilted his head, the oak beams and shadows from the vases of sunflowers on the shelves behind Haru gave the strange illusion that he had sprouted ram's horns, his smile turning demonic.

'Fine, don't tell me,' Jamie huffed, taking his place back at the door and refusing to bite what was obviously bait. 'I'm not interested anyway.'

'I am not lying,' Haru protested, leaning down to return the box to the drawer. 'I will show you what's inside when we are closer.' He seemed to ponder for a second and then changed his response. 'When you've earned it.'

Jamie frowned, trying to figure out what was going on behind Haru's easy-going smile as he continued to rummage through the drawer. He was so lost in his thoughts that he jumped when Haru shot up, presenting him with a brightly coloured packet that was covered in Japanese text. 'Here it is.'

Haru was so pleased that it took Jamie a moment to register what he was holding.

'Are those . . . cat treats?'

This only seemed to amuse Haru, who gave Jamie a mischievous look. 'They're for the little beast you brought back with you from Tokyo,' he said, tossing it at Jamie who caught it one-handed. 'The cats at Takeshin always loved that brand.'

Jamie hardly had time to wonder if it was safe for Haru to know about Vampy when Haru read his mind.

'Don't worry – I will not tell anyone about your little beast,' Haru assured him, before stepping round him and blocking the exit. 'Where will you go when you are old enough to take your sabbatical?'

The question came flying out of the blue, and Jamie was sure he saw Haru's smile curl a little at the edges, like the sly grin of a fox. Waving him off, Jamie moved to duck underneath him, but Haru didn't budge.

'I doubt I'll ever take one and, quite frankly, I'm surprised you took one yourself. How does Sayuri feel about you leaving her?' Jamie asked confidently. 'And for you to pick Rosewood . . . Why would you want to spend your sabbatical here, another school?'

Haru didn't even blink. 'It's part of the job that we are allowed to take a sabbatical. Or are you suggesting you don't respect this rule?'

'No,' said Jamie, 'I respect the rules, particularly the one where I make sure my master is secure at *all* times.'

'And does your master feel secure knowing you feel that way?'

Haru's words conjured up an electric cityscape in Jamie's mind, with static in the air that hinted at a storm. No longer was Jamie in Dame Bolter's orange-peel-scented room but on a rooftop in Tokyo, his nostrils filled with the smoke from celebratory fireworks. The Goat Man had asked him something similar that night, cornering him with questions they both knew the answer to. Not long after, he had found out that the Goat Man was no demon or mysterious stranger – he was Claude Wolfson.

'It's not the same for me.' Jamie stopped short, surprised that the words had left his mouth at all, and, like a reward for his honesty, Haru finally moved.

Shuffling past his fellow Partizan, Jamie swiftly headed towards the building's reception room where only a set of glass double doors separated them from the rest of the school.

'You're still a Partizan,' Haru called after him. 'You're entitled to time –'

'I owe the Maravish family for taking me in.' Jamie stopped and turned to face Haru. He felt his shoulders sag, not realizing how tense he'd been. 'And that's why I can't relax until I find out what Leviathan are planning and I can stop the man responsible for all this. I need to find where he's hiding.'

The shadowy figure of the goat-masked man morphed in Jamie's mind, transforming into the painting of Claude from the palace hallway, inky-black hair and leering eyes the elegant and flamboyant green of a peacock feather. Those eyes haunted his dreams. He had to make sure they never turned themselves on Lottie.

'Is that how they make you feel, Jamie-kun? That you owe them?'

Jamie scowled, snapping out of his thoughts with a jolt, his fingers uncurling as if Claude were escaping his clasp. He looked at Haru leaning casually against the wall and he remembered himself, turning hot at how rude he'd just been to a superior Partizan. He was at once distracted by his shoes, noticing that the laces had come undone on one foot.

Haru noticed too.

'Maybe I am misunderstanding,' Haru continued, kneeling down to tie them before Jamie could stop him. 'But it seems to me that if you're trying to stop the man who has caused you all this trouble and you haven't made any progress so far, perhaps you are looking in the wrong places . . .'

Haru held his hand out for Jamie to help him up, regarding him with an inquisitive look in his eye.

Jamie paused before reaching out to take it, mulling over Haru's words. They only reiterated a thought he'd already had: that he was missing something. That if he was going to keep Lottie and Ellie safe and figure out Claude's plan, he had to prepare for the possibility he'd find out something unpleasant. The writing in his wardrobe appeared in his head, and the question Lottie had been so worried about swam into his mind.

Why is Jamie your Partizan?

Looking in the wrong places, he thought. Like the words were a mantra or an important clue.

'To answer your other question,' said Haru, 'I wanted to be close to you.'

'What?'

'The reason I came to Rosewood.' Haru's fingers locked around Jamie's, their palms pressed together, skin smooth and rough in all the right places. 'I wanted to get closer to you.'

In all Jamie's life he had never had anyone say anything so honest to him. He was shocked that someone would expose themselves so willingly. He became hyper aware of the touch of Haru's fingers on his.

At Rosewood he'd learned how his appearance and attitude affected other students, who giggled and blushed when he walked past. It was only since being away that he'd admitted to himself that he might be capable of having these feelings for other people, for people like Lottie, but Partizans were not supposed to get distracted. Not in a million years would he have considered that Haru might be added to that list of distractions.

Jamie pulled away in one swift movement. 'Haru, I'm not sure I –'

'Looks like my time is up.' Haru's eyes were looking out through the glass doors into the grounds.

On the other side, blue from the shadows of the final seconds of sunlight, Lottie was sitting on a bench, waiting for Jamie. She gave him a wave when his eyes landed on her, round cheeks turning into ripe apples as she gave him a beaming smile, the kind that made his chest hurt and his stomach twist in a way he'd given in to.

'I've stolen you away for well over an hour now, Jamie. You should go back to your princess.' He gave Jamie a soft push towards the door, ignoring his protests, and despite himself Jamie thought of the box again, part of him wanting to open it. 'We'll train again next week.'

As usual, Haru left him feeling confused. But Lottie, and most likely his princess, were waiting for him. The crown always came first.

12

Walking through the school in the last hour of curfew felt like travelling through a city preparing for imminent disaster, everyone rushing to do whatever they needed. Ellie was no exception. Scurrying through the grounds, she felt like a rodent, not wanting to get caught on her private scavenging mission, and since learning about Haru there was never a moment when she didn't feel watched.

She ducked her head irritably as she stepped past another security guard in a black jacket on her way into the art block, his presence a reminder of everything she'd caused. The school didn't feel safe any more; it felt like a cage – one that Lottie was getting blamed for, one in which Lottie and all her friends were also trapped, with Haru as their keeper. And it was all Ellie's fault.

It had been hours since the incident in Anastacia's room. The images in Ellie's mind of Jamie on the field with their enemy and Lottie's crumbling face as she admitted to yet another secret she'd been harbouring to protect her burned a hole in Ellie's chest, leaving her feeling hollow. Round her neck like a lead, the wolf pendant and her family locket tangled. She ignored their heavy pull.

With quick, echoing steps through the grand mezzanine where Rosewood displayed its most prominent art pieces, Ellie shuddered at each looming shadow from a statue or dead-eyed stare from a painted portrait. Picking up her pace, she glanced around to make sure she wasn't being followed, and squeezed herself through the double doors at the very back of the hall. The doors closed behind her with a heavy groan; the sound was ominously similar to a tomb being shut.

No longer was Ellie surrounded by the bright, open space of the modern art block; what lay in front of her was the winding, dusty labyrinth of the old building and, if she completed the maze, she'd find who she needed at its centre.

Every school has a notorious clique. Students with crocodile smiles and predatory stares, whose presence inspires rabbit-hearted fear. At Rosewood this clique was a group of art enthusiasts. They called themselves the Artistocracy, and they delved into the more shocking extremes of artistic expression. Theatre of cruelty, gory prosthetics and – the reason Ellie was here now – tattoos.

This is what she had to do if she was ever going to make everything right again – leave a mark that wouldn't let her forget, that would stop her from caving in the moment she saw Lottie. She had to stop being selfish, no matter how much it hurt.

With confident strides, Ellie pushed through corridors of discarded and damaged art, dismembered hands from statues and wispy sheets of torn canvas brushing her skin with curiosity, until she reached the winding stairs to the now-unused photography department, and made her ascent.

At the top of the stairs, the floorboards were misshapen from water damage, twisted in a way that gave the illusion of wooden waves, their current pulling all who entered towards the black door of the old darkroom on the opposite side.

Ignoring the boarded-up doors in her peripheral vision, Ellie headed straight to the one with little baby-doll arms reaching out, beckoning her forward.

With no thought of turning back, Ellie knocked on the door. Rustling and murmurs could be heard from the other side, and finally the first of the two-door gateways opened with a sigh like an airlock.

'What do you want?' A mismatched pair of white and black irises appeared from a sliding peephole in the second door, eyelids heavy with blood-red shadow and intricate swirling eyeliner like spiderwebs.

The Rosewood art department was not a realm Ellie usually ventured into; she preferred the simple, straightforward worlds of sports and science. Art was confusing. It didn't have solutions or finite methods, instead consisting of abstract ideas that were intimidating to engage with.

'I'm here to see Stephanie Gallo.' Ellie refused to be intimidated by this stony un-welcome. 'I heard she can help me with something.'

The sliding panel slammed shut, followed by more murmurs and whispers, louder this time, until the panel opened once more, this time to reveal a set of dark brown eyes and marker pen eyebrows decorated by an array of metal bands and rings.

'You're that little pink princess's sidekick, aren't you? The one that turned the school into a prison,' Eyebrows asked, tilting her head back, nostrils flaring around a septum piercing as if she were sniffing her out.

'Don't talk about her like that – unless you want to take this outside.' The response was instantaneous, an electric current that she couldn't stop. She could never control herself when it came to Lottie, and that's exactly why she was here.

'OK, OK, we won't make fun of your little girlfriend,' Eyebrows said, relenting, but Ellie could tell by the way she scrunched her nose that she'd learned her lesson. 'Do you have payment?'

'Yes,' Ellie said quickly. 'But I'll only give it to Stephanie.'

Once more the panel slid shut and once more the murmuring started up, until the door opened again, revealing the full extent of Eyebrows and Spiderwebs. Ellie didn't have much time to take them in, only catching a glimpse of their torn uniforms and brightly coloured hair. She stepped inside and Eyebrows shut the door behind them with a thud that left the tiny corridor in total darkness. The two of them strolled towards a second door with ease, and Ellie could almost believe they could see in the dark.

The loud groan of the heavy darkroom door was followed by a flood of red and blue light.

'Welcome to the Parlour,' Spiderwebs said with a grin, revealing a surprisingly elegant gap tooth.

The Parlour, as they called it, was one of the darkrooms that had been commandeered by the Artistocracy. The windowless room was hazy with bergamot incense that scarcely covered up the smoke that clung to their clothes. Displayed proudly was a selection of shock-value art pieces, ripped-up baby dolls whose limbs grew out of the furnishings, their dead eyes cut out and glued to the walls, watching all who entered. There were two others in the room. One of them was someone Ellie knew from her maths class – Max. Their hair was shaved short and dyed in red and white stripes. And finally there sat their leader, leaning back casually in a black-velvet chair with her legs flung over the armrest. This was who Ellie had come looking for.

Stephanie Gallo was large in both height and build, and all of her was intimidatingly gorgeous. She wore her black hair in a styled beehive with flicks of her natural tight curls peeping out round her neck like an elegant necklace. Rumour was that hidden away beneath her shirt, only visible in private, was a secret garden of floral tattoos. While the other members of the Artistocracy were the children of models turned actors turned philanthropists, and heirs to organic superfood brands that were only affordable to the wealthiest clean-livers, Stephanie was different. The story went that Stephanie's mother was an ex-Bollywood star from Jaipur, who had the most beautiful voice in the world, capable of creating music that could make the toughest man fall madly in love. She'd made her fortune by marrying a string of wealthy men who'd mysteriously died in tragic and un-expected ways. Ellie doubted the story was true, but Stephanie certainly walked around with enough confidence and flare that it was easy to believe she'd inherited her mother's golden tongue and could talk herself out of any situation.

'I always wondered when you'd pay me a visit.' Stephanie's voice was deep as the sea and equally as mesmerizing. 'You know, you'd fit in pretty well with us. We're all queer and angry too.'

'I'm terrible at art,' Ellie said coolly.

'No one's terrible at art,' Stephanie chided, fixing her hair in a clamshell mirror. 'I hear you want one of my henna tattoos.'

Ellie nodded, trying not to be drawn in by the push and pull of her voice.

'You have payment?'

'I do,' Ellie said, crushing the screaming doubt in her mind.

'We'll see about that,' Eyebrows cackled, taking a spot on a purple beanbag.

'That was Gem and Paris who greeted you at the door,' Stephanie said, gesturing for Ellie to take a seat in the wooden chair next to her. 'And this is Max. They've told me lots about you.'

'They're in my maths class,' Ellie replied inanely, giving Max a little wave. She was relieved when they returned the gesture. Having someone she recognized was a small comfort.

'So, what's your payment?' Stephanie asked, leaning her plump chin on her hand, her smooth sapphire-painted lips pursing with anticipation.

Money is boring to people who already have an endless supply of it, so Stephanie Gallo offered tattoos for payment in kind. What Stephanie wanted was secrets – and Ellie had the perfect one.

Reaching to her chest like she was reaching for her very heart, Ellie grabbed the locket that usually sat on her bedside table and, ignoring the static that stung her skin when her fingers brushed her wolf pendant, she freed it from under her shirt. 'Open this.' Looking away as if she were committing some unspeakable act, Ellie dropped the locket in Stephanie's hand.

With a barely audible click, the locket popped open. Stephanie leaned in closer, face contorting to get a better look. 'What? This is just you as a little girl and . . .' Stephanie's echoing and sultry voice trailed off like the tide drifting, realization dawning. 'Holy crap!' she said, her eyes shooting up to get a better look at Ellie. 'This whole time you were the real princess.' She was practically hissing, although her expression made it clear that she was thinking that no one in a million years would have guessed Ellie was royalty.

'Is that a good enough secret for you?' Ellie asked.

Stephanie's eyes stayed firmly locked on Ellie, until she laughed. A gorgeous, hearty cackle.

'What tattoo do you want?' she asked, still smiling. 'Though I must warn you for health and safety reasons, on extremely rare occasions people experience reactions from henna.'

'I know,' Ellie said. In fact, she had first-hand experience of being one of those 'extremely rare occasions' that had left a tiny scar on her foot, and secretly she hoped her tattoo today would also burn a permanent mark.

Ignoring the way Stephanie's eyes narrowed on her suspiciously, Ellie pulled a scrunched-up bit of paper from her trouser pocket and flattened it out on the desk to reveal the simple calligraphy depicting the Maravish word *bol'shbrota*.

'What does it mean?' Stephanie asked, already reaching for a silvery cone filled with henna mixture.

'It means to do something painful for the sake of someone else.'

'Like cruel to be kind?'

'Sort of,' Ellie replied, watching the sharp point disappear beneath the earthy mixture. 'Except this means you're being cruel to yourself as well.'

'So what are you doing that's so cruel?'

The smell of the henna caught in Ellie's nose, a thick scent like clay, and she chewed her lip before answering. 'I'm going to rescue a little princess from a nasty pack of wolves.'

Ellie made it back to the dorm just before curfew.

Easing the door open carefully to not make a scene, she found Lottie locking something away in her bedside drawer.

'Ellie!' Lottie rushed over to wrap her up in a hug she didn't deserve, but she leaned into it anyway, filling herself up with the sweet smell of roses that clung to Lottie's hair. 'Where were you? It's nearly curfew.'

'Sorry about earlier,' Ellie whispered, ignoring how her tattoo hissed at her. 'I've sorted my head out.'

Lottie beamed. 'Good. I knew you would. Do you want to get started on your Florence Ivy tribute for the PoP?' she added, already rifling through her books. 'It'll be a nice distraction, and we can talk about Haru tomorrow.'

'Sure.' Ellie smiled back, allowing herself this moment to take her in, her golden curls and tickled pink cheeks, the way she spread warmth around her like she was the sun itself.

Of course she was still hiding something. Ellie knew that. Lottie was always worrying about her, always trying to help, and that was Ellie's fault for dragging her into her world, but it wouldn't matter soon – none of this would matter soon. Not now that Ellie had made her decision.

13

An entire week passed before Lottie received her first reply from Claude. Class had ended and it was time for another of Jamie and Haru's get-togethers when she saw the telltale manila envelope winking at her from her cubbyhole. The moment Lottie saw it, she grabbed it – along with her other post – without looking too closely at it and headed straight for Binah's.

'It's here,' Lottie said, as Binah opened the door to let her in.

Stratus House had the most modern dorms, the building having been entirely refurbished recently. Binah's room was an oddity with its modern architecture and furniture paired with her collection of old books and enough plants that you might think you were in a greenhouse. Her room smelled of tangy incense, rainbow reflections dancing around the room where the light from the large circle window hit her collections of crystals.

Sitting down at a low table where Binah was already pouring cups of chamomile tea from a frog-shaped teapot, Lottie felt more like they were about to perform witchcraft than go over a letter.

With surprisingly steady fingers, Lottie pulled out the letters she'd shoved in her bag and got to work on ripping open the manila envelope. She pulled out elegant parchment paper, the heady scent of spiced wine catching in her nose. She peered into the envelope. 'There's another card.'

'Let's read the letter first.'

Nodding, Lottie lay the paper out flat on the table, ready for her next correspondence from the Master of Leviathan.

To my ever-curious niece,

I'm glad your youthful humour can prevail at this difficult time, although it does not give me hope that you are adjusting to my terms gracefully and with dignity.

Haru keeps me well informed, and it would take only one less-than-accommodating reply for me to decide this arrangement is not working. In light of this, perhaps you will try to refer to your uncle, who is responsible for the well-being of your friends, in an appropriate fashion.

Your desire to see the wolf in the crown is rather ironic. The joke will be lost on you, of course, so until it becomes clear perhaps this image and message will tide you over.

Remember, wolves are hunters too.

PS Your Partizan is the wrong that needs righting.

'Well, this is entirely useless,' Lottie grumbled, pushing the letter away.

Binah chuckled. 'Oh, Uncle Wolfson, you aren't generous with your clues, are you?' She grabbed the letter and Lottie couldn't help conjuring up an image of Claude and Binah having tea together, something so unfathomable that it made her shiver. 'What's the clue?'

Lottie snapped out of the bizarre thought and emptied the rest of the envelope's contents on to the low table.

The card that landed in front of them was much the same as the one she'd received before, only this did not depict a majestic and regal creature. Instead of a stag, a snarling wolf was drawn in gold ink wearing the same crown as the stag. It's what she'd wanted, to see the wolf in the crown – yet there was something grotesque about the image, as if this wolf had been feasting on the deer from the other card.

'What are you trying to tell me, Claude?' Lottie whispered at the wolf.

'Is there any way you could tell Sayuri or the rest of Banshee? Maybe they'd have some more information?' asked Binah. Lottie had filled Binah in about Banshee, Sayuri's secret biker gang who had sworn to get revenge against Leviathan, and how they'd come to be allies. It was clear that Binah was itching to meet them. 'What about that girl Emelia you told me about?'

Lottie cringed. Although she'd never met the girl, Emelia had become something of an idol in her mind, and part of Lottie desperately wanted to meet her. After having been kidnapped by Leviathan a year ago and deemed useless, Emelia had taken it upon herself to get to the bottom of the kidnapping, figuring out completely on her own that the princess of Maradova was at the centre of Leviathan's plot. Emelia and Sayuri had practically handed her everything she'd needed to figure out that Claude was the

Master of Leviathan, and all she'd done was walk them right into a trap. If Lottie was ever going to pay Emelia back or get her respect, she had to bring her something useful and prove to her that she wasn't simply the bratty princess that had inflicted Claude upon them all. Finding out what Claude's goal was; that was the only way she could help anyone.

Lottie sighed, already packing up the letter and clue. 'I'm sure that Haru will find a way to intercept any letters I send. It would ruin their cover and they've been through enough.'

Watching Lottie with narrow eyes, Binah began to stir her tea in an almost hypnotic way, like she was trying to extract something from Lottie's head with the pull of the hot water. 'Well, why don't you open your other letter?'

Lottie stared at the other post she'd thrown on the table.

'It looks like Ollie's handwriting,' Binah said casually, and Lottie paused, wondering how she could know such a thing, but she didn't have time to dwell on it.

In some strange parallel, inside was a letter and a card, the first of which was indeed from Ollie, her oldest childhood friend. His handwriting was as messy as ever, which would have been funny if not for the words.

Dear Lottie,

I hate sending you this, because I know you don't want it and I thought about throwing it in the bin and not even bothering you with it, but then I thought that if I was you, which I'm not obviously, but if I was, I'd want to be

112

prepared, so here it is and I'm sorry. Feel free to throw it away. If he comes round, I'll tell him to go away.

Apologies again. Hope you're OK.

Your pal (who will absolutely throw an egg at anyone if you asked him to) – Ollie

Blinking, she slowly removed the card from the envelope, the smell and the memories getting stronger. In gaudy yellow text surrounded by a beach covered in palm trees the postcard read *Havana*. She knew who it was from and what it meant, her eyes skimming the words in time with her thumping heartbeat.

You have not been living in the old house.

Thump!

It's become necessary to sell it.

Thump!

Your father.

A world she'd locked away came tapping on the door, asking to be let in again.

Like a phantom coming back to haunt her, the room filled with the smell of cheap alcohol that could almost be mistaken for hairspray and with it came a flash of shutter-speed memories: crying on the baggy trouser legs of a gloomy unshaven man, her mother's sold belongings, the bedding at Ollie's house when they took her in, the first time she saw her stepmother's blood-red hair, the quiet in the attic when she was all alone.

Lottie blinked, unsure how long she'd been gazing into nothing.

'This is useless to me,' she said simply, locking her eyes with Binah as if expecting her to agree.

Binah, having clearly read the card, stared at her with curious confusion, her mind untangling the scene in front of her. 'Perhaps if you told Ellie about this, and Claude's letters,' she offered, testing the waters. 'It seems like something you should be tackling together.'

'No.' Lottie stood up, stony-faced, and shoved the postcard in her bag with all the care one might give a used tissue.

'But, Lottie, that postcard is –'

'It doesn't matter.'

It was impossible for Lottie to pinpoint what was happening in her mind. The door slammed shut as she bolted up the memories and locked them away again. That wasn't her life any more. As long as she could be useful to the Wolfsons that would never have to be her life again. She just had to stay focused.

'The only thing that matters is that I find out Claude's plan so I can protect everyone,' she said firmly, downing her tea and making her way to the door. 'This is my duty.'

'What are you going to do?' Binah asked.

'I'm going to get info on Haru. He must have something we can use against them.'

And, with that, she left Binah to ponder how much was changing without Ellie or Lottie realizing.

With every step away from Stratus Side, Lottie reminded herself that she was a Portman – Ellie's Portman, playing the role of princess in order to protect the real princess from harm – and with burning fingers she latched on to her wolf pendant, her heart thundering beneath it. There was fear there, a creeping, foul voice that whispered how her life might look without Ellie and her job, but she squeezed the pendant tighter, pushing the thought away. This was not something she needed to give any attention to as long as she did right by the Wolfsons, which is what she was doing right now.

Lottie decided it would be best to wait for Jamie to finish his allotted hour with Haru. Trying to leech information from Jamie after their little 'dates' was probably her best bet to find something she could use against the other Partizan.

It was easy enough to find the pair, Jamie having told her he'd be helping Haru water flowers in the rose garden, and, sure enough, she spotted them from a distance.

Jamie instantly saw her, pausing where he was gently misting something, and Lottie felt an odd pull in her chest. There was something so candid about it, nothing like his recent intensity. Before she could dwell on it, Haru locked on to her, smiling fox-like while he waved his fingers in a taunting greeting. It took all Lottie's strength not to roll her eyes.

Haru patted Jamie on the back, dismissing him from the flower cage in which he'd trapped the unsuspecting Partizan for the past hour.

Jamie's face heated up with that intensity again and he marched away with a sheen of sweat on his brow. Lottie took a cautious step back when she saw how furiously he was walking towards her. Something was wrong and it made her heart flutter in a way she couldn't make sense of.

'What's wrong?' he demanded. 'I thought we were going to meet back at the dorm.'

Lottie baulked, realizing Jamie had assumed she was in trouble and the fire surrounding him was purely protective. It made her feel weird, her stomach twisting. When had Jamie started making her feel so nervous again?

'It's nothing. I just thought it would be nice if –'

Jamie let out an exasperated sigh, completely cutting her off. 'Why didn't you tell me?' he demanded.

Lottie froze. *Did he know?* 'What are you talking about?' she asked innocently.

Avoiding his eyes, Lottie found her gaze resting on his chest and, as she watched its gentle rise and fall, it was impossible not to notice the angelic curve of his muscles, a testament to how powerful he was under his usually stoic demeanour. Before she could stop herself, she was thinking of how he'd cradled her against that powerful body on the lip of the Rose Wood only weeks ago, and ever since then she couldn't escape that look he gave her, that stare she couldn't get out of her head. She snapped back up to face it in full force.

'You had a fight with Ellie,' he said matter-of-factly, and she winced, partly in relief and partly in guilt.

'It's fine. Nothing we won't get past.' She shrugged, hoping he wouldn't push it further. 'Having the occasional fight is an occupational hazard when you're friends with Ellie.'

This didn't seem to satisfy Jamie, but he kept his lips tightly shut. The two of them quickly fell into a rhythm beside one another and made their way back to Ivy Wood.

Lottie was just about to begin her subtle questioning about Haru as they cut through into the empty dining hall, when Jamie paused, turning to her.

116

'Have you started on your PoP presentation?'

Lottie's brain stalled, having entirely forgotten that was even a thing she needed to do. 'Oh, that . . .'

'I thought as much.' Jamie tutted under his breath. 'What about the twins? Have you spoken to them? Percy says Micky's having a really hard time at the moment.'

Lottie recoiled inwardly. She hadn't spoken to them; it was like the whole thing had slipped out of her mind, blocked by Claude and Leviathan and Haru. 'I haven't even asked them how they're doing,' she admitted.

This was not how Lottie had intended this conversation to go at all.

Embarrassed, Lottie made her way to the door, only for Jamie to slam it shut again, leaning over her where he held it down with his arm, leaving no way out.

'That's not like you.' His voice was soft, despite the fire in his eyes. 'You're kind and thoughtful. You always worry about your friends.' Jamie's tone made her feel like an apprentice who'd disappointed their master, and it stung enough to make her flinch.

'I've had a lot on my mind.' Lottie raised her head to meet his gaze, and he had that look in his eye again, the golden stars in his irises burning intensely like they might set fire to the whole world.

It was dark in the dining hall with all the lights off, the space feeling odd at this time of day with no one else around.

Trying to understand what he was thinking, Lottie's eyes wandered over parts of him she didn't usually notice, the fading scar on his eyebrow, his slightly crooked nose and then down to his ever-frowning lips. Like Pandora's box, they quivered ever so slightly, a curious lock on whatever words were inside his head, and before she could stop herself she asked a question to try to open them up.

'Why do you keep looking at me like that?'

The words slammed into him, his skin prickling, the stars in his eyes dimming.

'Like what?' Jamie countered, voice pitching, something she was not used to hearing from him.

'I don't know. You tell me?' Lottie could hear the way she sounded, like a bratty child, but she couldn't stop herself.

'Lottie,' he began, ironically raising an eyebrow in a way Lottie totally deserved, 'I assure you I have no idea what you're talking about.'

'You and Ellie,' she spluttered, her hands flying out in exasperation. 'You both keep looking at me and it's starting to, I don't know –' she sighed, knowing she'd never be able to explain it properly – 'it's starting to make me nervous in a weird way.'

For a split second Jamie's mask dropped, and beneath was a pained look, not angry or fiery like before but sad. It was the kind of sadness you feel when you're a child and you find yourself alone and lost, and it made Lottie's heart lurch because she knew it all too well. And then it was gone, blinked away as fast as it appeared.

'So let me get this straight,' Jamie said, the curve of a smile sneaking on to his lips. 'You want us to stop looking at you?'

'I –' Lottie felt at a loss, sure she'd seen something deeply personal pass over Jamie and not sure how to engage with it, so instead she breathed out sharply, sending the thought floating away. 'No, that's not what . . . Forget it, everything's fine, me and Ellie will be fine, you and me are fine, and you two can both keep looking at me as much and however you want.'

She made for the door, but once more Jamie stopped her. 'Wait, I didn't mean that.' He shook his head, disappointed in himself. 'I'm being as bad as Haru and his ridiculous box.'

Lottie's ears pricked. 'Box?'

'Yes, he has this box he says he keeps his –' Jamie made little inverted commas with his fingers – ' "secret diary" inside, and made this whole ridiculous spiel about how he'd show it to me but only after I've earned it.' He rolled his eyes. 'It's entirely annoying and childish.'

'What does the box look like?' She tried not to sound frantic, but she was desperate, itching for anything she could use, anything that would help the Wolfsons and keep her useful.

'It's plain oak, no bigger than a jewellery box, with a lock at the front,' Jamie relayed, finally opening the door, and the two of them walked out together. 'He keeps it in the drawer Dame Bolter gave him in her office.'

Lottie smiled up at him, determined not to let anything slip. 'Sounds very annoying. But it also sounds like you two might be becoming friends,' she added, testing the water.

'Maybe,' Jamie replied, and Lottie's blood went cold. 'If he'd stop being such an insufferable tease.'

They walked in relative silence the rest of the way back to the dorm, Lottie pondering everything Jamie had said. Excusing herself once they arrived, she headed to her room to change into some more comfortable clothes for dinner, trying not to dwell on the fact she'd hardly seen Ellie all day. She felt overwhelmed with information, everything floating around her head with no way of pinning it down. The only thing she knew for certain was that she had to get that box and see what was really inside.

With the box still on her mind, Lottie slipped on a sweater, but she paused on her way out, staring at the open bag on her bed.

Lottie grabbed it and pulled out the postcard from her father. Without a second thought she marched over to the bin and let it fall into the trash.

14

It was a Thursday in the first week of October when the weather started to turn. The air was no longer heavy with sweet pollen. Instead a fresh, earthy chill had taken its place. Soon the leaves would turn, the ground would harden and another year would be over.

Jamie had always thought his favourite time of year was winter, when the world was still, calm and orderly. It wasn't until he'd started to spend more time away from the cold and desolate Maravish landscape that he'd begun to realize that, in fact, summer was his favourite season. He liked how unpredictable it was, the juxtaposition of the storms and heat, the way the days lasted forever, and how the citrine light spread into every dark spot with unstoppable resolve.

Why do you keep looking at me like that?

Jamie glanced up at the phantom sound of Lottie's voice, his ears playing tricks, to see Raphael staring at him from across their table outdoors. Vampy sat to the side, greedily nibbling at one of the Japanese treats.

'Jamie,' Raphael repeated, rubbing the top of the cat's head. 'I said, why don't you look it up? The Milton quote.'

'Yes, of course,' he replied, shaking his head clear. 'One second.'

It was lunchtime at Rosewood and Jamie had promised to help Raphael and Percy with their English coursework, not realizing Raphael wanted to study by the Ivy dorms so he could spend some time with the devil cat. Jamie was starting to wonder if Vampy had put some kind of spell on everyone, because he certainly couldn't see what everyone loved about the spoiled little beast. As if he could hear his thoughts, the cat turned to him, big yellow eyes like moons dipping in and out of view when he slow-blinked.

'*You OK?*' Percy signed, raising an eyebrow. '*You still haven't really talked about the run-in with . . .*' He paused to make pretend horns with his fingers, his pale skin and black hair making a surprisingly convincing image of a demon.

'*I'm fine,*' Jamie signed, swatting the conversation away. '*Nothing I'm not trained to deal with.*'

The truth was, he hadn't really thought about what happened in Tokyo since they'd found out his attacker had been Claude. The image had become warped, like the whole event had taken place underwater. Claude's face was so familiar, always watching you when you entered the palace, that he'd become as grounding as gazing at his reflection. To think that emerald-eyed friend was the man behind that Goat Mask didn't make sense.

'*Whatever you say,*' Percy signed, scoffing. He and Raphael shared a glance.

'*I can see that there's something bothering you two,*' Jamie signed and said at the same time. '*Just say what you need to, so we can move on.*'

Percy and Raphael gave each other one more look, before Raphael cracked.

'We're worried about you.' He ran a hand through his coiffed hair. 'Ever since you got back from Tokyo you've been so intense. Even more than usual, as though you're constantly on the lookout for an enemy, or someone to fight.'

'*And it's not just that,*' Percy continued, his sharp features contorting into a scowl. '*We don't think you're processing what happened properly. We just want to know you have someone you can talk about it with. Lottie, maybe?*'

'No!' His protestation erupted too fast, and they shared a look of exasperation, not even bothering to hide it from him.

'She has far too much on her mind right now after the discovery about her uncle, don't you think?' Jamie posed the question with sincerity, watching their faces cloud with shame, which he refused to feel bad for inflicting. This was a promise he'd made to himself – that this year he was going to protect Lottie from everything and not be the cause of her problems.

Why do you keep looking at me like that? He heard her words again, and a well of disappointment opened up in his stomach.

'Then what about Haru?' Raphael offered. 'Didn't you two get close while you were out there?'

'Perhaps,' Jamie said.

Haru was busy; he had sports classes to teach and files to organize, and Dame Bolter made sure she was getting the most out of her assistant, which meant they only got to spend about an hour a week together. Since their conversation at the Conch House gym, he hadn't pushed Jamie on more sensitive topics, the two of them steering clear of any complicated

123

Partizan talk or mention of Haru's desire for them to become closer. Instead they either trained in silence or worked on quiet tasks like tending the Rose Garden, all the while keeping their relative distance – yet even now, at the sound of his name, it was as if Jamie could feel the phantom warmth of their entwined fingers.

The truth was, if anyone was going to be able to help him find his enemy so he could finally find peace, he was sure that Haru would be more than happy to help. He always was. After all, he was the one who'd suggested Jamie was looking in the wrong places.

'*I think you should speak to him,*' Percy signed with a knowing, caustic gaze. '*Because if your vocation is to protect your princess, then I'm sure she'd feel safer knowing you're OK too, wouldn't she?*'

Jamie nearly laughed, impressed at how quickly Percy had turned his argument against him, but more so he was amazed at the absurdity of all this. *Protecting his princess* was indeed his vocation, except now he had two princesses he needed to protect and they were the most confusing, stubborn girls he'd ever met.

Just then Raphael and Percy looked up. Someone was approaching from behind him. From the heavy step of boots, he knew it was Ellie before he even turned round.

'Hey, Jamie, can I speak to you?' Her voice was hard, the kind of hardness she only had when Lottie wasn't around to soften her.

'Is something wrong?'

'I just need to talk to you.' Her face was bare and her eyes puffy, a sign she still wasn't sleeping. 'Come on – it's important.'

He picked up his bags and shrugged a goodbye to Percy and Raphael. 'Where's Lottie? I thought you two had made up.'

'We did, but . . .' She looked over her shoulder, making sure Raphael was out of earshot and Percy couldn't see her mouth. 'That's who I need to talk to you about.'

Seeing him tense, Ellie rolled her eyes. 'You don't have to kill anyone just yet.' She tried to laugh, but the sound was hollow. 'Come on.'

She led him to a quiet spot on the top floor of Ivy Wood, the two of them nestled in a bay window, looking out over the Rose Wood where the trees writhed in the wind, branches swaying. They sat for a while, Jamie allowing his princess to mull over what she needed to say.

'I've been thinking,' she said at last, her voice as fragile as a lullaby. 'About our conversation in the woods in Japan, and everything that's happened with Claude and Leviathan and my family, how it's hurting everyone and . . .' She paused to take a breath. 'I don't want to do this any more. Especially not to Lottie.'

Jamie could see how hard it was for her to get this all out. 'What are you saying?' he asked, wanting to make sure he really understood before weighing in – only he didn't expect her answer to nearly knock him over.

'I think we need to accept that we can't act on what we feel for her. I know you like her too, in the same way I do, as more than a friend.' The words hit him like a freight train. The fiery pit in his stomach that raged constantly with a thirst for revenge, a desire to hide Lottie away from the world and keep her safe began to hurt, burning his heart and searing his skin. But he put the fire out, closing his mind off until he felt nothing.

Ellie has to come first, he told himself.

'I understand, but . . . where has this come from?' He steadied his voice, choosing his words carefully.

'One day I'm going to be queen, Jamie. I have to accept that, and when that happens she's not going to be there any more for either of us.' Ellie looked down, her face disappearing into the shadows. 'She doesn't realize it, but you were right all along. I've been bad for her; this whole Portman agreement has been bad for her.'

It was so strange to hear Ellie saying what he'd wanted her to realize when Lottie had first come into their lives. But now all he felt was senseless.

'I will always support you and your decisions, Ellie, you know that. Seeing you finally take this seriously is excellent.' Each syllable felt like being flayed alive; he was disgusted at himself for failing so fantastically at his job. He shouldn't care how he felt; he should only be pleased that Ellie had come to this conclusion on her own.

'I want to make a pact.' Ellie spoke firmly, her mind already made up. 'A royal bond to make sure neither of us go back on our word.'

With only one final fleeting ache of hesitation, Jamie nodded.

They both knew nothing would ever be the same after this.

As he got on his knees in front of his princess, Jamie felt the world sink down with him, every experience and moment they'd shared with Lottie plummeting into depths they would not recover.

Ellie took her place in front of him. Bathed in the light from the window, she was only a black silhouette, the sky behind her rolling too fast and grey, the sun vanishing.

'As your princess and your master,' she began, placing her middle and index finger over his forehead, 'I hereby command you, Partizan Jamie Volk, are not permitted to act on your romantic feelings towards the Portman Charlotte Edith Pumpkin – and nor shall I, Eleanor Prudence Wolfson, Princess of Maradova – and that we shall commit to only a professional relationship from here on until the end of time. Bound by the blood of Alexis Wolfson, this is an order that will never be disobeyed.'

And so it was done.

Instead of heading back outside to join the others, Jamie found himself wandering to his bedroom, a siren's call pulling him towards a box hidden away in his wardrobe that he hadn't touched for longer than he cared to admit.

The door let out a long, moaning creak as he eased it open, the box sitting at the bottom, still locked away in his bag. He reached for it and the blue velvet brought back painful memories. The small box made a popping sound as he opened it, the wolf pendant still sitting there untouched, still sleeping, waiting for him to feel ready to wear it again. The only problem was that he'd lost all sense of what exactly he was waiting for. He didn't think of Ellie and the Wolfsons and what he owed them any more when he saw the winking silver of the snarling wolf. He only thought of that same chain round Lottie's throat, binding her to the Maravish royal family.

He quickly shut the box, his gaze drifting to the back of the wardrobe, thinking about the spiderweb of clues hidden behind it.

'*Where is my enemy hiding?*' he muttered.

Haru was right. He'd been looking in all the wrong places. All this time the greatest threat to Lottie had been sitting under his nose.

It was the Wolfsons.

He put the box out of sight again and wondered if he trusted Princess Eleanor Wolfson to keep her promise.

15

'A box?' Binah repeated, leaning back into Lottie's frilly pink pillows and looking comfortable enough to start purring.

'Not just a box, a secret – one he wants to share with Jamie.'

Lottie was pacing back and forth on one of the purple rugs of the Ivy dorms, absently biting at the chipped nail polish on her fingernail, a bad habit she'd picked up.

'Isn't that odd? And why is he waiting to show it to him?' Sitting down on the floor with a thump, Lottie stared up at Binah as if she might magically know the contents of the mysterious box. 'It has to be something we can use, right?'

The room was getting warm from Lottie's frantic energy, only the slight breeze coming from the half-open balcony keeping the temperature bearable, but it came at the price of occasionally blowing Claude's letters about. Both of them were starting to look like little creatures, rustling for attention if she ignored them for too long.

'Oh, absolutely,' Binah agreed, 'but how on earth would we get it?'

Lottie had secretly been hoping Binah would suggest something reckless like breaking in and grabbing the box themselves, and to hear her discuss it so cautiously was a reminder of how serious this was. Even Binah wouldn't tempt fate when it came to Haru.

Claude's most recent letter fluttered again, and Lottie quickly put a book over it in an attempt to force herself to stop worrying about it.

She wasn't any closer to solving anything, not Leviathan's plan nor Claude's goal, and now she was fixated on that box and what might be inside it.

What would Sayuri do? Lottie thought, spreading out on the rug and seeing the dark spot under her bed where her sword – or, rather, Liliana's sword, was wrapped in cloth and hidden away. It looked lonely, out of place and useless, everything Lottie was afraid of becoming.

'What's this?!' Binah exclaimed, her voice full of curiosity.

Lottie sat up just in time to see her pluck one of the postcards Lottie had displayed on her wall by the bed.

It was the one she'd got from Sayuri back at the palace, the front illustration depicting the bamboo forest where they'd found the first sword, Sayuri's sword.

'It's a postcard from Sayuri.'

'You two became quite close, didn't you?'

Lottie nodded. 'I promised her I'd help figure everything out and that she could trust me, but so far all I've done is push us into a corner.'

Binah hummed thoughtfully to herself, carefully putting the card back. 'What did you do with the postcard you received the other day?'

The question made Lottie pause, having buried the thought in the bin along with the postcard. To her relief, footsteps sounded on the landing, and Binah and Lottie quickly shoved the letters and notes they'd made under Lottie's pillow just as the door creaked open. Ellie stood there, looking sweaty but invigorated in her fencing clothes.

'Well, I'd better go.' Binah grinned at Lottie, but Lottie hardly noticed; she was too caught up in seeing Ellie looking so well after her class.

'Oh, yes, thank you for the science help, Binah. I'll see you later.' Lottie could have kicked herself for how terrible the excuse sounded, and Binah rolled her eyes as she made her way outside.

'Have a pleasant evening, you two,' she called over her shoulder, leaving the two girls alone.

Ellie looked back at the closed door, lifting an eyebrow suspiciously, but she didn't say anything, instead letting out a tired but satisfied sigh as she stretched her neck out.

'You look pleased,' Lottie announced, unable to stop herself smiling at the way Ellie's flushed skin made her look like a valiant prince returned from winning battle.

'Yeah, I beat Anastacia.' Ellie threw her fencing gear on to her bed, and began fiddling with her suit.

'Let me help you with that.'

As she'd done many times before, Lottie reached for the zip at the back of Ellie's neck, coming close enough to smell the cocoa scent of her shampoo, close enough to feel the warmth of her breath against Ellie's porcelain skin. Carefully she pulled down the fabric, which fell away to reveal the hard white breastplate beneath. Her hands reached for the straps, muscle memory taking over, pulling on each tie with delicate calm attention.

It was just as the breastplate fell away that she saw it, a flash of dark markings, angry as a scar, the skin puffed up and sore around a deceptively elegant script. She didn't have enough of a view to see it in full, but it looked to be the Maravish word, *bol'shbrota* – which Lottie knew meant 'painful self-sacrifice'.

There was no time for her brain to be sure she'd seen it correctly, when abruptly, like an animal caught in a snare, Ellie grabbed her wrist with so much force it made Lottie jump. 'I can do it myself.'

She pushed Lottie to the side, hard enough that Lottie caught her leg on the bedside table, and her water glass fell, smashing as she landed on her duvet.

'Ellie, what was that?' she asked. 'And . . . and . . . you pushed me!'

'It's nothing,' Ellie replied. 'Lottie, I didn't mean to, I just . . .' She swore in Maravish. 'I'm sorry.'

'Ellie, calm down, it's OK.' Lottie scrambled up to start clearing away the glass. 'I'm fine.'

'No, no, Lottie. I'll clean it up. You stay right there.'

Her head still spinning, Lottie sat back down to watch Ellie pick up the broken glass, and from the way her dark eyes glittered it looked like she was fighting back tears. She sat there for a while, replaying the event over and over and the sore-looking mark on Ellie's skin, not believing what she'd seen or understanding what it meant.

'Lottie, what's this?' Ellie called over from the bin where she'd put the glass.

Lottie turned, blinking away the last of her shock, when she saw what was in Ellie's hand.

'It's nothing,' Lottie said, staring at the Havana postcard.

'It's not nothing . . .' Ellie's voice caught. 'It's from your dad.'

'I know.' Lottie marched over to take it. 'I'm not interested. I have you guys and my Portman job; why would I want to see him?'

'Why didn't you tell me?'

'Why didn't you tell me about that thing on your ribcage?' Lottie countered, throwing the postcard in the bin again.

'This is ridiculous, Lottie,' retorted Ellie, ignoring Lottie's accusation. 'It says he's selling the house? Where will you live?'

'Why does that matter?' Lottie demanded. 'I live with you.'

They stared each other down, chests heaving. Lottie looked at the wolf pendant that dangled over Ellie's chest, knowing that as long as they shared it they were bound together. Just as it should be.

'Because,' Ellie said at last, sounding colder than Lottie expected, 'you need a family beyond me. You need to have a place to go if all this stops.'

Lottie felt her stomach drop. Ellie *was* her family. The idea of there being anything else beyond what she felt for Ellie was as impossible as the sun rising in the west.

'But I only want you.' Lottie could hear her voice break.

From the way Ellie flinched, Lottie knew she felt the same way – that there was part of their relationship they'd never acted upon, full of wonderful possibilities.

Ellie looked away first, sighing. 'Sometimes,' she began, 'what you want isn't what you actually need.'

And, just like that, the fruit of possibility shrivelled into dust.

Before Lottie could ask any of the burning questions she had, a knock sounded at their door. Both of them looked to one another, waiting to see who would answer.

'Hello?' Saskia's voice carried from the other side of the door.

'Hey!' Ellie answered, opening the door to reveal not just Saskia but Percy too, and with them a flood of worry so thick they could smell it like smoke from a forest fire.

'What's happened?' Lottie asked.

'Is it Leviathan?' Ellie added, both of them already preparing for a fight.

Instead Percy and Saskia looked at each other in slow gloom, totally at odds with Ellie and Lottie's energy.

Saskia shook her head, putting a hand on Percy's shoulder in comfort, squeezing ever so slightly. 'It's Lola and Micky,' she said, and Lottie already knew what awful news was coming. 'Their dad has passed away.'

PART TWO

The Kiss

1907 painting by Gustav Klimt

16

To the Man in the Goat Mask,

I do hope this address will suffice, for I'm afraid I know you
only as the man in the goat mask who tormented my
Partizan on the roof in Tokyo, or perhaps you'd prefer the
'Master of Leviathan'? Or do you only let those you deem
useful enough refer to you in that way?

   With regard to the new puzzle pieces you have so generously
gifted me, I find the image of the wolf admittedly disturbing,
although it's not hard to remember that they are also hunters
when you yourself are one. In spite of this, I feel I am getting
nowhere with these clues and would hope you would see it
time to give me something more substantial, perhaps a corner
piece? Something to build the rest of the puzzle from?

Your ever-curious and increasingly frustrated niece

PS I understand the story you weave to your lackeys about
Partizans, but, I assure you, Jamie is content in his position,
which you will undoubtedly learn soon enough.

In spite of the light-hearted wordplay, the handwriting had an almost unnoticeable quiver, a secret hidden in the words that told of nervous shakes or agitation; either way, it meant the princess was scared.

Sipping his bitter coffee, Claude traced the letter with bemused satisfaction, feeling the parchment under his fingers like butterfly wings, pinned down and exactly where he wanted them.

'May I get you anything else, sir?' The valet finished placing the breakfast items on the table, his voice sounding odd and hollow, a typical side-effect of the Hamelin Formula.

Claude didn't even know the man's name, though that was no concern to him. All that mattered was that he'd wanted this cabin and he'd wanted a servant to ensure that his sojourn would be comfortable, and, most importantly, he could get all this and more with just a drop of poison. The only problem was it was terribly boring. Claude much preferred when people did what he wanted because they revered him, as it had been when he was a prince.

'No,' Claude replied, watching where the housekeeper stood corpse still, constantly waiting to be told his next move with a plastic smile on his face. 'Go and clean the cabin.'

The morning mists that clung to the mountain lakes of the Bavarian Alps spread up to the tips of the ferns, trapping the landscape in the illusion of a wildfire. The air was fresh; the cold had never bothered Claude, having grown up in the snowy landscape of Maradova. He was perfectly content to welcome the brisk dawn barefoot on the decking of the cabin. It reminded him of the palace, waking to eat breakfast on the balcony, nursing away whatever trouble he'd found himself in the night before. In those days he'd had the whole world at his fingertips, and he wanted it back. The palace, the adoration that gave him unlimited control, everything owed to him as the rightful king of Maradova, and he knew the country would not be whole while that mangy lying pack was in charge. The country needed the true wolf to lead the pack.

Holding the princess's letter up to his nose, he could smell roses. It was the one thing that threw him each time. The delicate scent did not fit with his memories of the palace, as if his brother's daughter had been grown from a different garden. He folded the letter away. 'I've always detested roses.'

A soft tapping on the glass screen of the decking let Claude know that Ingrid had arrived. The sound was muffled, as if she didn't want to disturb him, even though he'd requested her presence.

Without looking behind him, he gestured for her to come.

'You wanted to see me, Master?'

There was always a neediness to Ingrid's tone like a mewling cat, a hungry longing for his favour that both pleased and irritated Claude depending on his mood. In truth, he didn't want to see her at all, after what she'd done in Tokyo, pushing too hard at Jamie until he had been forced to throw himself to the ground just when Claude had him in his clutches.

'Did you bring what I asked for?' He still didn't turn round, focusing on the writing set he'd laid out on the table.

Ingrid was clearly trying her best to stay composed, but Claude could always sense the quirks and twitches, glances and fidgets that most people would miss; they were as clear as the mountains before him, screaming the person's weaknesses.

'Here.' Ingrid laid a wooden box beside him on the table. Claude could tell that she was desperate to have his attention, but looking at her right now would only annoy him, so he waved her back a few steps. 'I'm going to make it up to you,' she uttered, a venom in her voice that he knew was only poisoning herself.

'You are,' he replied simply, and this time he did turn to look at her, locking on to those furious grey eyes with sharp focus that made the girl flinch.

Ingrid was short for a Partizan, hair black like an oil spill, and since her tantrum in Tokyo she'd not been caring for it. The strands fell in cobweb clumps over her delicate feline features. It bothered Claude immeasurably to see someone who served him looking so unkempt, shivering and red-nosed in the cold air, and he made a note to have his valet fix her appearance.

'Come,' he demanded, gesturing to the wooden chair on the other side of the table. 'I want to show you something.'

She hesitated, but Claude caught it. Usually she jumped at the chance to be near him, and he knew exactly what this meant. Despite his continuing irritation with her, it was time to bring her back in, remind her why she served him. He'd learned from Saskia that it was better to let them in than keep them at a distance.

He'd always suspected Saskia would be the weak chain in their group. She was never loyal only to him. Her heart belonged to her Parisian master, and it's precisely why he was wary of letting her in on their plans, demanding that she prove herself first.

His first clue that she'd never truly be his was her desire for payment in exchange for adhering to his list of demands, and there was always the expectation that when she had acquired the money he'd offered to lure her in, she'd leave them to run away with her girlfriend. Having factored this into his plan, he'd kept her in the dark about most of their operations, eventually deciding that the pros of having someone close to the princess outweighed the cons.

Claude hadn't expected Saskia to turn on them so soon and was now left wondering if she might have stayed had he not alienated her from the group. Her betrayal was still a humiliating mark on Leviathan, one that he would be sure to make her pay for. He would not be making the same mistake with Ingrid.

Lifting the lid, Claude reached into the box, careful not to disturb the rest of the items, and pulled out the two new clues he intended to send his niece.

'Do you know who this is?' Between his fingers, Claude held out an old photograph. The colour had faded with time, yet the faces in the picture remained clear, their purpose sharp and vibrant.

Ingrid swallowed, her eyes flicking over the photo with nervous speed. 'Yes.'

'I'm going to send this to the princess,' Claude explained. 'It will be my second-to-last letter to her before the truth comes out. Do you understand why I am doing this?'

Ingrid nodded, and Claude raised his eyebrows, waiting for her to say it out loud.

'You want to give her a chance to put things right,' she said quickly, looking down at her lap like a petulant child.

'I can see that you are once again doubting my choices.'

Ingrid's hands began to bunch the fabric of her skirt up so tight in her fists that it looked as though she might claw through her skin. 'I don't think she deserves it,' she finally spat out, her mouth closing quickly to lock in anything else that might spill over.

Occasionally Ingrid was able to say the right thing; it was rare, and usually unintentional, but nonetheless it pleased Claude immensely when he was able to coax her into doing what he wanted, especially when she believed it was her idea.

The truth, of course, was that Claude had no intention of giving them the chance to make amends, but it was important that his followers believed him to be a benevolent and forgiving master.

'I agree – she might not deserve it,' Claude said, and his lips twisted at Ingrid's whiplash response. Like putty in his hands, she softened so easily, and her fingers uncurled. 'I do not do this because she deserves it. I am doing it to prove our point.'

As if on cue, his valet set down two cups of coffee between them. Gently pushing one towards Ingrid, Claude signalled for her to join him, knowing the gesture would be the last bit of bait to reel her in. 'Once she knows the truth about her family, and she inevitably chooses to side with them, Jamie will come to us of his own free will.'

Ingrid swallowed down the bitter coffee and the effect was instant. Her eyes widened like a cat focusing on her prey, and that impulse was precisely what Claude needed to keep in check.

'I am giving you a chance too, Ingrid,' he began, and, from the way her lips parted in hunger, he knew she needed a reminder that his favour would not be easily won back. 'Not because I think you deserve it, but because you still have lessons to learn.'

As expected, she flinched, the words getting the message across without alienating her.

'Now, if Jamie should choose to come to me, what will you do to fix the awful impression you've made that has not only damaged your relationship with him but mine too?'

Ingrid's shoulders lifted, and she shrank in on herself.

'I'll be good.' Her voice was barely above a whisper. 'I'll be quiet and stay out of the way. I can do that.'

That was not the answer that Claude wanted.

'No, no, Ingrid,' he said, tutting, shaking his head with a weary sigh one might expect to give a child. 'Jamie needs to see that we are a family, that we are patient and make amends.' Ensuring that Ingrid was really paying attention, Claude dropped his voice until it was almost a growl, a clear sign that what he said next was an order. 'When we bring Jamie in, you will be present; you will cook for him, clean for him, be helpful and accommodating. Can you do that?'

In the distance a murder of crows set off from the high top of a tree, their rasping, haggard cackle taunting Ingrid over such a humiliating demand, but Claude knew she'd agree, because it was the only way to get back in his good books.

'Yes, I can do that.' Her voice had diminished, weighed down with defeat, the only indication of her usual gutsy attitude coming through in the way her jaw tensed as she spoke. Another subtle twitch that did not escape Claude's attention.

'Very good.' He clapped his hands together for good measure, applauding the behaviour he wanted to see. 'Feel free to take the coffee tray to the kitchen when you go.'

17

Alfred Tompkins's funeral was at Sweetmill Crematorium on a rainy Saturday morning in October. The service was quiet, only attended by his remaining family and closest confidants in a lily-lined chapel, preceded by the matter of the will. Lola and Micky did not return to school the week following their father's passing, nor did Percy. Their two family businesses, Tompkins and Butter, had recently merged to become the world's largest confectionary empire, and, to honour Alfred, the Butter family joined the Tompkins in grieving their loss.

Without the twins around, Rosewood felt bitter, their absence a constant gloomy reminder of what Lottie's world would be like should any of her friends get taken away from her. This vision of her world splintering only made Lottie that much more determined to give them the perfect welcome home, and she wasn't the only one striving for perfection.

'I said yellow, green and *pink* icing, not yellow, green and orange.' Anastacia spoke sharply, pointing at the tray of fondant fancies and macarons being held out by the Conch girl before her, who was supposedly top of the food-tech class in their year.

'These are lovely, thank you,' Lottie said, taking the tray off the gaping girl.

Rolling her eyes, Anastacia picked up another tray of cakes, falling in line behind Lottie to head to the Conch House reception room they'd commandeered for Lola and Micky's return to Rosewood.

'I clearly requested pink, not orange,' Anastacia mumbled to herself as she laid out the tiered cake tray and teacups, indicating to Ellie and Lottie where to place each item while continuing her rant. 'Everyone in the whole world knows pink and yellow are the twins' favourite colours. I mean, what kind of idiot confuses orange with pink?'

'Ani, they're going to appreciate it regardless.' Saskia wrapped a supportive arm round her girlfriend, before laying out the remaining teacups on the round oak table.

'I just wish . . . you know . . .' Anastacia's mouth quickly zipped shut when she met Lottie's gaze.

Lottie did know, they all did, that Haru's rules meant they had to stay within the school grounds. None of them could so much as offer to attend Alfred's funeral or ask the twins if they needed help at home, and they couldn't risk dragging them into this situation with Haru and Leviathan when they were already going through so much.

'I just want to see them happy again,' Anastacia continued, winding and unwinding a strand of mahogany hair round her finger.

'Ani, the most important thing is that everyone's safe – and, besides, we also made a gift for them,' Lottie said, grabbing a cloth-covered canvas by the table and holding it up, but her attempt to add a positive spin was only met with blank stares.

'Yeah, *safe*,' Ellie mumbled drily, and there was something sharp in her tone, like she was coughing up needles. 'Everyone is so safe.'

Lottie chose to ignore the remark. A degree of unpleasantness had continued to linger since their argument the week before, and if Lottie thought about it too much she'd have to think of that postcard from her dad again.

Seeming to know exactly where Lottie's thoughts were going, Ellie exhaled sharply.

The door squeaked open in a welcome distraction, revealing Jamie and Raphael with a gaudy candyfloss-coloured collection of party hats and decorations, which to anyone else would have seemed wildly inappropriate, considering the circumstances, but made perfect sense for the twins.

'Percy and Binah are going to be here with the twins in ten minutes,' Jamie relayed, already setting up a welcome sign.

There was something distinctly odd about watching Jamie, dressed in a black shirt and trousers, with all the gloomy concern of an Edvard Munch painting, meticulously putting up bright decorations covered in glitter. The two things were so at odds that Lottie stared at him until Raphael came over and shoved a party popper in her hand.

'Set this off when they come in the room.'

'Five minutes,' Jamie announced, stepping down to take his place round the table.

Lottie found herself sandwiched between Jamie and her princess, the three of them not quite touching, like they were opposing sides of a magnet. When she looked at them to try to grasp their odd behaviour, both of their eyes were firmly focused on the door, as if even looking at her might break some unspoken rule she wasn't aware of.

What on earth is going on with them?

Lottie remembered the strange blistering she'd seen on Ellie's ribcage and the odd look in Jamie's eye. She wanted so badly to call them out right then and there, only now was not the time. Then the door was opening, with Binah rushing in to give them the signal.

'Welcome back!' they all called, pulling on the party poppers and spreading confetti and glitter in a colourful explosion.

Standing stiff as statues in the doorway, Lola, Micky and Percy were three ghostly figures, their blank confused stares obscured by streams of coloured paper and ribbon. They didn't move, and for a white-hot moment Lottie wondered if they'd completely misjudged what they thought would be a good way to welcome them back, until, like a rainbow emerging from the grey, an apple-cheeked smile spread over Lola's lips and her beaming aura scattered through the air like sugar powder.

'You guys, you didn't have to do this.' Lola's eyes were glittering, and she squeezed her brother's hand.

'We made this for you.' With one swift motion, Lottie pulled off the cover, revealing a detailed oil painting of Alfred Tompkins surrounded by all his marvellous candy creations, their father immortalized forever in the golden frame. She didn't need to let anyone know that working on a picture of someone else's father had been a welcome distraction from thinking of her own.

Binah laughed. 'She's being modest. Lottie painted it; we just got it framed.'

'Your dad was clearly an amazing man, so we wanted to pay our respects however we could.' Lottie handed the portrait to the twins, delighting in how it made them light up.

'Come, sit, eat.' Binah pulled a chair out for them, everyone following suit to take a place round the overflowing table.

'And let us know if we can help with anything now that you guys, you know –' Raphael shoved a Florentine in his mouth, the chewy caramel distorting his words – 'own the biggest confectionary company in the world.'

'Raph, please, what did I teach you about tact?' Jamie scolded, only to be met by an impossibly charming shrug, the kind that only someone as unfairly attractive as Raphael could make look endearing.

Percy rolled his eyes but there was humour behind the gesture as he took a seat next to his boyfriend and plated up cakes from the tiered tray.

'We're not taking over until we finish school,' Micky said, methodically adding three sugar cubes to his tea while Lola picked up the rest of the explanation.

'Nadia – you met her at the factory tour – she's going to handle the company for the next few years and finish all the legal stuff to do with the company merger.' Lola looked between her brother and Percy, lifting her shoulders as she grinned contentedly. 'And then the three of us will take over once we graduate from university, together, as a family.'

Both Lottie's and Ellie's eyes shot up at the mention of 'family', it having become a dirty word since their dispute, and Lottie shifted uncomfortably under her princess's piercing dark stare. It took only a second for Jamie to catch on, his eyes narrowing between the two of them with such intensity she was sure he could read their minds.

'You were lucky to have such a wonderful father.' Lottie couldn't help the pointed tone as she spoke, and prayed that no one but Ellie would pick up on it. 'A close family is very special.'

Stirring her tea, Lola hummed an agreement, the sound strangely melancholy. 'It wasn't always a perfect family, though.' She didn't look up from the whirlpool at her fingertips, like she was stirring up a memory. 'Alfred had to make his own family. That's what happens when you have a bad parent sometimes.'

The room went still and Lottie felt Ellie stiffen, her fingers twitching with the strain of not looking at Jamie or Lottie. It was no secret that Lola and Micky's grandfather was the man behind the twisted Hamelin Formula, and, although he'd tried to make amends for it and hide it away, nothing could ever make up for the terrible acts he'd committed. Some evils are simply too great.

'When you're a little kid, all the stories tell you how important family is, how they matter above everything else, but it's not true,' she said, her voice soft. 'Sometimes you're lucky and the family you get given is great, like us with our mother and father, but sometimes you're less lucky and you have to find your own family.'

In perfect unison, Lola and Micky looked up at the painting and, as if like minds had melded together, Micky finished the sentiment.

150

'Alfred found his own family, with our mother, and everyone who helped to build Tompkins Confectionary.'

Their words settled over Lottie's skin with the gentle touch of blossoms in spring, sweet and fleeting, and she was captured by it, not wanting to let the feeling go.

'I think, for some people, the family you find is just as important,' Lola went on, looking round the table with Micky, a shared look of warmth in their sky-blue eyes. 'For some people, that family you find, they're your real family.'

The twins beamed, bringing everyone in, and spoke together: 'All of you, you're our family too.'

The stillness continued to creep over everyone, the dust of the twins' words settling over the room, and Lottie wanted to smile back, to say yes, but all she could think of was the postcard from her dad and its scent of cheap alcohol. And right behind her was a shadow she could never get rid of – the Goat Man, telling her that even these happy moments were only a mask.

'I'm going to tell my dad that Saskia's my girlfriend,' Anastacia announced, immediately covering her mouth, as if she was shocked at what she'd said.

Saskia nearly fell backwards off her seat in surprise.

'I want to give him the chance to accept us, to do the right thing,' Anastacia explained, a blush creeping on to her face that was entirely out of character.

'But what if he doesn't?'

'It doesn't matter any more. Lola's right – we have other family.' Anastacia tried to hide her red face behind her teacup, and when that failed she gave everyone a stern look. 'You can only give people so many chances, even your parents, and I want to know for certain if there's no hope with him.'

For Lottie, the cakes and candies began to slip out of focus, their sweet smells replaced by the sickly scent of rum, the room blurred and she caught a glimpse of herself in the black Assam tea. She didn't look anything like her father. All she could see staring back was her mother's side of the family and the wolf round her neck sparkled white in the sunlight from the window.

Lottie knew Ellie had been right, that she couldn't ignore the postcard from her father, that doing so was only prolonging something she should have done a long, long time ago.

'That's a really brave and good idea, Anastacia.' The look Lottie gave Anastacia let her know she understood, only Lottie had already reached her threshold when it came to chances, and it was time to stop pretending otherwise. 'Now, would you excuse me? I'm just going to pop to the girls' room,' she announced.

Ellie immediately clocked on to her. 'I'll go with you,' she said, standing up and following Lottie out of the room so fast that the door barely had time to shut behind them before Ellie began her tirade.

'I could practically hear the cogs turning in your brain in there.' Ellie's voice followed her while Lottie continued firmly on to the bathroom, shuffling awkwardly between confused Conch students while Ellie pushed past them, indifferent to the scene she was causing. 'What are you thinking? Did what Anastacia said get to you? Are you going to speak to your dad?'

Sighing, Lottie rounded the corner of the corridor, the oak floorboards creaking under their fast steps. She didn't know why Ellie was so desperate for her to build bridges with her father. She could only assume it was to do with the guilt she felt around her uncle and Haru. But Ellie had to understand that she was everything to Lottie, the most important thing in her world, her princess and her best friend, the reason she carried the weight of Claude's letters and why she could stay strong in her role as Portman. She'd always choose her, no matter how hard it got.

'Ellie, I've thought about what you said in our dorm the other day, and you're right – I do need to speak to my father – but Lola's right too.' Lottie pushed the bathroom door open, relieved to find it was empty, and she turned fast to Ellie to make sure she was really listening. 'I know who my family is.'

'Wait, what?' Ellie shook her head in confusion, her fist coming down hard on the tiled wall, trapping Lottie in the corner by the sink. 'So you *are* going to contact your dad?'

The way Ellie glared down at her made Lottie understand completely why the royal crest was a wolf. She was practically panting, a hunger in her eyes, determined to get her way.

Lottie's gaze flickered down to Ellie's ribcage, knowing that odd blister probably still lay there, and seeing the bubbling clump of stretched red skin in her mind's eye only confirmed that she was making the right choice. She had to get to the bottom of this sickness that Ellie had inflicted upon herself and help her.

'Yes, I'm going to get permission to call him,' Lottie said simply, and Ellie's whole body seemed to go slack.

'Lottie, that's great, that's . . . that's really fantastic. I –'

Lottie took the opportunity to dive out from under Ellie's arm before continuing, looking Ellie right in her dark stormy eyes, making it clear what she said next was not up for debate.

'I'm going to talk to my dad and I'm going to tell him that he can sell the house in Cornwall and that I never expect to see him again, because I've found my real family.'

18

This was not good. In fact, this was precisely the opposite of what Jamie and Ellie had hoped would happen. On the other side of the door, Lottie was leaving a voicemail for her father, one that would make it clear she didn't want anything to do with him any more, and it filled Jamie with so many conflicting emotions that he felt like a piece of blown glass about to shatter.

Deep under his skin he could feel two versions of himself clawing at each other. There was the Partizan: disappointed in this outcome, knowing that eventually Lottie would need to step down from her Portman role and return to a regular life so Ellie could make the transition to queen and let Lottie go. This was the version he was clinging to, not wanting to give the other a moment of consideration, because the other was selfish: a demonic, confused version of him that wanted to wrap his arms round Lottie and pull her in so close that the rest of the world couldn't touch her. He wished that he could whisper against her cheek how proud he was of her for doing this, that she didn't need anyone else because he would protect her forever.

Through the cast-iron keyhole in the old door, Jamie saw Lottie put the phone down, finally turning round, which revealed absolutely nothing. She smiled her sunshine smile as Jamie pulled the door open for her.

'Is it done?' he asked, watching her with the same hard focus he might use on someone he suspected was a threat, scanning for any tiny movement that would give an insight into what she was really thinking. 'Did you speak to him?'

'No, he didn't pick up, so I left a message,' she replied, setting off to the courtyard, a bounce in her step that spread to the ends of her golden hair.

Jamie felt his jaw twitch, unable to pick up so much as a wane in her smile. When did she get so good at hiding things from him?

'And that's it? You plan to never have anything to do with your family again?'

'I've told you, and I've told Ellie – he's not my family any more. There's nothing complicated about it.'

'If there's nothing complicated about it, then why do you continue failing to make any semblance of a start on your PoP project? Seems like you don't want to think about your family at all.'

There it was, blink and you'd miss it, but Jamie caught it like the sun in his eyes, the light vanishing from Lottie's pupils for a panicked second, and it told him everything he needed to know.

'Looks like you're more confused than you're letting on.'

'I'm Ellie's Portman,' she said stubbornly, and as soon as the words left her mouth he felt his gaze land on the chain round her neck where the wolf's head kept guard.

'That's not a family; that's a job.' He knew it was harsh, but it bubbled out of him nonetheless, a terrible poison he'd been harbouring since his pact with Ellie.

Lottie suddenly turned to him. 'You're going to be training with Haru for the next hour, right?' And once again she did something he couldn't read, recoiling after she spoke, like she was disappointed in herself.

'Yes, and if I didn't know any better I'd think you were trying to get rid of me.'

Lottie shrank under the accusation, round cheeks going pink in that oh-so familiar way. 'No, I just need some privacy for a little while.'

They were at a stand-off, neither of them wanting to be the first to break away, but it was as plain as day that there was somewhere she needed to be. Seeming to realize he was on to her, Lottie was the first to cave, plastering on that fake smile he could always see through.

'I'll see you in an hour, OK?' She began to skip off before Jamie could protest, calling behind her, 'And I promise I'm fine so you can stop looking at me like that.'

Jamie froze like he'd been burned. He didn't know if she'd picked the words intentionally, but they sent a surge of fire through his belly. They were a searing reminder that she'd noticed there was something different in the way he approached her, something he couldn't control, ever since Tokyo, ever since she'd found him at his most vulnerable. Ever since he'd met the Goat Man.

Without a second thought, he marched to the Ivy dorm, knowing exactly what he was going to do, despite his misgivings.

As if he'd read his mind, Haru was there, drenched in the golden sun, waiting for him at the gate to Ivy Wood.

'I was coming to find you,' Jamie said stupidly, knowing full well they always met there. 'I know we usually meet up today and . . .' It wasn't often that Jamie found himself unable to finish a sentence but Lottie's words were still burning in his chest and he was at once overwhelmed by them.

'What's wrong?' Haru tilted his head in curiosity, one lock of his curly hair spilling forward, like a tiny ram's horn.

Jamie was unable to look at Haru directly, the light behind him was too strong and made him think of Lottie. 'I'm not sure,' he confessed, only realizing it was true after he'd said it out loud.

'I don't have any work I need help with today and I'm not in any mood for training,' said Haru. Jamie's shoulders sagged in disappointment, and Haru gave him a thoughtful look, likely taking note of his reaction. 'Do you want to go for a walk instead?'

With Jamie's mind in the state it was, he knew he shouldn't put himself in a position where the older Partizan might have a chance to dissect him. Training or working was fine – they were too busy to talk – but this was different. He could sense an intimacy in the offer that made him squirm, and yet wasn't this precisely what Percy had told him he needed to do, to talk to someone who might understand some of what he was experiencing? Wasn't this exactly why he'd sought him out?

Percy was right. He couldn't protect anyone when at any moment he felt like he might catch fire. And, just like that, the irrational part of him won. Jamie nodded, and let Haru lead the way.

In expectant silence they wandered all the way down to the long-closed outdoor pool for which Haru had a key. The whole area had become one with the surrounding nature, curious flowers and weeds peeping out from between the stone slabs, the emptied pool filled with emerald puddles, the crisp oranges and browns of leaves resting on the surface.

Last time Jamie had set foot here, he'd been poisoned by Leviathan's makeshift Hamelin Formula. It had made him drowsy and persuadable, honesty spilling out of his lips that he cringed to think about, and he was glad he could hardly remember it. Now the dappled topaz light hung in streams over the void of the empty pool, everything drenched in the calming scent of wet earth and pine.

'What is troubling you?' Haru asked, taking a seat on the damp ground.

Surrounded by the natural quiet, with only softly chirping birds and rustling leaves, Jamie allowed himself to exhale some of the tension in his shoulders, settling down beside Haru, their legs dangling over the edge of the pool.

'Percy said I should talk to you. He *asked* me to actually, because he thinks we have a lot in common,' Jamie blurted out. 'He and Raphael – they think I'm not processing what happened in Tokyo properly, which is ridiculous because we're trained for moments like that, which they don't understand.'

'Those are very good friends you have.' Haru looked up, the sun drenching his freckled face. 'It's a shame they've had to go through so much simply because of who they know.'

'What do you –'

Haru turned back to him, his face warping in a way that Jamie hadn't seen before. His expression was no longer warm. It flickered like a roaring flame, surging just enough for Jamie to catch a glimpse. 'It was very scary,' he said, sounding strangely childish, 'when you fell off the roof.'

'Excuse me?'

'You fell, didn't you? That's what the nurse said. I'm amazed you made it to Takeshin. Do you remember how?'

'No, it's a blur.'

'Maybe someone helped you home.'

'The only people that knew where I'd fallen were Leviathan, and they . . .' Through the flashes of lightning and the biting rain Jamie could feel something else, a memory of being carried, the weight of another human, strong and tall, accompanied by soft murmurs making sure he was OK, with all the care and worry of a parent doting over a child.

'What is the matter?' Haru asked.

'Nothing, my brain is just getting confused. Making stuff up to save me from the trauma, I assume.'

Even as he said this, though, he relived the sensation of being carried, and the smell caught in his nose, nearly overpowering him. It was the scent of spiced wine and burning.

When he looked back to Haru, the sky behind him was red over the dense wall of trees. The sun was so low on the horizon it stretched their shadows, and the distended forms twisted and pulled until they morphed into demonic reflections in the space below their feet.

'Tell me about your parents,' Haru said, his voice soft and hypnotizing.

'I don't know them; the Wolfsons are my family,' Jamie replied, listening to Haru's steady breathing beside him like a swinging pendulum.

A smile that almost looked like a private joke spread over Haru's lips, and Jamie had the strangest desire to touch them, like they might tell him everything he wanted to know and fix what was broken.

'What about your mother? What do you know about her?'

'My mother?'

Jamie was confused. Why was Haru bringing up his mother? He knew he should get up and walk away, that he should kill this conversation dead before it could do any harm, but the way Haru looked at him instilled a sense of trust in Jamie that he had never felt before. The words spilled out of him, bringing her to life after years of keeping her locked away.

'Her name was Hirana.' He felt her name on his lips like a prayer, awakening something deep inside him. 'She was an immigrant from Pakistan; she worked at the palace in Maradova for a while. In the gardens, I think.'

'Aren't you ever curious about your heritage?' Haru pondered, his heavy eyelashes fluttering and coaxing him to keep uncovering these things he usually buried. 'Perhaps you could use your sabbatical to visit her home country?'

'Haru, I've told you – I'm never taking a sabbatical,' Jamie grumbled, whatever spell he was under breaking as the last of the sunlight slipped beyond the horizon.

'I'm sorry,' Haru said earnestly, placing his hand dangerously close to Jamie's. 'I only find it confusing that your princess and her family do not encourage you to explore your, how to say

161

this –' he paused, tapping his fingers in thought, one of them brushing very softly against Jamie's hand – 'your personal identity. Sorry if I am misunderstanding.'

Haru's words had the world melting away, a memory forming, not of his princess but of Lottie and the gift she'd bought him for his birthday before she knew his preference not to celebrate it. It was a book about Pakistan, filled with recipes and stories and history, which he'd been so angry about, so afraid. But, despite his disapproval, he'd found himself unable to part with it. Ellie had never given him such a thing, nor had the rest of the Wolfsons. All he had from them was the silver wolf they all hung round their necks. Biting down hard on his cheek, Jamie reminded himself that they'd also taken him in and, most importantly, trusted him.

'I have a question,' Haru said, his summer-breeze smile returning, eyes creasing like a fox. 'It's about your princess, and her friend Ellie – they are very close, are they not? Closer than most friends?'

Jamie froze, torn between his relief at the change in topic, and the prickling feeling on his skin at the mention of Lottie and Ellie in the same sentence, knowing they were skirting dangerously round the truth.

'Yes, they are very close.' Saying it out loud made the phantom burn in his chest surge.

'It is only my observation, but the two of them seem so different, like night and day.'

Jamie winced once more. It was his greatest fear to see that light in Lottie snuffed out by the darkness of the Wolfsons' burdens.

'Sometimes opposites are good for each other,' he replied through gritted teeth, furious with himself for having all these awful thoughts.

'Then why does Ellie make your princess so unhappy?'

Somewhere a twig snapped, and Jamie turned sharply in the direction of the sound. However, there was only Haru staring back at him, his dark brown doe eyes black as charcoal in the encroaching night.

No more was what he saw in Ellie and Lottie his own bias; it was fact, observable to those around them. Jamie knew that Lottie had been good for Ellie once, because she'd showed her the damage her carefree attitude could inflict. In that split second the Maravish royal family no longer felt like his saviours. They were not benediction, kindness and salvation. They were a disease, one that had already claimed him. And when he searched deeper into the feeling he could not see Ellie as his princess. It was only Lottie that he wanted to defend, and Ellie was what she needed protecting from.

'Jamie-kun? Are you OK?' Haru said, his voice softer now, and Jamie felt as if he were landing in it, a pillow to cushion him after such an awful thought. But then Ellie reformed in his head, standing over him with the light at her back, more like a prince than a princess, making that promise, swearing them both to protect Lottie by distancing themselves. He had to trust her; he had to believe she could hold up her end of the agreement.

'I'm fine,' Jamie said, standing up in one swift movement. 'Come on.'

Holding his hand out like an invitation, Jamie gestured for Haru to take it, not shying away from his touch any longer.

This was his way of saying thank you, of letting Haru know he'd earned his trust. The Partizan smiled up at him, the empty pool where his legs still dangled looking like an unknowable, unending void. It was easy to pull him up, and in seconds Haru was looking down on him again and the intimacy between them was palpable, their warm breath mingling like perfume in the air.

Haru had done him a huge favour. He'd offered him an ear and given him more clarity than he could know, so it was time for Jamie to return the favour.

'About what you said,' Jamie began, facing it head on. 'Back in Dame Bolter's office . . .'

'Does it bother you?' Haru asked, taking a small step back.

'No, it's just . . .' Feeling shy in a way he didn't know he was capable of, Jamie pushed his hair out of the way, thinking about all the times he'd seen Ellie do something similar. It was a peculiar and unknown realm to know that someone else had feelings for him in that way, someone he admired. 'The truth is I don't think I'm in a position to be thinking about anything like that,' he said, feeling strangely guilty for the vague response.

Haru smirked down at him, clearly finding Jamie's unexpected bashfulness far more funny than he did. 'That's OK. I'm happy if I can simply give you some comfort. I don't like to see you lost, even if my persistence for us to get closer has been an annoyance.'

'Well, you've done that.' Jamie tilted his head to the side, the corners of his mouth inching into a smile. 'I'm glad you were so persistent.'

Having reached a comfortable truce, the two boys walked back through the nearly deserted school with only the moon watching them, and Jamie thought with a sigh what a relief it was to finally have someone who understood him, someone he could trust.

19

Lottie had never felt so guilty in her whole life. She needed to go somewhere she knew would cause suspicion. Unfortunately the only distraction she had was Jamie, even if it made her feel like the worst person in the world. So she'd sent Jamie to Haru, knowing it was the only way to guarantee he wouldn't follow her.

It had taken a little bit of snooping, but it wasn't long until she heard about an Ivy student resembling Ellie's description who had been seen wandering into the mysterious back buildings of the art department, with rumours spreading that perhaps she'd joined the secret underbelly of Rosewood's cult artists.

The Rosewood art facilities were some of the best in the world. The clear white hallways with their introspective abstract paintings and marble statues were more like a museum than a school. Every piece was an insight into the creative minds that dwelled within the school. On a regular day walking through the echoing mezzanine was peaceful, with soft chatter coming from the classrooms and the smell of wet clay or sulphur spilling over from the pottery room's kiln.

But this was not a regular day, and with begrudging acceptance Lottie ventured past classrooms she knew, and through the doors at the back that would take her to the old building. As soon as the doors boomed shut behind her, the world turned tight and claustrophobic, rooms overflowing with junk and old art pieces that could be scavenged and claimed by other students like an ocean of debris blocked her path.

Still Lottie went further, imagining Ellie making this same trip weeks ago, until she found herself at the centre of the maze, at the winding staircase leading up to what used to be the photography department. The wood was misshapen into waves, and chains hung over most of the doors, and others were barred like they were keeping in some terrible Kraken. Only one door showed any semblance of use, with three baby-doll arms reaching out of the cast-iron fixtures round a closed peephole, looking like trapped souls in a witch's den.

I will be kind, I will be brave, I will be unstoppable, Lottie repeated to herself, lifting her fist to knock at the cursed door. However, before she had so much as made a single tap, the door flew open and Lottie nearly tumbled into a girl with blood-red hair and eyebrows covered in piercings, drawn on so thick they looked like creatures with tiny metal legs.

Blinking away her shock, the red-haired girl's face split into a wide grin, a tongue piercing glinting. 'Well, well, well, if it isn't the little princess herself.'

'I need to talk to you about someone who came to visit a few weeks ago,' Lottie said, refusing to let herself be intimidated.

'You're in luck,' the girl said, moving out of the way to let Lottie through into the pitch-black corridor beyond.

'Stephanie said we were to let you in immediately when you finally came.'

Lottie gulped, a cold chill running through her at the idea they'd been expecting her, but nonetheless she went on, feeling around in her satchel for the box that held her family tiara, the shape of it through the fabric reminding her not to back down.

When Lottie pushed the second door open, she was at once consumed by a kaleidoscope of deep blue and emerald lights, the air turning cool with the salty-sweet smell of brine, like she'd been submerged under the sea. Along the walls, doll limbs reached out from where they were trapped.

'Back so soon? Oh!' And there she was, one of the most beautiful girls Lottie had ever seen, looking up at her through feathered eyelashes as she leaned back in a black-velvet throne covered in twisting shells glued over the fabric.

The sea witch.

The thought flared in Lottie's head without warning and her hand shot up to her neck like she was in danger of losing her voice, and she had – her throat was so dry she could hardly make a squeak.

'Oh, Gem, you've caught me a little fish,' Stephanie cooed. 'Paris, Max, say hi to the little fish.'

Lottie found herself being pushed further into the Parlour, shoulders being pressed down, forcing her into a seat opposite Stephanie. Her vision swimming at the flickering lights, Lottie was vaguely aware of two people raising their heads in greeting before returning to their gruesome pieces of art, but her focus stayed trained on Stephanie.

'I need to ask you about a henna tattoo I think you gave a friend of mine,' Lottie began, swallowing down her nerves like she was gasping for air. 'I need to know what tattoo you gave to Ellie Wolf.'

She had to know for sure what the tattoo said. If Ellie had really got the Maravish for 'painful self-sacrifice' etched on to herself, then Lottie had no choice but to confront her princess about it, no matter the cost.

Stephanie's eyes pinged up to hers like an elastic band, black fingernails coming up to wind in hair darker than the bottom of the ocean. 'I deal in secrets, little *princess*,' she murmured, a wry smile awakening on her lips at the taste of the word. 'And that also means keeping the secrets of others.'

It hit Lottie like a cannonball, knocking the breath out of her. *She knew.*

One thing was clear – it was important enough to Ellie that she'd traded her secret identity, which meant the girl in front of her knew Lottie was a fake.

'Now, if you have any secrets of your own, we have plenty of services we can offer you.' Stephanie gestured to a board at the back of the room, bullet points marks with skull motifs.

- *Tattoos*
- *Piercings*
- *Acquisitions*
- *Removals*
- *Grades*
- *Contraband*

Lottie squinted at the board, as if focusing harder on it might make it make sense.

'She's confused.' The boy – Paris – turned and laughed, revealing duplicate eyes painted immaculately below his own, giving the illusion of a spider's face. 'Why don't you give her a demonstration?'

Appearing like a cloud of smoke, Max kneeled in front of Lottie's chair, their height making them at eye level with each other, even though Lottie was sitting. So mesmerized by Max's long eyelashes, Lottie took an embarrassingly long time to realize that they were holding her family tiara.

'Well, that is very pretty,' Stephanie mused, her blue lips curling in wonder.

Lottie didn't give a second thought to how they'd got it, or when; she only felt a white-hot panic that she had to get it back.

'Give me that,' she demanded, reaching out, but Max only cocked their head to the side as they pulled it out of reach, the opal glittering.

'Give you what?' they asked, feigning confusion, and Lottie watched in horror as their hand passed over the tiara and it vanished.

'Ta-da!' Gem declared, holding her arms out like a magician's assistant showing off the amazing trick. 'Cool, huh?' There was a thrill in her eyes as she gazed at Max, enthralled by this mean little trick.

'OK, stop teasing the poor thing.' Stephanie's voice rolled through the room like the tide, making her three minions stand to attention.

'Here!' With one swift movement, Max held a mirror in front of Lottie, revealing the tiara on her head, nestled in her tousled hair.

Lottie could only gasp at her own reflection, speechless.

'Acquisitions and removals,' Max said, shrugging as if it were all very simple. 'We steal things and we make things disappear.'

'If you ever have anything you need us to get for you, or anything you need to disappear, all it takes is a good secret and it's done,' Stephanie explained, clapping her hands in a way that felt as if she were casting a spell. 'So, what will it be?' she asked, flashing her teeth in a shark-toothed smile.

It was so obvious that Lottie could see it laid before her – Haru's box. Her tongue tingled with the desire to ask them to steal it for her. One secret and she could solve this and finally find out what he was hiding in there. But there was one problem; she couldn't bring herself to share the only secret that would be good enough for such a job.

'I think I'll take my leave,' Lottie said, standing up quickly.

'Suit yourself,' Stephanie called after her. 'I'll be here when you change your mind.'

Wandering out of the art block in a daze, Lottie was disorientated to find it was already dark. The paths were lit up by soft orange floor lights, but in this part of the school there was something creepy about them, like an anglerfish was leading her into its jaws.

Her head was still sore over her failure to get any information about Ellie's tattoo. She was lost, no closer to solving Claude's strange letters or figuring out how to help Ellie.

'Excuse me, Princess.'

Lottie turned to find a Year One girl staring up at her, a vacant expression spinning in her eyes, not quite focused, and all Lottie's nurturing instincts kicked in.

'What's wrong? Are you OK?'

The girl continued to stare up at her, her blank face like a fish out of water, and strangest of all was her dried lips and out-of-place hair, almost as if she had lost all sense of her body.

'Are you hurt?'

Without warning, the girl's hand shot out as fast as a frog's tongue, her fingers wrapping tightly round Lottie's wrist, and with a jerk she pulled Lottie behind the art building.

Lottie tried to prise herself free, clawing at the girl's fingers, but she kept pulling, dragging Lottie with surprising strength past the walls and windows of classrooms and through the school grounds, far away from other students. That's when Lottie smelled it, the sickly-sweet smell making her nose crinkle in disgust. It was a scent she loathed to recognize – the Hamelin Formula.

With one last tug, the girl pulled Lottie into a narrow gap between the old and new art block where only a sliver of light could reach them, and where two eyes glinted out at her from behind brown glasses.

Haru grabbed Lottie's shoulder, righting her before she fell to the ground from the girl's aggressive thrust. She was so shocked she could hardly move, slowly coming to terms with how stupid she'd been. She'd got cocky, been lulled into a false sense of security, forgetting that Haru was still a threat, that he was always there, watching them, and at any moment he could use that formula on one of the students like the poor Year One girl who continued to sway on the spot.

'Stay right there,' he called over Lottie to the poisoned girl behind them and Lottie glared up at him. 'Don't worry.' He shrugged, letting go of her at last. 'It'll leave her system completely in about a week.'

Shaking off her confusion over why Haru had ended his hour with Jamie early, she became angry at what he'd done to this girl. 'You promised you wouldn't hurt anyone else.' Lottie had never considered herself the type to growl, but right now she was dangerously close to it.

His gaze hit her hard and sharp, pinning her in place. 'And I seem to remember you promised you wouldn't tell anyone about my involvement with Leviathan.'

There was not an inch of the sweet, soft mask Lottie had become so accustomed to. This was Haru at his core, simmering and dangerous, and it had Lottie wondering what he and Jamie had talked about to get him so worked up.

'What are you –'

'Come now, Princess – let's not waste time lying.' He waved away whatever she had been about to say, leaning against the wall, his long limbs blocking her way out. 'I know you've been discussing the letters with your little friend Binah. What I do find curious is that you don't seem to have told any of your other inner circle about them.'

Lottie felt her knees going weak and a sick feeling in her stomach at the realization of just how much Haru knew. For a nauseating moment she feared he might even know the one thing he must never learn, that Ellie was the real princess.

Haru began tapping his chin, pretending he was thinking. 'I'll allow this one, I suppose, if it helps you solve it faster, but let me do a little demonstration for you,' he declared, his arm shooting out and making Lottie flinch. 'Watch what happens. This is how I could have all your friends look at you, so let this be a lesson not to tell anyone else, OK?' He gave her a wink like this was just a fun class, but Lottie recoiled.

The younger student came forward to stand at the Partizan's side, and like a doting parent Haru beamed down at her. 'Repeat after me,' he commanded, and the girl nodded along. Her dead-eyed stare made her look like a mannequin. 'You hate the princess of Maradova.'

'I hate the princess of Maradova,' she spat back with all the venom of real revulsion.

Until now Lottie had only ever seen the effects of the Hamelin Formula from a distance, the awful lingering symptoms, the way it made people sick and confused, but this, up close, was scarier than any nightmare her brain could conjure.

'She's mean and scary, and we want her gone,' Haru went on.

'She's mean and scary, and I want her gone.' Upon repeating this, the girl turned to Lottie and began to shake, taking fearful steps back until she'd planted herself behind Haru for protection.

'No, this is wrong. Stop!' Fists balling at her sides, Lottie said the only thing she could think of that might get through to Haru. 'Stop it or I'll tell Jamie.'

This seemed to grab the Partizan's attention, his head cocking to the side curiously, until another sickening smile cracked his face like a scar. 'You'll tell him what exactly?' he taunted, taking a step towards her. 'How you made a pact with me to throw him under the bus?'

'That's not what –'

'Certainly looks that way to me.'

He stared down at her, his dark eyes glinting in the moonlight, and she could taste the guilt, bitter and sharp, because maybe Haru was right.

'I can see this has upset you.' He almost whispered the words at her, his mask gradually climbing back over his face until she hardly recognized the happy-go-lucky boy in front of her. 'Perhaps this gift will cheer you up.'

From inside his jacket, Haru pulled out two manila envelopes and held them out to her. They were numbered. 'These are your last clues before we reveal the truth and take action.'

Lottie felt a panic she hadn't been prepared for course through her. She still wasn't even vaguely close to solving the story – how could this be the last of them?

'You will open the second only after you have solved the first. Good luck, Princess.' Haru pushed the envelope into her hand, his mouth coming close to her ear so she could feel his voice like a curse. 'And remember I've got my eye on you.'

20

Dear Princess,

These are your last clues, and I do hope the pieces will all come together with them.

I have built this puzzle around you, and everything I know about you, so I will tell you now that it is your knowledge of fairy tales that will guide you.

Let it not be said that you and I have nothing in common; in fact, your grandmother used to read one story in particular to me and my brother growing up, one that has become very special to me over the years. It is exactly this fairy tale that will be the key to uncovering the truth. Search for Salten, 1923.

Time is ticking on your chance to put things right before I take it into my own hands.

Your uncle, Claude

'Yep, there it is!' Binah pulled the faded book by Felix Salten out from the shelf in the library, the ancient jacket nearly coming clean off.

They were in the dark and dusty rear section of the library where the oldest books were kept, and it was only Binah's prefect status that had got them permission to nose around freely. Gently, like holding a baby bird, Binah lifted up their find, an original copy of a book Lottie had always had an odd relationship with – *Eine Lebensgeschichte aus dem Walde,* or, as most people knew it, *Bambi.*

'Why *Bambi*?' Lottie mused, staring at the book like it might be able to answer her question. 'We had a stag with a crown, then a wolf with a crown, and now *Bambi*.'

'The stag makes sense, but I don't remember there being any wolves in *Bambi*, let alone any royal wolves.' Binah delicately flicked through the pages, the nostalgic illustrations making Lottie wince.

'No, there aren't.'

Binah tapped her chin. 'Maybe they're trying to say the wolves aren't meant to be in power.'

'A *usurper*?' Lottie exclaimed, shocked by the idea.

'Whoa!' Binah held her hands up. 'Slow down – there's no point in jumping to conclusions.'

'I just . . . I don't get it,' Lottie groaned. 'Claude didn't *want* to take the throne of Maradova. That's why he was exiled and Ellie's dad took the crown.' Lottie shoved the letter in her pocket. 'Why's he doing all this? What does he want?'

'Maybe that's the whole point,' Binah said. 'That there's more to it.'

Lottie tried to focus, but her brain was still fuzzy after her run-in with Haru. He had left her feeling paranoid. She felt as if she might look up to see floating eyeballs staring at her. Even working with Binah no longer felt like a weight off her shoulders. Now it was another thing she'd been given permission to do, and, worst of all, the book had to be *Bambi*.

'I always hated this book,' Lottie confessed, tucking it underneath her arm so they could find a quiet spot at the back. 'It was the one story I'd never let my mother read to me.'

'Because of what happens to Bambi's mum?'

The moment they were seated beneath the library's skylight, Binah turned to her inquisitively, the crown of curls arranged on top of her head bouncing like a little exclamation mark.

'Surprisingly no.' Lottie flicked through the yellowed pages to find the part that always made her so upset, and she wasn't sure if it was her residual frustration at Haru cornering her, or her anger at Claude and his terrible game, but she found herself scowling at the pages.

'See here.' She pointed down at the image of the great stag looming over the young Bambi, antlers like a crown above his head. 'This is the prince of the woods; he is the stag that has survived the longest in the unpredictable forest, evading all hunters, humans and predators. He is wise and ancient, and Bambi is his son.'

Binah listened attentively, so Lottie went on.

'Yet, for all his wisdom and knowledge, when Bambi loses his mother, he still doesn't tell him he's his father; he waits until Bambi has learned everything there is to know, passing on the title, and the cycle continues with two young fawns, Bambi's children, who he promptly ignores in the same way as his father.' Slamming the book shut sent a large cloud of dust into the air and Lottie squeezed her eyes shut. 'I hate it,' she whispered.

Binah's reaction was not what she expected.

'You really have a way with stories, Lottie. I can't wait to see what you'll offer the world after we finish school.'

Lottie spluttered out a shocked laugh, her cheeks going pink as a rose at the compliment. 'You're the one who's going to do all the amazing things when school ends.'

Binah looked away now, turning to a blank page in her notebook where she drew a few question marks around the word 'Bambi'. 'Actually Ollie and I are thinking of travelling across East Africa and South America after school ends, to visit my cousins in Kenya and his grandparents in Brazil, see the Big Five, walk the Inca Trail. We've already started planning.'

Lottie's head shot up. 'You and Ollie, as in *my* Ollie?'

'Well, yes. I've been exchanging letters with him ever since the summer.'

So, not my Ollie any more, Lottie thought, and it felt like part of her was coming loose, the image she had of her life sliding a little further out of view.

'You're taking a year off?' she asked quickly, trying to expel the unpleasant thought from her mind. 'I thought you were heading to Oxford to study law. Aren't they weird about gap years?'

Binah shrugged. 'I've spent the last fourteen years being the perfect student and perfect daughter. I'm the poster child of queer Black girls; I get the best grades, excel in all sports and clubs, not to mention my prefect duties. I need a break.'

'But it comes so naturally to you. I thought you had a whole plan?' Lottie felt the words tumble out of her, unable to understand why the idea of people changing their original path was so distressing.

'I suppose –' Binah sighed, giving Lottie a sideways glance – 'but I realized I'd like some time for me, where I don't need to think about being a perfect role model, where I can just go wild. So, before I throw myself into saving the world, I want to explore it a little.'

Lottie mulled this over, feeling embarrassed that she was floundering while Binah had such a clear idea of her own identity and what she wanted.

'The truth is, the more I think about it, the more I realize,' continued Binah, 'that I think perhaps what I actually want to do is go to King's College to study physics or astrophysics. You know, something to do with space and the universe, where we're all working together – not a subject where we're competing with each other.' An excited grin erupted on Binah's face, a plan forming while she brought the idea to life. 'Maybe you could apply there too? They do a great English course.'

Lottie nearly choked on her laughter, as if Binah had made a very funny joke.

'Don't be silly, Lottie – you'd get into King's easily.'

'No, I mean, I'm going to Maradova, of course, continuing my Portman duties. I'm sure the work will truly start once school ends and we've defeated Claude once and for all.'

'But what about when Ellie takes the throne?'

The question was so unexpected that it felt like someone had pulled the ground out from underneath her feet. An image of Ellie came into her head, but it wasn't the princely figure she usually saw. It was scowling down at her, trying to get rid of her, and it was so painful it made her eyes sting.

'I don't . . .' Her words dried up. Without Ellie and the Wolfsons, what did she have? 'I don't know.'

Above them a slow pitter-patter began, the world beyond the skylight shifting with the building rain.

'I have to go. Looks like it's going to start chucking it down any minute now, and, silly me, I don't have an umbrella. So I'd better get back, shouldn't I?' Lottie laughed. 'I need to get back to solving the rest of this puzzle anyway.'

Binah's eyes narrowed, seeing right through the excuse.

'May I ask, have you told her about these letters yet?'

Lottie waved off Binah's concern, hiding her face. 'It's part of my Portman duties to handle all the tricky stuff,' Lottie declared, packing up her things. 'Thanks for the help, Binah. I really appreciate it.'

'But don't we need to open the other letter?'

'It's fine. I'll handle it on my own from here.' Throwing her bag over her shoulder, Lottie marched off, desperately needing to get out of the suddenly stuffy library. 'I shouldn't have dragged you into this anyway.'

Using her satchel as an umbrella, Lottie rushed to the exit before Binah could say any more. Surrounded by others running to shelter, Lottie's path was clear, and she was determined to get back before any of that rain could get to her. She knew what she was doing, didn't she?

Lottie marched through the Ivy Wood gate, nearly bumping into another boy on his way out. It made her jump – too many eyes, too many people, everyone watching.

Without hesitation, she headed straight to Room 221.

'Please!' she whispered, needing something, anything to distract her, to anchor her back to the Wolfsons, to give her a purpose. 'Let me solve this.'

And there it was locked in her bedside drawer, something to keep the chain that tied her to Ellie strong and unbreakable: the second envelope.

She grabbed the manila envelope, running her fingers along the slit and pouring the contents out on her bed.

She was surprised to find only one item inside. She had been hoping for something more to sink her teeth into. Instead what fell on to her bedspread appeared to be a photo, an old one.

'OK, Goat Man.' Lottie let out a long puff of air to calm herself. 'This'd better make sense or . . .' Lottie trailed off as she held up the picture. It was a photograph of a group of women she didn't recognize. They were smiling cheerfully at one another and at the photographer. There was something familiar about their clothes and the background. One of the younger women in particular had a stern expression and a build that reminded her of . . .

Her eyes darted to the words at the bottom of the photo that were written in Maravish. *Wolfson Palace female staff with their children, 1998.*

She was wrong; she did know these women. The one who looked familiar was a younger Edwina Wintor, head of staff. There was also a short black-haired woman in a sensible maid uniform holding a serious-looking child, a child who was now all grown-up and worked in the palace herself. It was a baby Midori. And clutching the hand of a chubby red-headed woman in a matching dress and apron was a girl with a wide grin she'd become so used to seeing, Hanna, also a maid now, her face red and round and happy.

Eyes flickering over the photo, the room held its breath as her gaze rested over the last woman in the image, unknown yet entirely familiar. Once more her mind began to swim in the sea of disjointed clues, a herd of deer and a pack of wolves running along the edges of the room, and the whisper, over and over, of Ingrid's voice. *Why is Jamie your Partizan?*

The unknown woman stared back at her with an intelligent side smile, dressed in dirty dungarees with gardening tools firmly attached to her slender hips. Her features were long and elegant, giving her a delicate appearance. Her skin was a shining bronze, and her eyes were gold like the stars at the top of a mountain, eyes that Lottie knew so well.

She knew who this was, like she knew the sky was blue and the grass was green. The question was, why on earth had Claude sent her a photo of Jamie's mother?

21

Brush, brush, brush.

Every night before getting into bed Lottie brushed her hair in the bathroom mirror, a ritual that Ellie would watch from the door frame while she cleaned her teeth. It was hypnotic the way the yellow light made Lottie's hair look like sunshine, the soft humming from her lips, and the serenity that overtook her features, except none of it was calm now, only anxious.

Brush, brush, snag.

Ellie wanted to ask her what was wrong, what she was hiding, but that meant getting close to her, which was dangerous, and besides it wouldn't matter soon anyway.

Catching Ellie's eye in the mirror, Lottie beamed, a smile that would have fooled anyone else – and Ellie's stomach began to burn, the Maravish word she'd had written into her ribcage still not healed. She winced, putting a hand to her torso.

'Ellie,' Lottie said tentatively, 'I hope you don't mind me asking, but . . . did you get a tattoo?'

Ellie couldn't meet Lottie's eyes, but nodded silently. She could tell Lottie wanted to know more but she wasn't prepared to share any details. This tattoo, and what it meant, was for her alone.

Lottie understood the silence. 'It's so cold now –' she gave a little shudder to emphasize her point – 'might be time to sleep with an extra blanket.'

Lingering in the bathroom, Ellie could sense the plea in Lottie's tone; her Portman was desperate for her to make one of her classic quips, to prove everything was still normal. Ellie complied, always weak for that puppy-dog look. 'Doesn't Mr Truffles and your mountain of other stuffed animals keep you warm enough?'

Lottie's eyes lit up at the perceived olive branch. 'They need a blanket too,' she said, smiling.

Lottie finally headed to her bed, satisfied that Ellie had been appeased – but they both knew that things were anything other than normal.

There had been an unspoken discomfort hanging in the air since Lottie's decision to cut her father out of her life. The very thought sent a fresh wave of hot-needle pain over Ellie's tattoo, and she tried her best to cover up the wince, both she and Lottie pretending not to notice.

'Night, Ellie,' Lottie cooed, cuddling up with her stuffed pig.

It was too much seeing Lottie snuggled and sleepy with the squishy soft toy, the kind of cute that makes your chest feel like it's going to explode if you don't squeeze something.

'Sweet dreams,' Ellie murmured, rolling over to get the sight of Lottie out of her head before it made her tattoo hurt any more. And so she prepared for another sleepless night.

She could tell when Lottie was out cold, her breathing deep and whistling like a lullaby – the trigger for Ellie to begin her nightly routine. Sometimes she'd manage to sleep for a little while, but now that winter had arrived, with the Christmas holidays and time with her family slowly approaching, Ellie found her mind endlessly buzzing. So she did what she always did now, and got up and went to the bathroom to rub salve on the puffy area where the henna was slowly fading.

'Why do you hurt so much?' Ellie whispered to herself, staring at her reflection in the bathroom mirror.

Stephanie had been adamant that the tattooed area would eventually heal, yet so far no amount of creams or salves kept the flaring down for long. Ellie was starting to become used to the sting, the tattoo her conscience, reminding her of the pain she'd inflicted upon everyone by getting them tangled up in her family's messes, warning her against crossing the line with Lottie into a place they couldn't go back from.

One day you'll be queen and they'll be far away from the Wolfson sickness, she told herself.

Rubbing her hands through her hair, Ellie prepared to head back to the bedroom, knowing it would smell of roses and lavender and Lottie, Lottie, Lottie. As she left the bathroom, she heard the telltale squeak of the Ivy Wood gate. No one was allowed in or out of the dorm area this late at night, especially not since the doubled-down security.

Peering out of the corridor window, Ellie could see that the figure was tall, waving at the night guard as he made his way down the path towards their building, drifting with a ghostly gait. There was something in his arms, something Ellie couldn't make out. It wasn't until the mystery person stepped into the light from the path, that his signature fluffy

186

hair and glasses gave him away. It was Haru, and he was heading towards the boys' dorm.

Before Ellie could see what was nestled under his arm, he moved out of her sight. She knew she had to find him and stop him.

Ellie crept back to her room and switched her nightclothes for black T-shirt and leggings. As she passed Lottie's bed, the rose-pink bedsheets rising and falling with Lottie's steady breathing, her lips parted slightly indicating she was in a deep sleep, Ellie wondered if she should stay behind, that maybe doing this would only cause more trouble for her friend. The storm inside her began to calm until she saw a flash of metal winking at her from beneath the pink bed. Liliana's sword.

The storm bellowed inside her once more, directionless and confused – a great hurricane that had no understanding of its target or why it raged, only that it needed to unleash itself, and it had to be now. Ellie grabbed the sword, feeling the singing metal greet her, and together they flew down the stairs.

Sticking close to the shadows, Ellie tiptoed round the back of the building. Sure enough, she found Haru skulking at the back door to the boys' dorm where the emergency exit light shone bright crimson against the twisting ivy. There was none of that malleable and accommodating charm that Haru usually wore, no lulling summer-breeze smile. Only pure concentration.

He was on a mission, and Ellie was going to put a stop to it.

'Put your hands up!'

Before Ellie could utter another word, Haru effortlessly dipped under her blade, twisting with the slick movement of a shadow until he was out of the way. He shot his leg out, tripping Ellie, before grabbing her with his free hand and pinning her against the wall with such force that the air flew out of her lungs.

Haru blinked at her, confused, before quickly righting himself. 'I am so sorry.' He bowed low, and the moment he let go Ellie rolled forward, desperately gulping in air. 'It is my Partizan instinct to attack intruders.'

Ellie watched the Partizan-trained member of Leviathan raise his head, and this time she couldn't breathe for completely different reasons. There was something behind his mask, the illusion broken, and for the first time she saw what was hiding there and it was terrifying.

Is this what Lottie had been dealing with? The thought was so awful it made her feel sick.

'Your little princess should have made it clear to you not to interfere with me.' He spoke calmly, more like an adult affectionately telling off a naughty child, and it was so disarming that she nearly didn't register how sinister his words were. 'Unless you are intentionally trying to make things difficult for her?'

Ellie tried to hold her ground. 'What are you doing skulking around?' Her lungs still ached from being winded. 'You said we'd be safe if we behaved.' She was about to ask what he had in his hand when she saw the Christmas-pudding wrapping paper.

It was a Christmas present.

'I was going to leave a present for Jamie-kun. I wanted it to be an anonymous surprise. Something to take home with him when term ends.' He cocked his head to the side in faux innocence. 'Has your little princess got him anything yet?'

'She . . . What?' Ellie was thrown by the question, and she tried to move to the side where there was a clearer chance of escape, but Haru's hand shot out, holding her in place.

'Of course she hasn't – probably hasn't even crossed her mind.' The mask slipped further and his face tilted upward as if he were about to take a bite out of her. 'Jamie has told me about you and his princess.'

Ellie froze, shocked that Jamie would talk about her and Lottie at all, let alone with Haru . . . except Jamie didn't know anything about Haru, thanks to her. If she'd just let Lottie tell her parents when they had the chance, but her stupid obsession with having one up on her parents had ended up hurting everyone. She always ended up hurting everyone.

'You are a troublemaker,' Haru continued, squeezing her shoulder so hard that she winced.

'What are you talking about?'

'You and the princess you are so close to,' Haru went on, his voice not matching his cold expression. 'Your relationship seems to cause a lot of drama for everyone. Of course, this is only an observation.'

This time Haru didn't need to squeeze her shoulder to make her flinch. The words were painful enough. Everything she'd feared about herself, everything she knew to be true, was spewing out of her enemy.

'And you talked about this with Jamie?' It came out ragged and defeated.

'It has come up,' Haru replied.

It was the last push and sent Ellie over the edge.

'I know what you're doing,' she snapped. 'I know you're trying to get inside Jamie's head. I'll kill you before I let you do that.'

Haru took a step back. 'What do you mean?'

'I'm not going to let you get away with this,' she snarled. 'We're watching you too.'

When Haru narrowed in on her this time, he looked less like a mischievous fox and more like a bird of prey, who would swoop down at any moment and eat her alive, and deep, deep down there was just a hint of something human. 'Does Jamie know?'

Ellie hesitated, hot panic making her realize how stupid she'd been, that she was only digging herself further into her own grave. 'Maybe.'

Relaxing, Haru leaned casually against the stone wall, the gift still nestled under his arm. 'I didn't think so, although it's strange that his princess never told him,' he pondered, passing the present from one hand to the other.

Ellie gulped. 'Maybe you don't know her as well as you think you do.'

'Let me assure you,' Haru mocked, 'we know the princess of Maradova better than she knows herself.'

Haru took a step towards her now, and she bared her teeth, preparing to strike if she needed to. 'If I were you, I'd get as far away from the princess as possible.' His words came with a warning. 'She is not good for anyone.'

If only he knew who really needed protecting, Ellie thought, part of her wanting to laugh. The other part wanted to scream and destroy something.

'You think you know her, but actually it is you who is the most oblivious.'

190

'What are you –'

Haru patted her on the head condescendingly. 'It's simple, really,' he began. 'Every important choice she's ever made, everything she's ever done – it's all been laid out for her.'

'What?'

Haru smiled, pleased with her reaction. 'We started the rumours about her reckless behaviour that kept her locked away and desperate to leave. We sent her the information about this very school. We are the reason she went to Japan. The Maravish royal family are as predictable as the changing seasons; all we had to do was give them a little push and –'

'Stop it,' Ellie barked, not wanting to hear a single word more. The sword went slack in her hand, her shoulders dropping. 'I don't want to hear any more.'

'So,' Haru said, seeming satisfied, 'will you keep your distance?'

Head still spinning, Ellie mulled over everything, from the moment she'd set foot in Rosewood, meeting Lottie, inflicting the Portman job upon her, Leviathan, Jamie, all their friends and what they'd been through. There was not a sliver of doubt left about what she needed to do; she just hoped she'd have time.

'Yes,' she said at last, the tattoo on her chest screaming like a fresh wound as she stared herself down in the black window behind Haru. 'I think it's time everyone kept their distance from the princess of Maradova.'

22

Looking at the pictures of William Tufty, Lottie could hardly make sense of it. His features were constantly morphing until she couldn't find any trace of her own genetics in the image; instead, all she could see was Jamie's mother.

Why is Jamie your Partizan?

It didn't help that ever since she'd got the photograph she couldn't get rid of Ingrid's voice in her head, constantly whispering the same question.

Christmas holidays were only a week away, and out of the bay window in the Ivy common room Lottie saw students wrapped up in winter coats, giddy with the possibility of snow, while she stayed inside, preoccupied with Claude's puzzles.

'Lottie?'

'Cla–' Lottie nearly jumped out of her skin, imagining that Claude had called her name, but it was only Jamie, sitting opposite, patiently helping her find inspiration for her PoP piece. 'Sorry – I was just thinking, maybe I should try a different book?' she said quickly, hoping he hadn't notice her slip.

Lottie's fingers brushed Liliana's diary within the pile of William Tufty's books of poems and nursery rhymes, the feel of it sending her hand back like an electric shock.

'You seem very distracted,' Jamie said, his eyebrows furrowing in a familiar way. 'You're supposed to be submitting your Tufty tribute soon,' he reminded her; the fact that she'd made virtually no progress lingered unspoken in the air.

'Sorry, I know this won't look good for the Wolfsons if I don't get a move on and submit something impressive.' She sighed, annoyed with herself. She couldn't exactly tell Jamie that he and his mother were the very reason she was distracted.

'That's not what –'

'Honestly . . .' Lottie began, her eyes wandering to the window, where a flurry of browned leaves danced in a chaotic circle above them, casting strange shadows over the common room. 'I'm worried about Ellie, among other things. The PoP feels like a pointless distraction.'

Jamie's jaw twitched. Turning to her, his eyes narrowed and she forced herself to look down at her hands. 'What's wrong with Ellie?'

'Haven't you noticed?' Lottie needed to talk about something, anything else – anything to get her mind off Jamie and his mother. 'She can barely look at me recently. Not since I made the choice to cut off my family. I know she's been blaming herself for everything, and I've tried to tell her it's fine. I don't understand why she's locking me out like this –'

'Your father,' Jamie interrupted, giving her a pointed look.

'What?'

'You said you cut off your family, but I thought you said your father wasn't your family.'

Confused, Lottie felt her brows crease, sure that Jamie must have misheard her.

'I'm sure I said –'

'I wish you'd give yourself a break,' Jamie said, interrupting again. 'This should be a big deal for you, researching your mother's ancestor. Liliana, Tufty, Rosewood, this is who you are. It could be your whole future.'

Flinching, Lottie struggled not to look away, but knew that would only make Jamie press her more. 'Since when are you so encouraging about discussions about family?'

It was a low blow, and Lottie instantly regretted it.

To her surprise, Jamie's face twisted painfully. 'I've been wrong about a lot of things.' Shaking his head, he picked up another book.

Something about his expression reminded her of when Binah had looked at her in the library the other day, sympathetic in a way that made her embarrassed, only Jamie's was harsher, a little of himself leaking into it.

'I know what I'm doing,' she said without thinking.

'If you know what you're doing, then why can't you even look at one of these books? Why can't you concentrate on anything that doesn't involve Ellie and her family?'

The words made her head hurt. Nothing fit right any more.

Above them an old clock ticked away, the sound of its hands turning an incessant reminder of how time was running out, and with great frustration she did the only thing she could think of.

'Jamie, can I ask you something personal?'

'Absolutely not,' he scoffed. 'You aren't getting out of this work so easily.'

'Please. If you answer, I'll focus on the assignment. I promise.'

Jamie watched her fidgeting, and she tried her best to put on an innocent smile.

Sighing, he leaned back into the wall. 'What?'

Lottie slammed her book shut, pulling herself up to sit with her hands clasped firmly in her lap until she was leaning forward towards Jamie, excited by the rare invitation to probe the Partizan and relieved to not be talking about her own family any more.

'It's just, I realized,' she started, pushing her hair back to hide how awkward she felt, 'you know every little thing about my family, and I don't even know your parents' names.'

Jamie blinked at her, eyebrow lifting. 'That's not a question.'

Rolling her eyes, Lottie puffed out her cheeks. 'Fine, OK.' She felt herself getting hot under his blank stare, and she wasn't sure if it was the discomfort of having to ask Jamie something she knew he'd hate or from the way he was looking at her, like he might burn a hole right through her head with the intensity. 'What's your mother's name?' She said it as fast as she could before she chickened out.

Jamie stared at her for a weighted moment, until the intensity in his face melted away, replaced with an inward contemplation, like he'd gone away somewhere she couldn't reach.

'You're the second person to ask me about her,' he said at last, and Lottie felt her skin prickle because she knew it could only be Haru that Jamie was talking about.

'It's OK if you don't want to answer. I was just curious, and –'

'Hirana.' Jamie didn't look at her when he spoke, but instead turned to the curved window, his face so close to the glass that his breath made angel wings of condensation. 'Hirana Rajput.'

He spoke as if he was reciting a prayer, soft and personal, more for himself than Lottie, and she didn't want to interrupt his thoughts but a question popped out of her lips before she could stop it.

'Why did they change your last name?'

Jamie turned to her with the panicked look of a trapped animal. 'I . . .' It was odd to see Jamie of all people scrabbling for words. 'I've never thought about it,' he confessed, only this wasn't his usual blasé attitude – instead his eyes turned fiery again and stared off somewhere far away. 'That book you gave me for my birthday last year. It said that *hirana* means "deer" in Punjabi.' Jamie's voice was low but his next words hit her ears like a screaming banshee. 'Maybe they didn't want any deer among the wolves.'

Jamie's mother was the deer. Lottie didn't know what that meant, only that she had to get to her dorm right now and figure it out. 'Jamie, I –'

Before she could finish, a ruckus outside the window pulled their attention away. Vampy was yowling from the other side of the glass with a dead rabbit firmly caught between his teeth. To Lottie's horror, the cat began tearing the poor creature to shreds in front of squealing students, all the while looking up at Jamie as if he expected praise.

Percy came up behind the cat, waving at them in apology, entirely oblivious to the enormity of their conversation. He scooped up Vampy, who yowled in protest when Percy, in a panic, kicked the still-twitching creature under a bush.

Jamie tutted, the flames in his eyes turning to embers as he watched the cat wriggle about in Percy's arms, who had a world-weary look at having to babysit the little monster. 'This damn cat.'

'*Give me a second*,' Jamie signed through the window, giving Vampy a sharp look. The cat sank like a lump of putty, his large head receding into his neck until he was more slug than cat. 'Sorry, Lottie.'

The moment Jamie was outside, Lottie packed up her books and headed to her dorm.

Ellie had left the balcony door ajar when she'd gone to fencing practice, making the room cold and causing goosebumps to come to life on Lottie's arms when she entered. Placing Liliana's diary back on her bedside table, Lottie leaned down, ignoring the way the floorboards groaned in protest when she shoved the rest of the books under her bed before turning to her bedside drawer.

Nestled inconspicuously inside the antique nightstand was Lottie's sketchbook. It looked quite ordinary, a plain, if slightly beaten-up, purple moleskin, but when she pulled it open the pages were filled with her private thoughts and sketches. Ink and watercolour brought to life everyone, and everything that resided in her mind. Ellie, Jamie and all her friends flickered past her fingertips as she flipped through, mixed up in the slideshow with the more monstrous faces of Ingrid, Haru and Claude. And right at the centre, held in the creases of her sketchbook, were the letters and clues Claude had sent her.

Moving on autopilot, she plucked out the puzzle pieces, laying them on the bed until she found the photo of Hirana, and with shaky hands she wrote down her new information in pencil on an empty page. But writing Hirana's name still didn't help Lottie to make any sense of the clues, and so she did the only thing she could think of: she drew what she was feeling.

The graphite pencil became an extension of her thoughts, and slowly the pages began to fill with likenesses of Jamie and Ellie. Ellie she drew as a wolf, snarling teeth, biting and snapping in fear. Jamie she drew above his mother's name, in flames, trying to capture the burning in his eyes, with thick stag antlers protruding from his skull. These doodles looked more demonic than human, ferociously at odds with the regal and princely ways she usually drew them.

It wasn't until her left hand brushed one of Claude's letters that she was pulled out of her trance, the rustling of the paper underneath her skin like a menacing whisper in her ear.

Right there, at the bottom of this letter, were words she'd shoved into a locked box in her head, and now they glared back. She uttered them in horrified rapture. '*Wolves are hunters too.*'

It ignited inside her like a bomb, with no way of stopping it from going off.

Hirana, *Bambi*, wolves and hunters, and the question that kept her up at night: *Why is Jamie your Partizan?*

She still didn't have the answer, she still didn't understand why, but she knew one thing now with crystalline certainty.

Turning back to her sketches, Lottie stared down at her depictions of Jamie, the stag, and Ellie, the wolf, a story so simple and all it had needed was Hirana's name to solve it.

What Claude was trying to tell her was that Jamie's mother had been murdered.

Lottie stood up so fast the world started spinning. She dropped her sketchbook as her legs buckled with the effort of holding her up, sending her crashing to the ground. Fumbling for something to grab hold of, her hands met her bag, its contents spilling around her.

'What does this mean, Claude?' she said out loud, fists balled on either side of the sketchbook where the photograph of Jamie's mother stared back at her. 'What happened to Hirana? Why are you telling me this?'

With no further clues she felt hopelessly lost, her mind grinding to a halt. She needed something, anything else, to explain Claude's message.

Pulling herself up, Lottie searched for her tiara. She stared at it, watching the rainbow orbs in the opal swirling in the light like a hypnotic spiral. It felt strange to hold, not giving her any of the soothing properties it usually did; instead it reminded her of another problem.

In the back of her mind, pulling at her for attention, she knew she'd promised Jamie she'd focus on her PoP tribute if he shared something personal with her, but how could she after this discovery?

The very thought of opening up those books and thinking of Liliana made her recoil, as if even touching the pages would pull her further away from Ellie and the Wolfsons – further away from the only real family she had left, at the very moment they needed her the most.

'I'm a Portman,' Lottie announced to no one at all, willing the bad feeling away.

The opal moon of the tiara winked rainbow light at her again and the beam landed on the wolf pendant that hung heavily round her neck.

'I don't need this. I've found a new family, and I need to help them.' Lottie tried to believe herself but the words felt like excuses.

Shoving the tiara into its box, she clenched her fists again. She was going to find the meaning behind Claude's messages, and that meant doing something completely irresponsible. It was time to find out what was in Haru's secret box.

Lottie shut her sketchbook and slotted it, along with Liliana's diary, into her bag, patting the fabric to check everything was safe and sound.

This was for her princess and Partizan; they were all that mattered. As long as she could solve this and do her Portman duties, everyone would be OK, and she would be part of the Wolfson family forever. Then she set off to a place she'd hoped not to go back to.

Outside was freezing cold, with Lottie's purple blazer and scarf barely keeping the frost from nipping at her neck. She welcomed the cold – it distracted her from thinking about whatever terrible fate had befallen Jamie's mother.

Making her way through the school, Lottie kept her head down because there was little doubt that Haru was keeping a close watch on her, but it wasn't until she was at the door to the so-called Parlour that the cold finally hit her. Her hands were sore when she knocked and Lottie had to remind herself to be brave, that this was for the people she loved.

'Oh, it's you again.' Paris stared at her through the peephole, white-out contact lenses making his eyes look like two moons through the gap. 'What do you want now?'

Lottie squeezed the bag she was carrying, in which was concealed her greatest secret, Liliana and her royal ancestry, which she'd had to hide away for the sake of her Portman duties, and now she was going to make it useful.

'I need to speak to Stephanie,' Lottie demanded. 'I have a secret to trade for your services.'

23

The next two days were excruciating. Every shadow made Lottie jump, every unexpected sound sent her heart racing, as if Claude was right behind her. Lottie had to keep smiling, refusing to drag anyone else into her awful discovery until she'd fully solved it.

A very loud part of her brain told her that Haru knew everything, and that she'd put the whole school in even more danger with her silly plan to steal his box, but as time went by there was no sudden ambush, no more students turning against her, and no word from the Artistocracy on Haru's mysterious box.

'Are you gonna eat that?'

Looking up from where she was nervously pushing her dessert around, Lottie didn't even have time to process the question before Saskia stuck her fork in Lottie's last piece of cheesecake and shoved it in her mouth, much to the shock of the twins at her side.

'Saskia, how could you?' Lola squealed.

Before Saskia had the chance to offer a snarky retort, Micky placed a small portion of his strawberry tart on Lottie's plate. 'Desserts are sacred,' is all that he said.

There was no irony in Micky's tone, and he nodded to Lottie as if he were some benevolent lord of dessert doctrine, and she supposed he sort of was now that he and his sister owned their father's business.

Most of the students, including Ellie and Jamie, were off helping to wrap up club activities for the term, so the lunch hall wasn't overwhelmingly busy. Sushi was on the menu and the smell of raw fish was making Lottie queasy.

'Actually I'm not really hungry.' Lottie smiled, pushing the plate back while the twins shared a suspicious look that she decided to ignore.

Clearly Lottie was not doing a good enough job of keeping face, and if the twins were seeing through it, then Haru might too.

'You're smiling too much,' Anastacia said at last, not even looking up from where she flipped through her fashion magazine. 'If something's wrong, you need to tell us.' There was a weight to her words that the twins wouldn't understand, a crushing demand to keep Saskia and her in the loop about Haru. 'Binah told us you walked off the other day when you two were supposed to be working together.'

The indictment made her stomach turn.

Anastacia wasn't stupid, and Lottie could tell by the way her eyes locked on to hers that she knew Lottie was keeping secrets. But she couldn't tell her, no matter how desperate she was to tell someone about Claude's letters and their awful messages. It was impossible. She couldn't do that to Jamie, not until she knew what it meant and what had happened to his mother.

'Nothing's wrong,' Lottie replied, continuing to smile through the lie. 'It's just the smell in here, and –'

A bump at the back of Lottie's seat stopped her mid-sentence. Everyone's eyes turning to an unapologetic-looking girl standing behind Lottie.

'Oops. I'm *so* sorry, Princess.' Lottie's ears pricked. She didn't sound sorry. Haru might have got a hold on her too. 'I walked right into your seat. I'm so silly.'

Lottie tried to get a whiff of the telltale baby-powder stench of the Hamelin Formula. But there was nothing, just a light sea-salt smell like the girl had walked out of the ocean. She had thick make-up on in an elaborate cobweb pattern that looked familiar, and as she turned round to walk off Lottie recognized her – she was from the Artistocracy.

Then she felt it. There was something in her blazer pocket that definitely hadn't been there before.

'What the hell was that?' Saskia scowled, everyone staring daggers at the girl walking away, giving Lottie a chance to peep at what had been sneaked into her pocket.

It was a long aquamarine crystal with a note attached with green string that curled round her fingers like seaweed.

Please return the book you borrowed from me.
I'll be waiting in the Ivy laundry room with what you requested.
The book is in your bag ☺

They had it – Haru's box was waiting for her; all she had to do was go and get it. The very thought had her hands shaking.

'Where are you going? Anastacia's said as Lottie stood up. 'We're supposed to be meeting Ellie to go and study.'

'I have to return a book,' Lottie said on autopilot.

Trying not to let the sweat forming on her brow reveal her anxiety, Lottie reached into her bag in a leap of faith, and, sure enough, her fingers met something that definitely hadn't been there before. She pulled the book out, the perfect alibi.

'See!' Lottie held out the black notebook marked with an Ivy emblem, lines of text declaring it was maths notes belonging to an Ivy student. 'Louisa in the year above let me borrow her revision plan from last year to copy.' The lie flowed easily.

This is for Ellie and Jamie, she told herself. *This is a Portman's duty.* 'I'll catch you all later.'

Without giving Anastacia a chance to probe her, Lottie left the dining hall, trying not to run and give away her anticipation. By the time she reached Ivy Wood she was panting but not from exhaustion. She was used to running; this was entirely different. She was desperate for answers.

When she got into the hot laundry room at the back of the dorm, her fingers and cheeks stung with the sudden temperature change, and her eyes instantly locked on to the person sitting on top of one of the drying machines.

'I got your note.' Lottie walked over to Max, who stared down at her from their laundry throne, the metallic hum from the wall behind them making it look like the world was shaking.

'As you requested.' The sultry voice came from behind Lottie, and the door slammed shut, revealing Stephanie herself, who tossed Lottie the box so suddenly that the wood hit her in the chest hard enough to make her wince. 'You'll need the key if you plan to open it.'

'What?' Immediately Lottie began grappling with the box, turning it over to see for herself. It was plain, a simple wooden box with a discoloured but perfectly sturdy lock. 'So I can't even get inside?'

'All you requested was the box, Princess Mayfutt.'

Lottie froze, turning to Max who grinned at her like a shark, waiting to lure her into their jaws.

No one had ever called her that, and it sent tingles along the crown of her head, as if something deep within her was calling out, willing her to put on her tiara and claim that hidden part of herself once and for all.

Shaking it off, Lottie shoved the feelings down into the back of her mind again, and turned on Stephanie. 'Neither of you can call me that.'

Stephanie rolled her eyes at Max, patting Lottie on the head like she might a yapping puppy. 'Play nice, Max. We need to respect other people's secrets.' She gave Lottie a once-over, smirking to herself. 'Even if the secret seems counterproductive, little missing princess?'

Lottie ignored her inquisitive tone. She was Ellie's Portman, and the Wolfsons were her chosen family, a real family that she could touch, not a ghost or a secret in her blood. That's where she belonged and where her attention needed to lie, and if that meant closing herself off from her royal heritage, then so be it. 'I have to get this open.' Lottie was surprised by how desperate she sounded, both Max and Stephanie visibly recoiling.

Jumping off the dryer, Max tapped a long finger against their chin in thought. 'What's in there that's so important anyway?'

'You won't understand. No one does, not even me.' Lottie shook the box, as if it might give her a clue. 'Something's going on and, if I can't solve it, terrible things could happen. I could lose everything.'

Lottie wished she had Sayuri with her, someone she could actually talk to about this, to help her figure it all out. Someone who understood the need to cling to and protect any family you found.

Max and Stephanie looked at one another across the room, until eventually Stephanie exhaled, a deep sigh.

'Listen, little guppy.' Stephanie stepped forward to wrap her cold arm round her. 'You gave me a very good secret, so let me give you some advice. You need something sharp, really sharp, and you should be able to wedge it under the box's lid and prise it open. Can you do that?'

'Where am I supposed to find –'

Lottie stared at the box as Sayuri's postcard turned over in her head like the key she needed. *Our fates are linked by the sword.*

Even from across the world Sayuri still found a way to give her the advice she needed.

'I know what I need to do,' Lottie said, side-stepping Stephanie. 'Wait for me here; I'll bring the box back in fifteen minutes.' She stopped in the doorway of the laundry room and looked at Max and Stephanie's stunned faces. 'Thank you.'

Lottie ran straight to her dorm. She kicked the door shut and dived to the floor. There, deep in the shadows under her bed, a silver light winked at her from between sheets of cloth. When her fingers reached round her treasure she freed it with a metallic whirr.

As Lottie unwrapped the sword, the strange but familiar sun-etched handle came into view. Why had she hidden it away? Lottie stared down at her ancestor's sword, her eyes taking it in for the first time in a long while.

Holding it made her chest ache, and she longed to embrace her heritage. But she knew that what waited for her if she followed this feeling was loneliness. There would be no family: no Wolfsons, no Jamie, no Ellie; only Lottie, alone, again.

It was the last push she needed to pull the box back into focus. As long as she could help the Wolfsons, she'd always have a place she belonged.

With one final bout of resolve, Lottie lifted the sword with both hands and struck it down hard through the middle of the box. The sound of the impact was a sharp twang followed by a small and satisfying click, the lock melting under the blade like butter.

It felt like magic, the sword hitting exactly where it needed to, and, like a chestnut, the box cracked open, the juicy insides peeking out.

There was no going back from here.

24

'There you are,' Lottie breathed, reaching hungrily for her prize, until her fingers froze, confused by what she was seeing.

Not in all her wonderings had she imagined that Haru had been telling the truth: the box did indeed contain a diary.

Humming in thought, Lottie picked up the red leather notebook, flicking through the pages, hungry for a taste of anything she could use against Leviathan. The contents were not the instant clue she'd expected; in fact it was entirely empty until about halfway through where the pages erupted with lines and lines of Kanji and Hiragana, all of which she couldn't read.

She only noticed her mistake once she reached a page with an upside-down sketch of a cat, and she couldn't believe what a fool she'd been. The back of the book was, in fact, the front, meaning it must have been a notebook Haru had kept since he was in Japan.

A part of her thought that perhaps, once she turned it over, she might magically be able to understand the foreign characters, but that was pure optimism. As she began making her way through the diary from the correct side, she realized how hopeless it truly was.

Everything was in Japanese, not a single line in English. Here it was, right at her fingertips, probably everything she'd need to figure out what Leviathan were planning, everything they wanted, and Lottie couldn't read a single word of it.

A sudden pain in her bottom lip let her know she'd bitten down too hard on it in frustration. Despite her efforts to remain calm, her eyes swam with tears that threatened to spill over on to the diary.

With time running out, she hurried through the pages, desperate to find anything at all that she could use, when her attention snagged on three numbers, ones that she knew very well because she saw them almost every day.

In elegant handwriting were four sets of three-digit Arabic numbers.

$$2 \quad 2 \quad 1$$
$$0 \quad 0 \quad 9$$
$$1 \quad 0 \quad 9$$
$$9 \quad 9 \quad 9$$

Underneath Haru had circled some Japanese text three times, clearly indicating that this was significant, but it was those three numbers at the top that had made her pause. They were the numbers of her dorm room.

Fingers shaking, Lottie grabbed a pen and jotted the numbers down on some scrap paper, along with the Japanese characters underneath. Even if she didn't know what the other three numbers were, it had to link up; there had to be a reason for them all being together.

Her mind racing at the thought that she might have found something actually useful, Lottie's shaking hands struggled to hold the diary steady as she placed it back in the box. And it was then that she felt it, the way the leather at the back of the notebook gave slightly, something hard underneath it, an odd feeling as if it were a creature trying to shed its skin.

Turning it over once more, Lottie ran her index finger along the seam on the inside of the back page to find that the paper tucked into the crease. All it took was a little push in the right direction and the inner page popped out.

The second it came loose, a dark obsession was revealed: pictures, drawings and notes tumbling to the floor, and every single one of them was connected to Jamie.

It was easy to identify Jamie's elegant handwriting on the smaller scraps of paper, poetic notes he must have written down absent-mindedly while helping Haru with work, meaningless but pretty thoughts that Haru had felt precious enough to hold on to. Lottie rifled through, finding a dark wad of string that she held up to her eyes, and gasped, dropping it immediately as she realized it was a lock of Jamie's hair.

Continuing to look through the items with a thundering calm, Lottie picked up each one with the same quiet dread of someone identifying a dead body.

Along with the scavenged musings of Jamie's were photos and drawings of her Partizan, each one distinct in its own way, including a rare depiction of his smile. It was like a ghostly, twisted version of Lottie's own art book. But there was one that stood out above the others, and the most confusing thing she'd seen so far. The photo was old, showing Jamie when he was much younger, no more than a child, yet

211

staring at the camera with that same stony face he still wore now. It was strange enough that Haru would have such a thing, and yet there was something else that drew her to it. Haru had adorned Jamie's head with gold ink to give him a crown of antlers.

Lottie picked up the photo with extra care, tilting it in the light to get a proper look, and, when she turned it over, the world stopped. Written on the back at the bottom in English were the words THE LITTLE PRINCE OF MARADOVA.

'No.' The word escaped her lips before her mind had even caught up, the truth of what she was seeing slowly emerging from the fog of denial in her head.

The evidence was there, whether she liked it or not, and what it was telling her was that somehow, though entirely unfathomable, Haru believed Jamie to be the prince of Maradova.

Why is Jamie your Partizan?

The question hit her so hard she jolted upright. Lottie stood up and immediately stumbled back to the door. She had enough sense to quickly place the diary and its contents back in the box and shove the other clues into her bag before she raced outside.

When she reached the laundry room, Max was gone, but Stephanie was there, picking at one of her long nails, which were decorated with a shell design.

'That was quick.' She looked as if she was about to make a joke, but her face fell when she looked at Lottie. 'What did you find?' Her voice had dropped an octave, a dark hunger there to know what could have terrified Lottie.

212

Lottie shook her head, shoving the box back into Stephanie's hands, not able to articulate any of her discovery. 'You need to get it back into Haru's drawer. He can't know I saw it.'

Raising an eyebrow, Stephanie looked down at the box in her hand like it was a poisoned apple. 'He was in the Ivy building not long ago.'

'What?' Lottie nearly choked.

'Max saw him just now. He had an envelope in his hand. They walked over to the gym so that we can make sure Haru doesn't return before we have a chance to put this back.' She waved the box in the air.

Lottie panted, adrenaline rushing through her body. 'I have . . . I have to go,' she managed to gasp out, only vaguely aware of Stephanie calling to her.

Her feet felt like they were made of lead as she ran, knowing exactly what was waiting for her.

There was a letter in her cubbyhole. A manila envelope that she knew must contain all the answers. She picked it up and when she turned it over the top simply read in Haru's writing: *Time's up*.

It was early evening as she dragged herself through the school grounds, students like ghosts in her vision fading in and out of focus, until she reached Stratus Side and the entrance to Liliana's study.

Usually it felt peaceful to be alone in the heart of the school, in her secret place, but now it was tinged with fear. She didn't want to be alone any more. She had to help the Wolfsons and fix whatever this mess was, no matter how much it hurt. That way she, Ellie and the Wolfsons could always be together, happy.

With all the pieces in order, she laid them out in front of her on the rug. The *Bambi* imagery, the stag, the usurping wolves and Jamie's mother.

In the very centre she placed the unopened envelope. The answers she'd been searching for.

Claude had called himself a victim in his first letter, and now she was going to find out what he was a victim of, and why Jamie's mother was part of this.

Tracing each image, Lottie caught her breath. Picking up the blank envelope and turning its contents out, she whispered, 'I'm ready,' but she knew it was a lie.

A single square of card fell out, and on it was written the exact question that haunted Lottie whenever she looked at Jamie. *Why is Jamie your Partizan?*

It was written in a seductively elegant script. The answer was on the other side, the ink bleeding through the card. She'd got the answer wrong in the summer when Ingrid had asked her, foolishly believing his tie to the Wolfsons was purely out of obligation. She knew better now, and she had the scar Ingrid had given her on her skin as a reminder.

Still, Lottie was too afraid to turn over the card. Instead she pulled out the folded paper that remained nestled in the envelope, and with shaky fingers she unfolded it.

Lines upon lines revealed themselves, each one forming a branch in a tree of names spanning back through centuries.

One name caught her eye in a flash: Eleanor Wolfson. This was the Wolfson family tree. But it wasn't Ellie's name that sent the world spinning. It was the lines that extended above and around her, threads like a spider's silk twisting around every name and trapping them in their web of secrets.

Ellie had always said she was the only heir to the throne. That she had no cousins or siblings. That it all fell on her. Yet the threads revealed the dark truth. Beside Ellie was the name of a boy Lottie knew so well, and now the strings on the paper linked them by blood.

The truth bloomed in front of her. The name beside Ellie's was Jamie Volk, and, above him, two names declared him their child: Claude Wolfson and Hirana Rajput.

There was no denying it. Claude was Jamie's father.

Claude burst forth in her mind. His eyes, Jamie's eyes. The fiery gold and emerald green swirling together like a forest fire. The two became one, the twitch of his lips, the demons that lurked somewhere beyond his stare.

Blinking away a tear, Lottie gripped the card, her throat thick. *Why is Jamie your Partizan?*

She choked, imagining she held the knife that would cut all their ties. Gritting her teeth, she bit down hard, bracing herself. On the reverse of the card, written like a stab in the centre, was the answer.

As punishment.

25

Lottie burst through her bedroom door, her heart racing so fast she thought it might beat out of her chest. 'We need to book a trip back to Maradova. You, me and Jamie. I must speak to your parents.'

'What?' Ellie nearly spilled the packet of biscuits she was opening, pulling the packet's edges with too much force. 'What about?'

'I . . .' Despite having rehearsed this over and over in her head, now that she was here, talking to Ellie, she felt Claude's hand on her shoulder again, his and Jamie's faces staring back at her through Ellie, and she rubbed her eyes to try to get him out. 'I just need to speak to them,' she managed at last. 'Please trust me.'

'What could you possibly need to speak to them about that you can't speak to me about?'

It was dark outside from a brewing rainstorm. Lottie looked into Ellie's confused face and realized this was the first time they'd properly spoken in longer than she could remember. When had they become so distant? How did she let this happen?

'It's not like that, Ellie,' Lottie spluttered. 'I do want to speak to you about it, but I have to speak to them first.' Lottie searched in Ellie's dark eyes, feeling the storm brewing there, the way it fizzed and charged. 'You're always my number-one priority,' she continued, hoping to calm it. 'You have to believe me that I'd only do this if I truly believed it was for the best. Please, I . . .' She knew immediately it was the wrong thing to have said and the words got lost on her tongue as Ellie recoiled.

'I've been meaning to talk to you about something too.' It was Ellie speaking, but her voice came out harsh. 'About our situation.'

It was Lottie's turn to be confused. 'Excuse me?'

Ellie looked up at her and there was nothing there at all, not even a spark, and then she spoke, and it was the most horrible sound in the world. 'I want to know what you plan to do when you're not my Portman any more.'

The words screamed in Lottie's skull like a banshee. She tried to make sense of what she was feeling, scrabbling for her voice. Everything she'd done, everything she was doing, was so she could stay with Ellie; she had nothing else.

'I'll be with you,' she mumbled, and Ellie cocked her head to the side, like a curious animal seeing how far they could push their prey.

'Not when I'm queen.'

Lottie felt herself swaying, her head fuzzy and confused. 'I don't. I can't.' It was all she could get out; it felt like her lips had been sewn shut.

This wasn't how this was supposed to go. Everything Lottie had done was so they could put this right, so they could be happy together at last. This was the last hurdle; she just had to persuade Ellie that returning to Maradova was the best thing to do, and they would take it from there, get the truth from the king and queen and finally bring this whole thing to light. So why was speaking to Ellie suddenly the hardest part?

'You need to think about this, Lottie,' Ellie said, but it wasn't Ellie; this was something cruel, her black hair clumped together like bug's legs, casting shadows that warped her face. 'You need to think about the future, about what you'll do without me.'

Lottie felt the room get smaller, the same feeling she'd had when she spoke to Binah in the library, like the world was crumbling around her, sucking the air out of her chest as it got tighter and tighter. This was the future, wide and unknowable and so large that it crushed everything under its weight. And it was so lonely she felt like she could die.

'I need some air,' she declared, staggering over to the balcony. She flung the door open, launching herself into the grey, and Ellie followed behind, a shadow at her back.

The soft drizzle began collecting on their skin and hair.

'Lottie?'

When she turned, she was face to face with her princess, the small of Lottie's back against the stone balcony wall with nowhere else to go.

'What do you mean?' Lottie asked, fingers tightening over the cold slab of mossy rock, surprised by the grit in her tone.

'You know . . .' Ellie replied, glancing at the cloud mass in the distance. With her face exposed to the broken light, she looked harsh, skin sunken, as if she didn't fit in her own body any more. 'Like, what universities will you apply to; where will you go?' She let out an exhausted sigh, staring at Lottie

218

with what almost looked like disappointment. 'You're the ancestor of Liliana Mayfutt, the only known relative of both a missing princess and the founder of Rosewood Hall, don't you ever wonder what that means? What else you could be?'

'I don't care about any of that,' Lottie said, her stomach twisting, like she'd just committed a terrible blasphemy. But it was true. She didn't want to be alone again. 'I just want to stay with you. I thought we both wanted that.' It felt like a stupid sentiment, plain and simplistic.

'Why would you think that?'

'Stop it, Ellie.'

Lottie tried to meet her princess head on. Both of them were almost completely soaked through, their white cotton blouses clinging to their skin, hanging off them uncomfortably, and she could smell the roses and the spice, dampened and moulding.

'I don't know what you're trying to do, whether you're trying to push me away because of some stupid guilt you've burdened yourself with, but you can't lie to me.' Lottie took a step forward, pushing herself out of the claustrophobic cave-in that made her feel like she couldn't breathe. 'We both know there's more to us than this arrangement. We were meant to find each other.' As the words left her mouth, it sent a tingle through her, the memory of a kiss doused in sugar, the sweetest moment she'd ever tasted, but it was ripped away, the sugar turning bitter on her tongue when Ellie looked down at her.

'I don't know what you're talking about,' she said, her voice like a cane on wet skin, and she stared at Lottie through hooded eyes, her wet lashes casting long lines down her face like tears. 'We're completely different people, from completely different worlds.'

It hit Lottie in slow motion, a gasping pain that took her head a while to keep up with what her body was feeling. Then she pinned it down; it was the distinct feeling of betrayal and abandonment.

'My whole life . . .' she whispered, but the sound wasn't weak; it was simmering. 'My whole life has been a mess of never knowing where I belonged, searching for it, working endlessly to get to it.' Taking another step forward, Lottie felt heat from Ellie's body, proof there was still some warmth inside her. 'And by some miracle,' she continued, 'I got into Rosewood, and I found you, and we found each other, and for the first time I knew what it was like to have a home.' Her voice was shaking now, their bodies so close she could feel Ellie shivering, and she looked her dead in the eye, past this cruel mask she'd donned and into her very core. 'That has to mean something.'

There was a shudder in the air, a coffee-breathed sigh escaping from Ellie's mouth, an animal flicker in her eye that lingered over the place where Lottie's heartbeat pulsed visibly under damp skin, her lips moistening as if she was going to kiss or bite her. It was only a second, but it made Lottie's body ache, and she leaned in, repeating into her princess's chest softly like a prayer, 'It has to mean something.'

Ellie's fingers found their way into Lottie's curls, toying with the ends that dripped, the rainwater building until it ran down her wrists, the two of them intertwining. 'Lottie.' She breathed her name and it was as if no one had ever truly spoken it before, the sound beautiful and filled with meaning,

220

until she broke the spell. 'The only reason we're even friends is because you're my Portman.'

The words were like a cut, trying to sever them, but Lottie had seen it; she knew it was real whether Ellie admitted it or not. She didn't gasp or recoil this time; instead she squeezed her fists, gritting her teeth, and she shouted, 'You're lying!'

Tears pooled in her eyes, the salt stinging her rain-dampened cheeks, and it wasn't just Ellie; it was Claude and this awful secret, and Jamie, and everything they'd been through.

'You're lying,' she said again, and this time her fists came down softly on Ellie's chest, trying to force the feeling back into her. Her voice barely above a breath, she demanded it once more, willing it to life. 'You're lying.'

'Lottie –'

Before Ellie could speak another word, Lottie grabbed her face, fingers hungrily feeding on the warmth of her body, and rising up on her tiptoes, she placed her lips over hers, forcing the lie and all her cruel words back down into her throat.

For a wonderful moment everything was right, their bodies melting into each other as Ellie stepped forward, the two of them pressed into the stone balcony like they might become one with the building, forging their feelings into the stone for eternity. Everything faded away with the taste of coffee and spice. There were no more secrets, no more awful truths or burdens; they were the only two people in the world, and she was safe.

Ellie made a noise halfway between a growl and a whine, and then she pushed Lottie back. As she pulled herself together, Ellie seemed to shrug off the kiss, licking it from her lips with a contemptuous look. 'No,' she said, and it dripped with the same unaffected bite as it had before. 'I wasn't lying.'

Lottie felt her body turn to ice and all the warmth ripped away from her, leaving her shivering and feverish. 'But that kiss?'

'It's all just a bit of fun, isn't it?' Ellie pushed a hand through her hair casually, the rain slicking it back in a sticky clump, and when she looked down her bee-stung lips twitched from the kiss like a horse kicking off its rider. 'Not my fault you took more from it than there ever was.'

Lottie pushed past Ellie, her body convulsing, warning that she might be sick, and each step felt like a hundred knives were tearing into her feet. 'I have to . . . I have to go.'

She gagged as she said it, feeling like her heart might fall out of her chest if she didn't cradle her stomach. She didn't want Ellie to see her like this. She needed to find someone who would hold her and not ask any questions, someone who understood without her having to say a single word. Running down the stairs, her feet clumsy, she knew exactly who she was looking for.

She was looking for Jamie.

26

The cold drizzle felt good on Jamie's skin, the sensation soothing some of the burning inside him, if only for a moment. He was sure it was getting worse, and, while difficult to pin down, he knew it was tied up with Lottie. There was something wrong; her light dimmed and fractured like an eclipse, and that's what hurt, the prickly heat starting in his chest and steaming through every crack and pore of his flesh, because he couldn't reach out to her, not with Ellie's pact – he could only watch and let it pass.

'I need to fight something,' Jamie said, barely even breathless from their run around the field.

Both cooling down under the cover of a large oak tree at the edge of the field, Raphael and Haru looked up at him, their faces dewy and pink.

'I'd volunteer, but I think you'd probably kick my ass,' Raphael said, laughing. 'Besides, I'm gonna go and take a shower.'

Patting Jamie on the shoulder, Raphael set off, giving a small wave to Haru before pausing to call back. 'Jamie, you still on to watch a movie in my dorm tonight with Percy?'

Jamie held up a thumb, but his sights had already turned to Haru, the Partizan coming to stand in front of him.

'You want to fight?' Haru's head tilted to the side, a lock of hair falling out of place that coiled in the damp air.

'I've got a lot of steam left in me,' Jamie said, pushing his wet hair back out of the way. 'This weather is making everything too subdued. I feel like . . .' He trailed off, embarrassed to admit the endless fire in his body. It wasn't controlled; it wasn't how a Partizan should behave.

But Haru didn't ask any further questions, and, with a curious half-smile that reeked of mischief, he adjusted himself, falling comfortably into a hapkido fighting position. Jamie followed suit, unable to stop the grin of anticipation. This was the first fighting style you learned in Partizan training, the one you had to master to be allowed to graduate, making it widely accepted as the preferred martial art of Partizans. Jamie had always been a natural, his body flowing with the moves like water in a stream. It's how he'd known he was meant to do this, that it was inside him, like it was in all good Partizans: a demon of strength that needed to be put to use. At least that's what they'd been told.

Bodies falling into years of muscle memory, they began to move in time with each other, mirroring one another like a strange dance. Haru made the first move, his right arm coming over his shoulder to meet the side of Jamie's face. He knew this move like he knew the palm of his hand, and with a small side step he transferred the weight over to his left leg and batted Haru's arm away. Usually at this point he would pull the Partizan over his shoulder, spinning his arm round and throwing him on to his back, but, just as he went to do it, Haru countered the move, his other arm coming to twist him away. Jamie tried to get his bearings, slipping his leg out in

224

front to block Haru's footing, only he didn't move how he anticipated. It was like fighting the wind, and it constantly changed direction, pulling him from one side before spinning him out, and just when Jamie was sure Haru would throw him violently down, instead he collapsed Jamie's knee with his shin and twirled him round, gripping his hand and pulling him up mere inches before his face met the mud.

Panting from both the thrill and the exertion, Jamie righted himself. He wasn't mad he'd lost; he was elated. This was the first time in all his years of being a Partizan that anyone had ever surprised him.

They both fell back into their stances, sweat mingling with the rain, making them glow with each heavy breath.

'Did you ever specialize in a weapon?' Jamie asked, suddenly curious.

'Rope.'

He laughed as Haru shrugged, the two of them still poised, ready for another round. 'Why does that not surprise me?'

Haru cocked an eyebrow. 'How about you?'

'I don't want to say.'

'Oh, Jamie-kun.' His lips twisted, freckled nose wrinkling to stop himself laughing. 'You didn't fight with fans, did you?'

'I was unbeatable,' Jamie asserted, not quite believing how easy it was to laugh with Haru, how good it felt to have another Partizan he could talk to. 'Let's do another round.'

Sprinting forward, Jamie barely gave Haru a moment to prepare. Slicing through the air, he reached out to grab Haru under the shoulder. This time Jamie expected the unexpected, waiting for Haru's body to show him where it was moving, like watching a wind chime move, every tiny sound and sway letting him follow the rhythm of Haru's form. They were nearly at an impasse, one grabbing the other, one spinning out, one nearly landing a hit, one deflecting, until one wrong breath had the sweet scent of marshmallow filling Jamie's nose, the smell so warm and inviting that he lingered a little too long, his hand flying out with too much force, so that Haru had to manoeuvre himself out of the way, but not before Jamie grabbed hold of his shirt.

With a great ripping sound, the fabric tore down the middle and Haru recoiled, but not quite fast enough.

Jamie saw it: a small scar on his stomach.

He felt the ground give way beneath him, taking him back to the end of summer, when he'd said goodbye to Haru and watched him recoil then too, but in pain, that scarred wound still fresh. 'It's you . . .'

Jamie tried to make sense of his thoughts. The seed had planted itself because he knew what the wound was, he'd known all along, and now his mind felt like it was plummeting again, the ground breaking away until he was back to the roof in Tokyo.

Haru tried to reach a hand out, but Jamie batted it away, stumbling backwards into a tree behind him, blinking up at the Partizan he'd grown so fond of, because his face was gone. The fireside smile and dark fawn eyes were cracked, and behind them he could see a bird mask, the one on the roof in Tokyo.

'You're the bird from the roof.' It was all Jamie could say.

There had been a boy in a bird mask, who'd been hit by a knife in that exact spot.

Haru had been his enemy the whole time.

226

Jamie shook his head, staggering back into the tree. 'You lied to me.'

He could hardly believe the sound of his voice, petulant, whimpering. It made him furious.

When his eyes finally focused, Haru had his hands up, ripped T-shirt leaving him vulnerable to the rain. Whatever look Jamie had on his face, it was enough for Haru to have his feet locked in a defensive pose, ready to fight. This was the real Haru, burning with the same fire Jamie had inside him.

'All that stuff you said before . . . was that a lie too?' Jamie growled. 'Trying to make me feel like I owed you?'

'No, Jamie.' Hands still in the air, Haru held his gaze. 'That was true. I chose to come here because I like you. We get to make our own choices.'

'How can I trust you any more?' Jamie snarled.

Seeing the drop in his defence, Haru took a cautious step forward.

'We never lied to you, Jamie. We've been waiting. Giving them a chance to put this right. One they haven't taken. I was going to tell you today, after training. I didn't want it to be this way, you have to believe me.'

Suspicion stirred. 'What are you talking about?' Jamie asked. 'Giving who a chance?'

The sinking feeling in his chest got heavier, his mind refusing to acknowledge what somehow he already knew.

'They sold you out, Jamie.'

'No, I don't trust you.' Jamie tried to stand firm but his voice wavered. 'You're lying.'

Haru took another step forward, but Jamie couldn't muster the sense to push him away, and when he spoke it wasn't at all what he expected.

'Jamie, you are so much more than you know. You think you are the knight, but you are the one who needs rescuing.'

The world seemed to rock on its axis. Jamie felt the earth beneath his feet, the drizzle christening his skin. He felt as though he was sinking into the ground, an open grave ready to swallow him.

'Your princess, she sold you out.' The very mention of Ellie made him even more dizzy. 'She made a deal with me at the start of the year and traded you and your ignorance in exchange for information.'

Jamie tried to cling on to the world around him, to the belief that Haru was lying, but he wavered. 'You're lying,' he repeated, but it felt more like he was trying to persuade himself.

The rain was getting heavier. He could almost see them in the haze. Lottie and his princess. Lottie who would do anything for his princess. Lottie who'd become so corrupted by the wolves of the royal family that they'd twisted all that was kind about her.

'Go. Ask her,' Haru demanded, snapping Jamie out of his vision.

'What does my princess know?' Jamie was shocked at the venom in his voice.

'Everything you don't.' Haru snatched up his jacket and began to pull it around himself, covering up his scar. 'This whole time your princess and her friends have known who I am, and I had to watch them keep you in the dark, waiting

228

for them to prove themselves, but they disappointed me.' Each syllable fell out of Haru's mouth like a poison dart. But they weren't painful; they were transformative.

Jamie felt the demons inside him coming to the surface. All the secrets, all the lies, all the misplaced trust . . . Before he knew it, he was a growling beast. He punched the tree behind him, his knuckles exploding with pain. It felt good.

'Strange, isn't it?' Haru continued smoothly like Jamie was a wild animal that needed soothing. 'Why would they keep such a thing from you? Why don't they trust you?'

'Why would they –'

'Ask her.' Haru said it again so simply, as if it were the most obvious choice, and it snapped Jamie's attention back to him. 'I'll be waiting for you at the main gate when you've learned what they're keeping from you. I'll take you where you need to go. And I promise that if, when you learn the truth, you decide to stay here, we will leave you alone forever.' He placed a hand softly on Jamie's shoulder, his thumb resting over the jugular until he could feel his heartbeat. 'It's time for you to know who you are.'

27

The school grounds were empty, fog hanging low and dense. Trudging through the grey, Jamie shivered in his limbs.

The chimes at the Ivy Wood gate welcomed him, their hollow sound echoing through his head. All the while Jamie sensed Haru lurking, his words following him through the baffling mist. He recognized the symptoms of shock, the numbing cold, the dream-like calm, all of them pushing his legs forward. All he knew was that Haru was waiting, and so was his princess.

The gravel crunched beneath his feet as he approached the side of the building with the girls' dorm. By the time he'd reached the front door he was already starting to feel his senses returning, as if he was waking from a strange nightmare.

What am I doing? Going to accuse his princess and the girl he'd sworn to protect of lying to him? None of it made sense.

Catching sight of his reflection in the glass of the door, he paused. His eyes had turned from golden to green, an emerald sheen like staring into the heart of a forest. There was nothing controlled about the figure staring back at him.

This was all wrong. He should tell Ellie and Lottie that he knew about Haru, demand they hand him in, and fly the three of them back to Maradova. Yet Haru had let him go. He'd trusted Jamie not to turn him in. He'd agreed to vanish forever if only Jamie asked.

As his hand hovered over the door handle, a familiar stubborn howling drifted over, and a big lump of spoiled cat appeared. Vampy began weaving round his feet, nudging his legs until he had to take a step away from the door.

A sound tore through the fog, setting his body on fire. A sound drenched in pain. Lottie.

'You're lying!' he heard her cry.

Jamie began running round the side of the building, following the sound like a beacon at sea. Skidding in the mud, he stopped at the corner of the building, peering round to see the girls' balcony door open. The two of them stood framed in the light of their dorm. Lottie and his princess intertwined, tangled together, locked in a kiss.

The fire inside him slowed to a simmer, and he felt it rising to his throat like acid. It boiled inside him: betrayal and treachery. He didn't realize how hard he was gripping his fists until he felt blood in his palms from where his fingernails had dug into the skin. He watched, sick to his stomach, as Ellie brushed Lottie to the side with a cruel smile. She mumbled something he couldn't hear, something that had Lottie gasping.

That was all he could manage. He stumbled back, and, before he could register what he was doing, he was sprinting away, his legs carrying him to his dorm, where he threw open the wardrobe, rifling through his possessions until he found the velvet box. Plucking it from its slumbering tomb, in his hurry, his elbow hit the side of the dresser hard enough that the makeshift back wall fell away. There, etched in the wood, was the question he'd been seeking the answers to all this time. *Where is my enemy?*

With the box stashed in his pocket, Jamie looked over his room, knowing Percy could return at any moment. The space at once felt too small, too much a false and cloying part of the lie he'd been living. He had to get away, somewhere soothing, where no one would interrupt. Taking off as fast as he could, Jamie ran from the Ivy Wood dorm, knowing exactly where he was heading. Each time his legs pounded the path, a different image would pound inside his skull. Haru in the rain, Ellie betraying their pact, Lottie screaming and finally his own reflection. Not until he reached Stratus Side did Jamie stop for breath. Then with methodical calm he began his descent to Liliana's study.

The hidden room was filled with the scent of roses and lavender, the same comforting aromas he'd come to associate with Lottie. She smelled of Rosewood Hall, its spirit in her blood. The room came to life with the pink glow of the fairy lights she'd draped along the walls, hanging stars twinkling above him as though he was floating in space. The whole room was Lottie, and right now all he wanted was to wrap himself in her.

Taking deep, slow breaths he tried to make sense of the mess in his head, knowing that Haru was waiting for him, that Lottie and Ellie were in the school somewhere, that they knew something he didn't, and that Ellie had betrayed him. And the most unforgivable part? Ellie had forced him into a pact that would protect Lottie, one bound by their allegiance to the throne, and she'd destroyed it – just like she did everything.

As he went over it all, he moved around the room, picking up items and putting them down. Liliana's old work and Lottie's blended together like a conversation centuries apart. He paused at the desk, one of the drawers still open a little, and, without a second thought, he tugged it the rest of the way. Inside was Lottie's sketchbook, the moleskin glistening, and the pages split like the slit of an eye in the centre where she'd shoved something into the creases. Usually he wouldn't dare pry, but he was so desperate for something to ground him, something of Lottie's, that his hands acted for him. The pages were filled with strange sketches of everyone and everything from her life, including Ellie and himself. But they weren't simple portraits – Lottie had drawn them in a myriad curious get-ups, mostly regal. One of them caught his attention. It was a sketch of Jamie on a throne. His eyes were pure green, the same green he'd seen in his reflection a mere moment ago; there were no flecks of gold. But strangest of all was the crown on his head. No, not a crown, these were great stag antlers. The image felt prophetic, and he could almost hear it whispering to him.

Jamie, you are so much more than you know, Haru breathed over his shoulder.

Trapped in the spell, he flicked through the rest of the pages, with more alluring images revealing themselves. Cats with horns, Jamie with horns, Ellie stuck in a cage shaped like a crown, Ellie smiling, Jamie frowning, and soon they all blurred together, until he fell upon what was hidden at the centre in the book's creases, something that was entirely out of place. Handwritten letters spilled out on to the floor as he pulled the papers free, the script elegant and seductive like a siren's call.

At first they made little sense. Cryptic messages. Then his vision began to focus, and bile rose to his throat. Choking, he read the name at the bottom: *Your uncle, Claude.*

The Goat Man from the roof in Tokyo. Slowly he realized what this meant, why it made him feel so dirty and ill. All this time Lottie had been corresponding with Claude. But it wasn't over. With his body shaking, the rest of the contents in his hands fell around him, a paper rainfall of secret: a photograph, cards with images he couldn't decipher, and a folded piece of parchment. It wasn't until he reached down to pick them up that he realized what he was looking at. From the stone floor his own mother stared up at him.

She was smiling, a wry intelligence, a curve in her lip that he recognized in himself. His trembling fingers moved instinctively to touch his own mouth, his nose, his hair, everything he could see reflected within the ghost of his mother.

Below her was the folded paper, and somehow he knew, from the way the edges fluttered in an impossible breeze, and the way his mother beckoned up at him, that once he opened it, he'd understand all this clutter around him.

'OK.' He spoke into the empty room. 'Tell me everything.'

He picked up the photograph and the folded paper that lay beneath, letting the pages fall open, a family tree unravelling in front of him. And there it was, screaming in his face, and the truth didn't feel like a slap as he expected; it was a caressing, delicate touch. It was Haru's hand on his shoulder, it was the way the king and queen shared a look he could never understand, and it was the shadow of Claude in the palace hallway. Jamie finally knew who he was.

The calm that took over him now was nothing to do with shock. It was thoughtful and decisive. He turned to the desk and wrote a brief note, then he tucked it into the dressing table mirror. Next, he pulled the velvet box from his pocket, opening it to see the chain he'd worn for so long snarling up at him. Laying it on the table with care, he grabbed the knife that was strapped to his ankle. The blade glinted in the light. He brought it down as hard as he could upon the silver wolf, severing it down the middle.

His link to the Wolfsons was torn asunder.

Making his way out, he paused where he lingered over the switch for the fairy lights with which Lottie had adorned the room. On a whim, he turned back to the room, looking around. Then he grabbed a blanket – one he'd seen Lottie curl up in so many times. He draped it over his arm, holding it up to his nose to inhale the scent, and took it with him up the stairs.

He didn't need to find his princess. He didn't need to ask her what she was keeping from him. She wasn't his princess at all; she never had been. He understood that now. As he stepped back out into the rain, he began to walk down to the cast-iron school gates. He laughed to himself. All this time he'd been looking for his enemy, looking for where they were hiding, determined to stop them from getting to Lottie. It turned out he'd been their prisoner all along.

Haru was waiting for him at the main gate, a bag over his shoulder and an umbrella held aloft for Jamie. He ducked beneath it and finally found shelter from the rain.

They didn't smile. Instead Haru waited for Jamie to speak.

'Haru,' he began, his voice hard and strange to his ears. He didn't bother to look back at Rosewood. There was nothing there for him any more. 'Take me to my father.'

28

Lottie had looked everywhere. Now she was exhausted from dragging herself around the school in the fog, searching for Jamie. It was like walking through a nightmare. Part of her wanted to believe what had just happened was all wrapped up in Ellie's misguided attempt to push her away, but it felt too cruel, the pain too harsh.

She came to rest on the bridge between the field and the main campus, staring down at the river below. She was sure she could see herself reflected in the water. Only it wasn't her face. She saw Liliana and William Tufty. They both lived inside her, in her blood.

'What do you want?' she asked, her voice echoing back at her.

Her ancestors stared up from the river, silently watching her, as though they were trying to tell her something. It hurt too much to look at them, a bitter reminder of her uncertain future. A well of shame overflowed as she remembered all the awful things she'd said to Ellie, embarrassed that she'd lost everything.

Picking up a pebble, Lottie tossed it into the water, scattering the faces. 'If you're not going to help, then go away!'

Feeling a sob rising, she turned violently, rubbing her face, and asked the only question she really wanted an answer to. 'Jamie,' she whimpered, 'where are you?'

She looked up to see a black shadow at the other side of the bridge, its tail moving from side to side.

'Mreow!' Vampy's head tilted to the side, his yellow eyes narrowing at her salt-crusted cheeks.

Shocked and confused, Lottie made a sound like a twisted laugh. 'Do you know where Jamie is?' she asked the cat, her feet propelling her forward.

Vampy purred in response, fur slick and wet. He began rubbing against her legs, pushing her down the path, before skipping into the main campus.

'Hey,' Lottie called after him, wiping her nose with her hand, not caring how pathetic and disgusting she looked.

By the time they reached Stratus Side, Lottie knew where they were going, and her heart thundered in her chest – not from the exertion but from something unknown – and a prickle on her skin made her feel like an animal in the woods, sensing danger that was out of sight.

Vampy stopped at the door, howling furiously.

'It's OK,' she cooed, reaching down to pick him up and cradling him over her shoulder. 'Everything's going to be OK.' Somehow it made her feel better to be comforting him. 'Now what's got you so upset?' She pushed open the Stratus door. 'You want to go down to the study?' Vampy purred at her neck, sending calming vibrations over her skin. 'Is Jamie down there?' She was met with another pained howl, which she quickly shushed.

Something was off. She could feel it in the way Vampy shivered in her arms, and in how her emotions had turned numb, part of her held captive, afraid of something she couldn't pin down.

As she'd done so many times before, Lottie turned the 'W' on the Elwin statue, and with Vampy purring nervously at her ear she made her way into the dark.

'Hello?' she called, a weak, naive part of her hoping Jamie might be down there.

Switching the fairy lights on, the room came to life with a rosy glow, only it wasn't the warm light she was used to. The light filled her with the same nervous dread as the flicker of a predator's eyes in the dark of the woods.

In spite of their argument, Lottie wondered if she should go and get Ellie. Then she saw the papers strewn across the floor by the desk. Her private sketches laid bare like a bleeding heart.

At her side Vampy began howling again. 'Shh, shh,' she cooed, frowning as she tried to make sense of the mess, but the cat kept on.

'Vampy, please, I –'

She looked up and she was sure her heart stopped.

In the centre of the dressing table was Jamie's wolf pendant, shattered, just as Claude's had been.

Laid out on the floor beneath the severed wolf were all her clues from Claude, a conversation that mapped out the terrible truth.

Jamie had got to it first. She'd been too late.

Vampy let out another wail, and it was as if it came from inside her own head.

239

Tears spilled down Lottie's cheeks, blurring her vision while her hands reached for the note tucked into the mirror.

Jamie's writing. The words caught in her mouth, each one like a kiss and a bite.

Lottie,

I have left to find my family. I'll come back for you and free you from the wolves.
I am your Partizan, and I promise I'll always keep you safe.

Jamie

She had to tell Ellie.

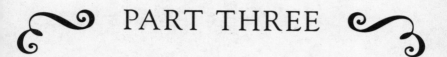

PART THREE

Truth Coming Out of Her Well

1896 painting by Jean-Léon Gérôme

29

Ellie stormed the Maravish palace hall. Abandoning her coat and scarf on the marble, she moved like a white tornado. 'How could you keep this from us?' she screamed at her parents, and Lottie was sure she saw the room rattle.

'Eleanor –'

'No!' Her voice boomed like thunder. 'You're going to tell us everything. Now.'

The king and queen shared a look, then they began to lead the way to the lilac quarters where Ellie's grandmother waited.

Everything had moved so fast once Lottie had found Jamie's shattered wolf. Within the hour they were flying back to Maradova. Here in the palace all the fear was starting to seep into her bones like the cold in the walls.

When they reached her grandmother's quarters, Ellie didn't pause to knock. She pushed the door, slamming it back on its hinges. Lottie jumped at the sound. Lying in bed, frail as an autumn leaf, Ellie's grandmother was propped up on a throne of silken pillows. Other than a knife-thin slit of light from a crack in the curtains, the room was dark apart from the glow of Willemena's eyes.

'No ceremonious crap,' Ellie said. 'You tell us both everything, right now.'

King Alexander draped himself over an armchair in the corner of the room, head resting in his hand, while his wife stayed in the slit of light, gazing out and away at something beyond the windows. And there was Ellie, stood at the end of her grandmother's bed, looking like death itself come to take her away.

Lottie remained by the door.

'Is it true?' Ellie stared her grandmother down, the storm simmering, ready to take a bite at any sign of a falsehood. 'This whole time, was Jamie just my Partizan as some messed-up punishment?'

Willemena tried to speak, but a cough cut her off, hunching her over while they watched.

Has she always been this frail? Lottie wondered. Had she always been putting on a show of strength or was this decline a recent development? Either way, right now, she was no match for her granddaughter.

'We did not mean for –'

'I don't care what you meant to do.' Ellie cut her off with a growl, turning to her parents to make sure they wouldn't attempt to intervene.

'I made a mistake.' The queen mother's voice was thick with guilt. 'I made a terrible mistake, and now we are all paying the price for it. Eleanor, please take a seat, and allow me to explain.' She shuffled over on the bed, so Ellie could sit beside her. 'You too, Miss Pumpkin.'

Lottie blinked, surprised to be called further into the room. Reticent, Lottie and her princess moved to settle on the bed.

Up close, Lottie could smell bergamot and lilac, a sleepy Earl Grey that covered up a dwindling rot like tooth decay which occasionally caught in her nose. It felt strange to be sitting here in such an intimate fashion, and Lottie kept thinking of the wolf in the grandmother's clothing, wondering if all this was only a ruse to lure them closer before swallowing them up. Looking at the yellow-eyed old woman, feeling the lump in her throat that wouldn't go away, she realized she needed to trust the queen mother. She had nothing else left.

'No one really knows what they're doing, Eleanor,' Willemena said slowly, her lips trembling. 'We can only keep trying to do the right thing, to retain the image of strength for others. This is what you have to do when you rule, when people rely on you.'

Lottie listened intently, hearing the words like an echo of her mantra to always be kind, brave and unstoppable. But it felt hard with Jamie gone and Ellie drifting away, the future uncertain.

'That's stupid,' Ellie said, her face still and emotionless.

'Perhaps.' The queen mother coughed and it almost sounded like a laugh. 'But that is the way it is.'

The sliver of light clouded over and Willemena's glance turned heavy. Lottie felt the shift in the room. A story was about to unravel, and this one would hurt.

The king and queen spoke quietly to each other, before silently making their way out. The moment the door shut, the spell was in place.

'Hirana,' she began, and the way she said her name, there was no hint of the malice Claude had suggested, 'she did not simply work for us for a little while as we have told you. She designed all the gardens in the palace.' There was a wistfulness to her voice that made her words feel like an ode to something beyond their understanding. 'She was a genius, and had a way with flowers and horticulture that was unparalleled. We were thrilled to have her finally bring some life back to the palace gardens, and she was as deep-rooted a part of the palace as any one of us.'

'But she wasn't good enough to be part of the family,' Ellie scoffed, nearly snapping the spell, but Willemena pulled the threads back together with one sharp look.

'Is that what that despicable son of mine has told you?' Willemena took the silence as confirmation. 'I knew he'd get to you sooner or later. I might appear a cold and bitter old hag to you, but what happened to Hirana was not my doing, although it is my fault.'

In Lottie's entire time working for the Wolfsons, she'd never heard the queen mother say something so honest, and there was something powerful in the admittance, like the chains of an old curse were finally coming undone.

'We always knew Claude enjoyed the company of beautiful people, and it was important that we kept it under wraps, because he had an arranged marriage, a tradition he was perfectly fine with if it meant he would be king. He understood this but he simply couldn't resist Hirana, and likewise she could not resist him.'

While clearly embarrassed, there was no disapproval in her tone, not a thread of the story Claude had woven.

'Something happened between them that caused Hirana to resign from her post rather dramatically. We begged her to stay, told her the gardens would die without her, but she said she'd seen what the future of the Wolfsons was, and she wanted no part of it. We had no idea she was pregnant with Claude's child.'

'What did he do?'

'What made her leave?'

Lottie and Ellie's voices came out in unison, and they leaned forward to find out more.

'That is still a mystery. All I know for sure is that there was something evil and ambitious in Claude, and Hirana had been unlucky enough for him to let it slip in front of her. I trusted her, and I had to take it seriously, so I confronted my son. For the first time his behaviour had had a serious impact on the palace and its workers.' She paused to look at Ellie, a grave expression that felt like a warning. 'This was my first mistake. I told him that his claim to the throne would be in danger if there were any more indiscretions that would hurt the family.'

'How did he react?' Lottie asked the question alone this time, Ellie too wrapped up in thought.

'He left the palace.' Willemena almost laughed, but it turned into a splutter. 'He packed a bag, like a child having a tantrum, and moved into one of our properties in the city.'

Stopping abruptly, Willemena gestured to a cup of water on the bedside table before she was racked with another coughing fit. After a few sips she patted her chest, preparing to continue.

'On the twenty-sixth of July 2000, Hirana arrived back at the palace, heavily pregnant and begging for help.' She patted her chest again, as if trying to pound the words out. 'Someone was trying to kill her – and they had already wounded her.'

At her side, Lottie saw Ellie squeeze the bedcovers until she had made angry clumps of balled-up silk.

'She'd escaped and found her way to us, but the shock and the injury she'd sustained was too much for her. She told us that she wanted the baby to be called Jamie. We promised we would raise him in the palace. It was the very least we could do.'

Rubbing her chest, Ellie's grandmother took in a long breath that sounded like a rattle, the last of the story still stuck inside her. There was another fit of coughing before she began to speak. As the last of the story finally emerged, Lottie felt the weight of this awful lie that had been kept for so long.

'You see . . . upon learning that Hirana was pregnant with his child, Claude – spoiled and obsessed with being king – ordered her death.'

The sick feeling in Lottie's stomach grew, the acid taste at the back of her mouth becoming unbearable.

Willemena went on. 'He believed her baby was an indiscretion that would endanger his claim to the throne. And I'd been the one to foster that belief.'

Lottie felt the room spinning, and, like a strange zoetrope, Claude kept flashing across her vision, his face melding with Jamie's.

'So you made Jamie a Partizan?' Ellie's voice was like a knife, coming down sharp on the image.

'That was my second mistake.' Willemena sighed. 'And one it has taken me much longer to admit to.' She closed her eyes, composing herself before continuing. 'I wanted to give Jamie a place in the family, but I was panicked, too afraid to let anyone know the truth about my son, and, above all, fearful of what Claude might do if he found out his son was alive.' Lottie wondered at what point Claude had discovered who Jamie really was, and how long he'd been plotting. 'I did not mean it as punishment by demoting him in social standing, and yet that is precisely what it became, my own grandson paying for the mistakes of his father, who he didn't even know, and by the time I realized what I had done we couldn't bring ourselves to tell him. We had persuaded ourselves he was happy.'

'Were you ever planning to tell him?' Ellie asked.

Willemena nodded, clearing her throat. 'Next year, after the completion of your school studies. But after you discovered Claude's link to Leviathan, I was scared Jamie might find out the truth on his own. And now he has. We are too late.'

The light from the crack in the curtain returned, stretching like a long pointed finger up to Ellie's grandmother where it split her face down the middle, one yellowed eye shrinking, and beside her Ellie's hand began to unwind itself from the bedsheets, the fabric turning slack again.

Lottie's head was still sore from the information and she was racked with exhaustion, but she watched Ellie, knowing it all fell on her. She seemed calm, and it was the simmering storm she was used to; it was decisive. She saw Ellie bring her hand to her ribcage, rubbing something that made her wince.

'Lottie,' she finally said, as soft as sleep, 'could you give me a moment alone with my grandmother? I'll come and find you later.'

Picking herself up, Lottie instinctively went to put a comforting hand on Ellie's shoulder, withdrawing it at the last second. Instead she put on the bravest face she could so they'd all have one less thing to worry about. 'Of course,' she said. 'I'll see you later.'

30

Someone had lit candles in Lottie's quarters. They flickered in their silver holders, casting the illusion of shivering leaves over her otherwise empty room. In the many hours since she'd found Jamie's wolf, this was the first time Lottie had been truly alone, and she knew if she didn't do something to distract herself soon, it would all catch up with her.

Lottie held on to the one thing of Jamie's she had – the gift he'd given her when she'd first taken on her role as Portman. The diary of an old Maravish Portman named Oscar Oddwood, who'd written down a personal account of as much history and gossip as he could uncover.

She'd read it hundreds of times, entranced by the exciting world of royalty; every detail in the book had been sucked dry. It was limp in her hands. It wasn't so fun reading about royal intrigue when you were part of it.

I have to make myself useful. I've got to help fix this. Kind, brave and unstoppable!

She couldn't stop now; she had to keep going.

Lottie wrapped herself up in her dressing gown. Too tired to go for a run like she usually would, she instead located an object that she hoped would help. Lottie found the clue from Haru's notebook she'd written down. Tracing the numbers gently, she moved down to the Japanese characters. They had been easy enough to translate, yet the words provided no clarity. '*Sū jū-nen*' it said – or simply 'decades' – but what that had to do with her dorm room number or the other three numbers, she had no idea. Thinking of everything they could be, she tapped the page, wondering if perhaps they were simply combinations he needed to remember: 221 – her room, 999 – the police. That left her with the middle two: 009 and 109. Were they safe combinations? Other room numbers? There were too many possibilities and no way to test her theories.

The numbers blended together in a meaningless blur, and the person who could usually solve a thing like this was gone.

'Jamie's gone.' She said the dreaded words out loud, finally admitting it to herself. 'He's gone, and it's just me and Ellie now.'

And Ellie didn't want her.

A drop of water fell on one of the numbers, the ink spreading like fur. She looked up, confused where it had come from, but when her eyes returned to the page there was another. It wasn't until a feral sound escaped from her throat that she realized she was crying.

Her face erupted into a mess of snot and tears while she floundered for tissues to clean herself up, only to find the box was empty. With wobbling legs, she pulled herself out of the plush room in a daze of messy grief, searching for something to fix herself. The hurt from Ellie's rejection and Jamie not being there overwhelmed her. She needed him and he wasn't there. He might never be there again.

Stumbling out into the hallway, she began wandering through the palace, clutching at her stomach.

'Miss Pumpkin?'

She paused, not wanting whoever it was to see her so broken up, her pink skin bright and irritated. She wiped desperately at her nose with the sleeve of her dressing gown before turning round.

'Hanna, Midori.' Her voice was shaky and raw. 'What are you doing up so late?'

They stood together like two magpies in their black-and-white uniforms. They looked at each other, concern etched on their faces.

'We're waiting for Eleanor to finish talking with the rest of the family.'

'They're still in there?'

Midori nodded, but it turned into a sigh, her fingers fidgeting with the hem of her apron, and without another word she marched over and wrapped her arms tight round Lottie. Her uniform smelled like freshly cut lemons and honey, soothing and clean.

'We're so sorry about everything.' Lottie could hear the cracks in her composure.

Squeezing back, she felt another body against hers – Hanna's, her big arms warm and pink. She melted, letting herself cry again, softer this time, each fresh sob dampened by gentle fingers stroking her hair.

After a while, Hanna pulled away, keeping one hand against Lottie's cheek. 'Let's go and get you something to eat and drink, hmm? I'm sure you haven't managed to have dinner with all this.'

Lottie nodded, following the two of them to the kitchen.

Taking a seat on one of the stools, Lottie silently accepted a tissue from Hanna. She listened to the low hum from a fridge, the ticking of the flame coming to life on the stove and soft singing from Midori while she went about stirring a bowl of batter.

'You guys don't have to –' Lottie wanted to tell them not to fuss over her, but her stomach rumbled, giving her away.

'Don't worry.' Midori attempted a smile. 'We're going to have some too.'

The room slowly filled with the thick, comforting smell of chocolate, and soon after Lottie was presented with hot chocolate and a chocorrito, a Frankenstein's monster of a dessert that Ellie had invented. Feeling like a child, Lottie grabbed a chunk of whipped cream and marshmallow, licking it off her finger, and letting the mushy sweetness wash away all the lingering salt round her lips.

'Thank you.' Lottie's voice came out as barely a whisper, her throat still sore from crying so much.

'We're sad about Jamie too,' Hanna said, taking the seat on Lottie's left with her own chocorrito piled high with ice cream and caramel sauce. 'Thought we needed something sweet.' Despite her attempt at a cheery expression, Hanna's nose wrinkled, the freckles scrunching together, and she sniffed hard as she took a bite, trying to ward off tears.

'He's like a little brother to us,' Midori confessed, pulling her hair up into a ponytail before delicately sipping on her hot chocolate. 'We always thought it was cute how serious he was as a child, but the older he got, the harder it was to see him like that.'

'So you knew? About who Jamie really was?' Lottie's fingers paused where they held the mug mere inches from her lips.

Eyes cast down, Hanna and Midori said nothing, their silence speaking louder than any words, and Lottie couldn't blame them; she hadn't told him either.

'We think Willemena was a bit afraid of Jamie,' Midori admitted, stirring the spoon in her mug until the cream had melted. 'He was always so smart and strong. It made her uneasy knowing what his father had done.'

Hanna began absent-mindedly fiddling with a curl of her orange hair. 'And after he was born, the gardens grew wild,' she said. 'The queen mother stopped bringing people in to tend them.'

'Why?'

'They are very superstitious.' The way Midori said it made it clear *they* were not the only ones who were superstitious. 'I suppose she feared invoking Hirana's spirit, that Jamie would seek retribution one day.' Pausing to lick a clump of chocolate sauce off her spoon, Midori's eyes clouded over. 'Now it seems that future she was so scared of may be coming true.'

Lottie imagined what it must be like for all of them in the palace to live with this awful secret, and she felt the burden heavy on her shoulders, that same feeling of guilt. 'I can't believe he's really gone,' she said at last.

The two maids shuffled and Midori looked up at the door.

'Lottie, we want you to have something,' Hanna announced, her voice pitching, as if she wasn't quite sure if what she was about to do would be allowed. She stuck her hand in her apron pocket and pulled out a small silver drawstring bag, its velvet skin glistening like mercury.

As fast as a kingfisher, she opened it and poured the contents into her hand, placing something in Lottie's palm with her eyes shifting constantly back to the door, as if this was all very secret and important. 'This is the ring Hirana left for Jamie,' she said, voice barely a whisper. 'They were going to give it to him next year when they told him the truth but after we found out he'd left we, umm . . . well, we took it. To look after it – for Jamie.'

'You what?' Lottie couldn't help baulking; even in her grief she had enough sense to be shocked.

'You do not understand – the queen mother was going to lock it away,' Hanna quickly explained. 'She thought it would become cursed because she failed to give it to Jamie.'

Lottie stared at the thick band of gold in her hand, tilting it from side to side where the buff metal revealed its stardust pelt. The whole Milky Way rested there, etched on its skin in painstaking detail; it wasn't the harsh, judgemental gold you found in the palace – it was candid and crisp like autumn leaves, warm and smooth. Angling it against the light, words exposed themselves, glowing from the inside, letters she couldn't make out.

'Why are you giving this to me?' she asked, matching Hanna's whisper.

'Because –' Midori sounded almost pleading as she closed Lottie's fingers round the band – 'out of all of us, we think you are the only one who can bring him back.'

They both stared at her – two sets of eyes, one blue and one brown, and both glossy like crystal balls, seeing a future that they believed Lottie could bring them. She could feel it as clear and consistent as the beating of her own heart, that despite finding her crying and scared and alone, they believed in her. She only wished she could believe in herself.

'I'll try my best.' The words woke something up in her she was afraid she'd lost. 'I'll do whatever I can to give him this ring and bring him home.'

Usually Lottie was so sure of herself, but now her voice wavered, pricked with fear, because she'd always had Ellie and Jamie with her.

She needed to get Ellie on board. She was her Portman, and they were stronger together. No matter what had happened between them, this was more important; they'd tackle it together, like they always did.

A sound from the hallway broke the moment, and Lottie quickly put the ring away while they all went back to their desserts.

Ellie's face appeared round the door, bruises from exhaustion under her eyes and lips chapped from the dry flight over. She seemed unusually uncomfortable under Hanna and Midori's gaze but shook it off. 'Hey, how are you –'

'What's the conclusion?' Lottie asked, still not sure she could handle talking to Ellie about how she felt; they had more important things to think about. 'How are we going to get Jamie back?'

Ellie pursed her lips, guilt turning her skin even paler than usual. 'We're staying in the palace for the rest of the Christmas holidays, then we're going back to school to finish our exams.'

Lottie's mouth fell open, dropping her fork on to her plate with a loud clang. 'You can't be serious? We need to act now; we don't have time to –'

Ellie held her hand up, gesturing for Lottie to follow her out of the room and away from the maids.

Once they were out of earshot, she turned back to Lottie, her expression blank and unreadable, like a mask of her own face. 'Samuel will be escorting us,' she continued, as if this was all completely normal. 'I know it seems unexpected, but the choice has been made that –'

'This isn't right,' Lottie snapped. Ellie was supposed to be on her team. They were supposed to save Jamie together. 'This isn't right and you know it. We need to be looking for Jamie. We can't abandon him!' She felt the ring in her pocket, her last remaining hope.

Ellie had her back to Lottie now, hiding her face.

'Ellie, listen to me,' Lottie said. 'We need to get Jamie back before –' Her words caught in her throat like a bone, as something she hadn't considered crawled up through her tangle of thoughts. Jamie would tell them that Ellie was the real princess, and if he did, where would that leave Lottie?

'Claude can't find out about you. This is urgent, and we need to act now before –'

Ellie turned on her, her robe whipping around her like a tornado. 'Don't you get it, Lottie? It's over.' Shaking her head, she rested both hands on Lottie's shoulders, pleading with her not to push the topic. 'It's already too late.'

What was over? What did she mean?

Ellie took a deep shaking breath, calming herself. 'My parents and I have made a decision that we think is for the best.' She paused now, squeezing Lottie's shoulders until it almost hurt. 'We've decided to handle Jamie and Leviathan ourselves. You are forbidden from going after him or Claude.'

Lottie pulled herself out of Ellie's hands. 'Why?' she whispered, but when she looked at her princess there was nothing cold or certain about her order; there was heat behind her eyes, tears ready to spill over, and the question soon got lost.

'Please, Lottie.' Ellie gulped, every inch of her working not to break down in front of her. 'Let's just go back to school and finish our exams before it all comes crumbling down around us, OK?'

Lottie was sure there was something more that Ellie wasn't saying, but the look she gave her was so painful, all her bravado chipped down to the scared girl that lay beneath, that Lottie was unable to push it.

How could she not go after Jamie? How could Ellie expect her to drop all her research on Leviathan's plan? It wasn't possible, yet the idea of fighting Ellie on this now was equally as impossible.

'OK,' Lottie said, swallowing down the hurt she felt, knowing that if she wanted to help Jamie she was on her own. 'If you think this is for the best, I'll do whatever you order.' She didn't bother putting on a smile; there was no way of hiding how she felt.

Lottie couldn't leave Jamie, and if the Wolfsons were forbidding her from going after him, she'd have to find a way round them.

'I think we should go to bed,' she announced, feeling the ring in her pocket and clinging on to the very last shreds of hope that they could one day go back to normal, that they could all be friends again, laughing and joking their way through homework and parties like regular teenagers.

Strange how a dream so simple could suddenly feel so far out of reach.

Ellie and Lottie began walking in time with each other, uncomfortable silence following them down the echoing hallways.

Lottie dropped Ellie at her room, who looked as if she were going to say something, but it only came out as a sigh. 'I promise you everything is going to be OK,' she said instead. 'I'm going to make it OK again.'

'I know,' Lottie replied, her hand going to the wolf round her neck, which felt delicate and rare now that hers and Ellie's were the only two left. She felt the same way. She was going to make it OK, whether any of them liked it or not.

Heading back to her quarters, the opulence of the palace felt stale; dampened silver and waning crystal decorated the dressers under the windows where vines and branches tapped at the glass. Lottie had never noticed the way the garden grew up around the walls before, its spindly green fingers creeping just out of sight. It was no wonder Willemena had been so afraid.

'I'm going to bring you back,' she said, gripping the ring tight. 'We'll be together again.'

31

Haru took Jamie to a remote log cabin situated by a lake in the Bavarian Alps, far away from any form of civilization. They travelled by train and car, using passports Haru had already acquired for them to keep their journey untraceable, until at last they arrived late in the night. A bloated and eager moon followed them up the winding path and deep into the mountains. Blanketed by millions of stars, the planet stretched out forever in front of him, the universe above reflecting in the giant body of water, endless.

'They will have food ready,' Haru said. 'How are you feeling?'

Jamie didn't answer, staring at where his feet met the blue grass at the edge of the lake, the light from the cabin glowing at his back, casting a shadow in his shape over the starlight mirror. For a moment he felt like the only person alive until Haru moved closer, their shadows melding together.

'Everything feels bigger,' Jamie said. 'It's a little overwhelming.'

Haru draped an arm round his shoulders. 'We can wait to go inside.'

Jamie knew he was exhausted, that his mind was playing tricks on him, but when they heard an animal howl in the distance he thought of Lottie crying on the balcony from the pain Ellie had inflicted upon her. Knowing she was still trapped in that small world, the wolf round her neck getting tighter and tighter. It set his skin on fire. He just had to hope she would be OK until he could put his own plans into action. Plans he'd need his father for.

Picking a rock out of the dirt, he threw it across the water where it scattered their shadows and the stars. 'Let's go.' Pulling away, Jamie gestured for Haru to follow. 'I have something important I need to tell Claude.' And without looking back he made his way to the cabin.

Haru was the one to knock – a specific sequence that let them know it was him. Locks clicked and turned on the other side, and faster than Jamie was prepared for the door swung open. The cabin looked like an upside-down ship, the dark rafters were the hull, with a great black fireplace protruding from the wall like a flaming rock through the bow. Opposite the door was a grand floor-to-ceiling window that looked over the lake, which from here seemed as vast and wide as the sea.

The woman who greeted them was tall and broad, with silver hair and gunmetal grey eyes, her stare as heavy and threatening as her powerful build. Her harsh appearance was baffling against the homely marigold glow from the fireplace and the calming smell of chicken soup. It only became more baffling when she bowed.

'My prince,' she said, her voice as deep as a grave.

It took Haru's hand at his back, gently pushing him inside, for Jamie to remember what he was doing. So many times in his life he had bowed to Eleanor, to the king and queen and queen mother, to his trainer Nikolay, but never had he had someone bow to him, and it made him feel like there was too much pressure on his shoulders.

'Now, now, Phi.' A man's voice drifted from the corridor to the left, soft and hypnotic like a snake's hiss. It was one Jamie recognized, and despite being here to meet him it made his skin prickle, a slow, building panic that told him to run far away. 'I'm sure young Jamie is not particularly comfortable with such displays.'

The floorboards creaked, and from the doorway, with no ceremony or fanfare at all, he appeared.

Someone closed the door behind Jamie, but he couldn't have said who, too preoccupied was he by the man in front of him. There was no mask this time, no cloaks or shadows. Claude stepped into the light with a warm smile.

Jamie had been brought up to believe that the man in the black-framed painting was something to be afraid of, that the green-eyed monster with his false charm and knowing smile was the very embodiment of betrayal and infidelity, the one thing Jamie must never become. Now he watched the so-called monster as he extended his arms out to Haru, bringing him into his robe where he patted him on the back and ruffled his hair like a father might a son.

A *father to the world*. That's what he'd said on the roof in Tokyo, and now he could see it.

'Welcome home,' Claude said, voice soothing like incense. 'You've done excellent work.'

Beaming, Haru relaxed, his expression softening in that way it did, where looking at him felt like a refreshing summer

263

breeze, then without warning both Phi and Haru left the room, leaving him alone with the man who was meant to be his enemy.

Claude turned to him now, their eyes meeting like magnets. Framed by the fire that burned behind him, shadows danced at his feet, his long robe dusting the floor, while rich crimson ate up the light. His black hair was tied back, a few strands escaping, reminding Jamie of his own untameable mane. There was nothing threatening in the way he stood or smiled, and yet there was a wildness to him. It mirrored the feeling Jamie had always had deep inside him, the one he had always been told to dampen and push down. It was fire, and it was ferocious.

Even though he'd come here to find Claude, he couldn't shake how peculiar it was to see him – the Goat Man, the Master of Leviathan, the scourge of the Wolfsons. This was the stuff of nightmares, but it felt like a strange dream.

Claude was the first to speak. 'I am sorry, please sit down,' he said with a sigh filled with regret. 'I'm sure this is all very unpleasant for you. I will get you something warm to eat.'

He swept out of the room again, leaving Jamie alone with the fire. He sat on one of the large grey sofas, his body melting into the cushions, and he had the strangest feeling he was swaying, the fire sending flickers across the exposed brick and wood, the ship cabin come to life, rocking him across the imaginary sea. He thought it curious that they trusted him enough to leave him alone, wondering also if perhaps they were spying on him, waiting to see what he'd do, but he had no plans to snoop; his only mission was to protect Lottie, and he needed Claude for that.

'Here we are,' Claude said, coming back in. 'Ingrid has prepared this for us tonight.' He placed a large bowl of soup and a plate of bread with cheese on the table. 'She wanted to do something special for you, a peace offering, if you will.'

'Are you sure it's not poisoned?' Jamie said.

For a second Claude blinked at him, and then he laughed. It was a big, booming laugh, his glance narrowing over Jamie as if it were their personal private joke. 'I see she's made a good impression on you.' Claude stole a piece of cheese off Jamie's plate and strolled over to a large armchair by the window, where he took his place.

Jamie could have killed him, and he must have known that; he was alone and exposed with no one nearby to stop him. They hadn't checked him for weapons or a hidden mic, so he could very well be there to slit his throat.

'Why are you trusting me?' he asked outright, not having time for any games.

Claude turned to him, a smile playing on his lips.

Jamie couldn't look away. *I am this man's son.*

It was that same caressing awakening he'd experienced when he'd found the letters, slow, methodical hands reaching inside him and putting pieces in place that he never knew he was missing. Something stirred in the man sat in the throne, his features warping, the shadows digging deep into the bones of his face.

'I am easing you in.' Claude spoke frankly now. 'You have been unleashed, freed from a sentence you did not know you were serving. I know the experience well. Eat.' He gestured to the food on the table, and without question Jamie followed the order. 'It is likely you are feeling lost, uncertain, the world stretching out larger than you remember it having the right to. Is that so?'

Jamie nodded.

'You are my son.' The fire ignited his eyes, the emeralds sparking with the power of the statement. 'You are the child of the woman I loved, and we have both been punished for it. All these years they kept you hidden from me. I only hope that now we are together we can make things right. Does that sound reasonable for now?'

Swallowing, Jamie felt burning in his stomach again, because that's exactly what he wanted: to right something that had been wrong, to free Lottie from a position she should never have been forced into, but first he had to be sure.

'Last time I saw you, you had me cornered on a roof. Why not tell me then?'

Claude answered immediately. 'I wanted to give them a chance to put it right themselves.' He shook his head, disappointment clear in his glum expression. 'I've only ever wanted to give them the opportunity to do the right thing. I never wanted to hurt anyone.'

'So what are you using the Hamelin Formula for?'

Jamie kept his questions short and quick, a lesson every Partizan learned, because it was the best way to make sure your subject had no time to consider their answer.

'It is our last resort. If they will not admit what they did themselves, forcing you to become a Partizan as punishment, banishing me, all for falling in love with the wrong woman, then we have the means to make them confess. I think the world deserves to know who really runs the world, what these people are really like and what they are capable of. Then the people can choose how they wish to be governed. If you had known all this, if the people working in the palace had known, I'm sure they wouldn't have taken these jobs of servitude. Do you agree?'

It felt like he was talking specifically about Lottie, that he'd reached inside his mind and located the very reason he'd come here.

'Yes, I agree.' Jamie already knew what he had to do next, all he needed was everyone else. 'Can you call in the other members of Leviathan?'

Claude tilted his head. 'Haru says you have something to tell me.'

'I do, but I need the rest of you here first, to make sure you understand how important it is. All of you.' He paused. 'Especially Ingrid.'

A smile crawled back over Claude's lips.

How had he been so afraid of this man, shivering at the idea of Lottie getting near him? The thought of Lottie reminded him why he was here.

Claude left the room again without a word. After a few minutes, the rest of Leviathan began filtering in. The first ones to come through after Claude were Phi, who prowled the room as if she expected a fight, and Haru, holding a plate of food. They were followed by two mousy teenagers Jamie had never seen. From their similar height and build he imagined they must be twins. Both of them stared at him in unison, giggling to each other, noses crinkling identically.

The last to enter the room was Ingrid, who stood in the furthest corner of the room from Jamie and crossed her arms, sulking.

So, this was the Leviathan. The monsters he and his friends had been fighting for so long. Their stance made it clear they were all Partizan trained.

'Where's Julius?' Jamie asked, looking over his shoulder, trying not to react to how the name tasted in his mouth.

'He's on an important errand,' Claude said quickly.

'I understand your plan involves bringing in the Maravish princess?' asked Jamie, looking straight into Claude's eyes.

They looked among each other, except for Claude who continued to stare at him.

'Is that a problem?' Claude's voice stayed level.

'Yes,' Jamie said, and all eyes trained on him. 'You can't go after her.' He paused, thinking of Lottie, the way she'd been betrayed by Ellie – the way both of them had been betrayed by the Wolfsons. He swallowed. 'You can't go after her. She's not the real princess.'

In the silence that followed only the fire continued to crackle, one of the logs snapping and spitting, and Jamie could feel it deep in his stomach, a furious blaze. There was no going back now. 'Lottie Pumpkin,' Jamie began. 'It's not a pseudonym the princess is using. It's her real name. She's Eleanor's Portman.'

The faces staring at him were almost comical. Like melting wax, their expressions couldn't seem to settle, mouths parting and jaws going slack, as if they were not able to contain the millions of mixed feelings. Haru looked particularly adrift, his gaze resting in the middle distance while he tried to make sense of his folly. Ingrid and Claude were the only ones who seemed to know exactly how they felt about this information. Ingrid's eyes went wide at the cold hard slap of humiliation, while Claude showed no hint of shock or embarrassment. For him it seemed as if everything were falling into place. Fingers swirling in his beard, he looked at Jamie once more, a hungry smile pulling at the corner of his mouth.

'So who is the real princess?'

Jamie's glance flicked over to Haru and he watched as his eyes widened in understanding.

Haru laughed, although the sound was more shocked than amused. 'Ellie. The bad influence.'

'You mean this whole time, some common little urchin has been causing me all this trouble?' Ingrid looked ready to rip out the throat of the girl she'd been continually bested by.

This was exactly why Jamie had come here. He turned to Claude. 'Lottie is a good person who has been dragged into all this. The real princess, Ellie Wolf, has brought nothing but trouble on her shoulders since the day they met.' Jamie couldn't believe he was saying these words, that it had taken him so long to see the truth. He felt a twinge of guilt. But he'd been denied his identity for his whole life; it was time for Ellie's identity to be revealed.

Something passed over Claude's face then, a spark in his emerald eyes that felt like, for a split second, he'd looked right inside him, down into the very depths of his most private thoughts until he was lying exposed. It made him shudder, but not from fear, but because he knew there was nothing he could hide from this man. They were the same.

269

'What do you need from us, Jamie?' Claude asked, but Jamie could tell his father had already guessed.

Looking around the room, he focused on each of them individually. They were his pack now.

'My conditions for joining you are simple.' He leaned back into his seat, mirroring his father. 'You are going to help me save Lottie from the Maravish royal family.'

32

A thick blanket of snow had settled when Ellie and Lottie arrived back at school after Christmas. It felt disconnected from the Rosewood they had left. Then, their world had been hazy with fog and rain. Now, the air was crisp and peaceful.

Slowly, her mind clearing with the cool air, Lottie began to realize something was wrong, something Ellie wasn't telling her.

They were accompanied by Samuel Petrov, who would be staying on campus. The school had assured them security would continue to be maintained at the highest degree since their Partizan and Haru had been 'called away on a confidential expedition by the Partizan Council' – or so Haru's note had alleged.

A routine quickly formed, and during classes Samuel would wait for Lottie outside the door, then escort her to the next class and so on. The blanket of protection quickly began to feel suffocating, but it wasn't until their third day back, when they were in the library studying, that Lottie started to become suspicious.

The instructions from the crown were simple enough.

Do not tell anyone what has become of Jamie.

Cease all research into Leviathan's plan.
Do not go after Jamie.

Lottie had no intention of following these rules, but she hadn't expected to find herself being watched so closely.

'He never showed up for movie night,' Raphael moaned for the hundredth time, an untouched mug of tea turning cold in front of him. 'He didn't even say goodbye; it doesn't make sense I tell you . . .'

Ellie didn't so much as flinch, her eyes cast down over her coursework, the perfect tableau of a high-school girl studying for her exams. It was creepy.

'Not to mention that he completely abandoned Vampy. It's just so unlike him,' Raphael continued, yet still Ellie didn't look up.

Lottie's heart wrenched at the thought of the cat.

Saskia, Anastacia and Binah's eyes flicked between the two girls, the only ones aware of what had really happened, all of them sworn to silence. They weren't what Lottie was worried about. Behind Ellie's chair, watching her pointedly, was Samuel.

Lottie gulped, trying to make her voice as calm and hinged as possible while feeling like her heart might explode at any moment. 'I've told you, Raphael. Jamie and Haru have been loaned to an important mission by the Partizan council and their whereabouts cannot be disclosed.'

Lottie felt like a robot, spewing out lie after lie at the whim of her programmers, and all the while Ellie stayed silent. Her role as Portman had never felt like such a prison.

Raphael finally picked up his tea and held it to his mouth. 'I just wish he'd said goodbye.'

Me too, Lottie thought. Part of her envied Raphael's obliviousness, wondering if it would hurt less if she had no idea where he was.

Lottie thought that would be it for the day, but once they'd parted ways with Raphael and the twins and stepped out into the frosty night, Saskia finally spoke up.

'Are you two OK?' she asked, red scarf whipping around her in the snow flurry. There was none of her usual humour, no raised eyebrow or smirk. She only looked confused. 'This all just seems really weird. You two must want to talk about it? I know your family said you're handling it but we could still do something, and I don't know why you're –'

'It's being handled,' Ellie said before Samuel appeared beside them once more, looming like Lottie's own personal shadow.

All three girls gawked at Ellie's response, Anastacia and Binah looking to Lottie like she might be able to explain it, but she could only shake her head. She didn't understand it either.

During the third week the lack of privacy was becoming even more oppressive, and it wasn't just Samuel that was the problem. The whole school seemed to be watching her with whispers and curious glances, no longer angry but pitying. There was not a single chance to let her emotions slip.

By the following Friday Lottie understood that she was being watched just as much as she was being looked out for, and if she was going to continue her research and start looking for Jamie, she'd have to be come up with a plan to avoid her new bodyguard.

'Curfew is in two hours,' Samuel reminded the girls as they laid their bags down in the library, settling down for another evening of studying.

'Yes, thank you – we're aware,' Lottie replied, the curtness slipping through unintentionally.

Ellie flitted over, brushing snow off her winter coat, and placed a white-chocolate mocha on the table. 'I got this for you, Lottie.' She beamed at her, the smile too full, too much like the ones she would give her when they first became friends.

Fingers still red from the cold, Lottie took the cup, her eyes locking with Ellie's, trying to find any sign of secrets that she was hiding. 'Thank you.'

The two of them nestled into the booth and Lottie had the oddest feeling of nostalgia, like they were playing happy families. The dark under Ellie's eyes didn't match her disjointed smile. This was make believe, but why? Why wouldn't she let them talk about Jamie or Leviathan?

Binah arrived soon after with some maths notes, cursing the cold weather as she shrugged off her coat. 'This must be the coldest February we've had in years,' she grumbled, slipping next to Lottie.

This was her chance.

The moment Binah put her bag under the table, Lottie let her pen roll off, and with a small kick of Binah's bag the pen landed exactly inside.

'Oops! I'll get it,' Lottie said.

She couldn't even look under the table because she knew if she did they might get suspicious. She'd hidden a message up her sleeve, so all she had to do was grab the pen and drop the paper at the same time.

If Samuel was looking at her face, he'd miss the small move. Something she'd picked up from watching Stephanie and the Artistocracy.

The note contained basic instructions.

Monday, 12:30, under Elwin.

Now she just needed to come up with a reasonable excuse that would give her twenty to thirty minutes alone, enough time to go over the numbers she'd found in Haru's diary with Binah and tell her she still planned to find Jamie.

It was Sunday, the day before Lottie intended to meet Binah, when she truly saw what Ellie was doing with all her cheeriness.

Lottie was alone in their dorm after curfew, books open around her that she could barely focus on, when Ellie pushed the door open with her hip, appearing with armfuls of snacks and that same plastic smile.

'Thought you might want some fuel.' Again Ellie grinned at her, a shadow of the old cocky smile she used to give her, and it made Lottie uneasy.

She sat beside Lottie, opening up a packet of spicy crisps while she leaned over Lottie's shoulder.

If anyone could see them, they'd think that they were simply two friends studying together. They'd never imagine the fight or the betrayal. So why was Ellie pretending?

'How's your PoP tribute coming along?' Ellie asked, and the question threw her.

Lottie had forgotten, again.

'I haven't really been in the right frame of mind to be thinking about it to be honest.' Lottie closed her book and allowed herself to dig into a jam tart, despite finding the situation extremely odd.

'Remember when we first found Liliana's study, on Halloween?' A soft smile replaced the plastic one on Ellie's face, a wistful yearning that finally felt real, and Lottie clung to it.

'I was so afraid,' Lottie admitted. 'I couldn't believe something like that was real, but I think I was more afraid of finding part of myself.'

Ellie leaned back against the bedside table, the tips of her toes touching Lottie's thigh, the contact making Lottie hyper aware of how little they'd touched each other recently. 'It's like you were always destined to find it,' she said. 'It's in your blood.' Tilting her head to the side inquisitively, Ellie fiddled with the hem of Lottie's skirt, not making eye contact. 'I hope you'll realize that when you start your tribute. I know it'll be amazing.'

Things Lottie didn't want to think about began surfacing, which was especially dangerous when she was feeling such a fraying connection to her Portman role and Ellie's family.

'Jamie would be so mad if he knew I still hadn't started it,' she said instead, letting a painful laugh escape her.

Ellie froze, pulling her fingers away, as she turned back into that strange plastic version of herself.

Lottie stared at her princess, feeling the weight of the silence finally crushing her. 'Ellie, I can't do this.' She let out a sigh, preparing herself for the worst. 'I don't know what's going on with you, but we can't just pretend everything is fine. I won't.'

Ellie didn't even look up, but Lottie could see it. Through that blank look there was a small flicker of light.

'Please, just for a little while.' Lottie wasn't sure she'd even heard Ellie speak. 'Humour me.'

It was the first honest thing Ellie had said since giving her orders back in the palace. She finally looked up at Lottie with that same pleading look, desperate for something Lottie couldn't understand.

With every bit of willpower Lottie could muster she shook her head, not letting herself give in this time. 'We can't do this forever.' It hurt to say but Lottie pushed through. 'We had a fight, and we lost Jamie, and Leviathan could be coming at any second, and –' Lottie's voice cracked and she took a second to calm herself. 'It's one thing to tell me I can't go after Jamie or Leviathan, but you told me you didn't want me, so why all this?'

It was the most painful thing she'd ever had to ask, and she could see it hit Ellie in the same way.

Her princess narrowed her eyes, sinking into herself like the moon disappearing behind cloud. 'Please, Lottie, I can't explain it. I just –' She swallowed hard and Lottie knew she was still hiding something. Lottie was ready to push her, ready to force her to reveal whatever it was, when Ellie said something shocking. 'Can't you just be my Portman?' she whined, sounding distressed. 'Like back in the first year we met, just me and you and no danger, please – only for a little while.'

Ellie's hand found Lottie's, warm soft fingers curling round her own.

Just being Ellie's Portman was everything Lottie wanted. It meant being part of a family. Even though it was broken and had parts missing, she still wanted somewhere to belong. But it was wrong. What Ellie was doing was odd, and there was something secret and twisted at the centre of it that Lottie had to fix.

Lottie sighed, feeling like a coward for playing along, but she couldn't let Ellie know what she was up to, and, more than that, she knew she could never say no to her princess. 'OK, I'll humour whatever this is until the PoP when we break up for study leave, but that's it. This isn't healthy.'

Ellie nodded enthusiastically, clutching Lottie's hands until they were sat like they were praying. 'And then I'll make everything right, I promise.'

Lottie watched as her princess put on that fake plastic smile once more, helping herself to another handful of food, all the while humming happily, like she'd just solved a problem. And in a dark part of her mind she wondered whether she was the problem Ellie needed to solve.

Lottie tried not to let slip the fear that had just settled in her stomach. Tomorrow, she told herself, tomorrow she'd get to work on Leviathan and finding Jamie.

She'd prove she was still useful as a Portman.

33

By Monday the snow had melted. There was not a single trace of it anywhere, leaving the world glowing with dew. The air smelled fresh and clear; spring finally starting to break through the harsh winter. Lottie would have been able to enjoy it, if not for her personal shadow, also known as Samuel.

She was taking a risk with her plan to get away from him, relying on an assumption she'd made about the bodyguard and her own ability to act.

It was lunchtime, with Ellie off at fencing practice, when Lottie made her move.

Walking past the Stratus building, Lottie stopped abruptly, letting Samuel walk a few steps in front of her until he realized she'd paused.

'What's the matter?' he asked.

Samuel was not a bad person. He did his job for the Wolfsons and he did it well. His only problem was he entirely lacked a sense of humour, and he was painfully shy when it came to anything personal.

'I can't say,' Lottie demanded, balling her hands into fists and doing her best to look embarrassed and angry at the same time.

'If something is wrong, it's my job as your –'

Lottie let out a grumble, looking down at the floor. 'No, I can't tell you; it's too humiliating.'

Samuel seemed confused. He took a step forward and she could already see the sweat building on his brow, and Lottie took her chance.

'If you insist on knowing and you're so determined to give me absolutely no privacy, I've had an accident,' she huffed, staring him down indignantly. 'The kind that only happens once a month. Are you happy now?'

Samuel baulked, his usual stoic and calculated appearance bursting into stutters and sweating, his feet betraying him as he stumbled backwards.

It was just as Lottie had suspected. Samuel was a prude.

'I, um, I can perhaps escort you, um, back to your dorm, if, um, that would help?'

Lottie let out an exasperated noise, rolling her eyes to make the bodyguard feel even more out of his depth. 'There's no time for that,' she moaned. 'I have a friend in Stratus. She can lend me a change of clothes and give me some personal products.'

'I'm so sorry, yes, of course.' Samuel tripped over his words, reaching for the Stratus tower door, which he opened for her, letting Lottie march through.

He looked as if he were about to follow when Lottie turned on him sharply. 'Can I have a bit of privacy?' she demanded.

Samuel was turning the colour of a tomato. 'You can have twenty minutes to find your friend and . . . sort this out,' he said. 'I'll be waiting outside.'

Lottie nearly let out a whoop of triumph, shocked that such a ridiculous plan had worked. She had to suppress a giggle, though; it was simply too much, the idea that someone could be so uncomfortable with such a thing.

The moment she was inside the second set of doors and out of his line of sight, she raced to the statue of Elwin, greeting him in relief like an old friend as she turned the 'W' on his name.

Making her way down to Liliana's study, she remembered the last time she had made this journey, her fear and pain, and she needed to fix that.

'What took you so long?' Binah asked, arms crossed where she sat on the floor, already laying everything down that they would need to start back up on figuring out Claude's plan.

'Sorry.' Lottie held up her hand in apology. 'I had to make Samuel think I was embarrassed about my period and didn't want him following me.'

'Why would anyone be embarrassed about their period?'

'I know!' Lottie almost laughed, plopping herself down on the rug. 'Jamie never even gave it a second thought. He always just carried a supply of products around for us in case we needed –' Lottie felt her throat close up, swallowing down the aching lump that had formed. All the good feelings she'd managed to muster evaporated as she remembered why she was there.

'I'm so glad you're here, Binah,' she said instead, reaching over to pull her friend into a tight squeeze. 'We have to find out what Leviathan is planning. You're my only hope.'

'Let's do this,' Binah said, squeezing her back.

After weeks of whispered conversations and secret notes, this felt like the first time both of them had been finally able to talk candidly again.

'I have a new clue,' Lottie announced as she pulled away, and Binah instantly lit up like a Christmas tree. 'We only have about twenty minutes until Samuel will get suspicious so we need to brainstorm quickly.'

She pulled out her notebook and opened it, sliding it forward. 'I found these numbers in Haru's secret diary, with a note next to them saying "decades", but I have no idea what they could be. The only one I recognize is my dorm room number at the top.'

Binah continued to stare at her, seeming to want to say something but changing her mind. When she finally looked down, her eyes narrowed, fingers tapping on her chin thoughtfully. 'Hmm, yes, these do seem important.'

'I was thinking they could be numbers he needed to remember. Maybe the middle two are PIN numbers?'

'Too short.'

'Or lock combinations?'

'Possibly, but without anything to test them the information is moot.'

Groaning, Lottie fell back against the rug, sending up dust. Binah was only voicing her thoughts. Everything she'd come up with was impossible to test, and she was starting to feel like Haru had intentionally let her find the numbers just to torment her.

Binah grabbed the notebook and adjusted her glasses so she could look at the four lines of numbers better. 'Is this an exact copy?' She waited for Lottie to nod in affirmation. 'The way they're spread out seems odd to me,' she said, pondering as she put the notebook back down again. 'What else have we got that we could compare it to?'

Lottie counted everything they knew on her fingers. 'We have the mystery numbers, the Hamelin Formula, Ingrid's mention of Alexis Wolfson and his link to Claude, and Ingrid's mention of the disposal of the king and queen.'

Binah let out a laugh that surprised Lottie. 'We have more information from Ingrid than we've managed to get ourselves.'

Lottie blinked, realizing it was true, but it didn't make her laugh – it only made her more worried. 'Yes, everything is very weird at the moment,' Lottie found herself saying, and Binah gave her an inquisitive look, silently asking her to explain.

'I'm sure you've noticed how Ellie is pretending everything is fine? It's worse than you could imagine. It's one thing for them to forbid me from going after Jamie or Leviathan, but Ellie won't even let me mention his name. She's acting like it was back when we met, when we didn't know anything about Leviathan or Claude.'

'How are Ellie's parents?' Binah asked.

'They're being strangely calm. It's a little unnerving. And none of them will tell me what the plan is. I feel like –' Lottie cut herself off, because she didn't want to admit that she was starting to feel obsolete.

Binah contemplated Lottie's words, chewing them over. 'Are we in agreement that whatever Claude's goal is he needs Jamie for it?' she asked.

Lottie couldn't answer. Her mask had slipped.

'Are you OK?' Binah asked, putting the cursed notebook to the side. 'We don't have to do this if it's too hard to think about right now. We can just talk if you want.'

'We do have to do this,' Lottie replied. 'Jamie is missing and Ellie and her family are locking me out and acting like nothing has happened, and it's making me feel like I'm going insane.'

Getting up, she made her way over to where she'd found Jamie's note. The room felt different now. It was no longer a home of stories and mystery where she could look in the mirror and see Liliana staring back; now the room was nothing but a dark reminder of how alone she'd be if she lost her connection to the Wolfsons. She had to make sure she fixed this.

In an attempt to bring a bit of herself back into the room she reached for the velvet box in her bag and placed Liliana's tiara under the mirror, hoping it would stop her thinking about Jamie's awful message when she saw her reflection. It didn't work; the tiara was not glowing like it was supposed to, and she felt like it was disappointed in her, like she was doing something wrong.

'I'm Ellie's Portman, and no matter what they say it's my job to solve this, so I won't stop until I have.' She tried to muster some of that unstoppable force. 'I have to for Jamie, and Ellie, and Sayuri and Saskia and Percy and everyone else Claude has hurt.' In her mind she pictured Hanna and Midori; they were counting on her too – they'd entrusted her with the ring. With Ellie behaving as she was, it all fell on her. 'I can't let Claude win and take it all away from me.'

The silence that followed made Lottie squirm and she was surprised to find she was panting. She caught sight of her reflection and it felt like she was spying on someone she didn't know.

When she turned back to Binah, her dark round eyes bore into hers, her head cocked to the side like an owl, and Lottie felt like a tiny mouse in her sights, waiting for her to make a move. She could smell the coconut body shimmer she used, and see the twinkle on her skin like gold dust.

Lottie paused before saying, 'Let's keep thinking.'

With a great sigh, Binah looked down at the notebook again, and Lottie thought of her tiara watching her, disappointed in something she couldn't pin down. 'What else might we find a clue in?'

'I brought Oscar Oddwood's diary back with me,' Lottie said, wanting to get them back on track. 'The old Wolfson Portman.'

'And?' Binah licked her lips now, her usual spark coming back. 'Is there any mention of Alexis?'

Swallowing, Lottie shrugged. 'All I could find is a throwaway line about a banquet they had to honour him in the nineteenth century, and he only mentioned it because it was the setting of some palace gossip.'

The flare in Binah's eyes fizzled out, a sympathetic smile resting over her face that made Lottie feel like a failure.

'Don't beat yourself up, Lottie,' she said, closing the notebook. 'It's a start. You can't expect to solve this overnight, especially not after what you've been through with Jamie.' Binah put a reassuring hand on Lottie's thigh, and it made

285

her jump. 'Why don't we go back to yours and think about something else for a while? Sometimes thinking about a problem too much can make –'

'No,' Lottie barked, the word jumping out of her like a hiccup she couldn't stop. 'I can't stop. I'll just keep at it myself.'

The expression that passed over Binah's face was unlike her usual self. The rosy glow of the hanging star lights made her small frame into a golden statue, a deity that needed to be respected and would not tolerate displeasure.

'You can't keep doing this to me,' Binah suddenly said, taking a tone Lottie had never heard from her before. She puffed out a long breath from her nose, the sound full of frustration. Binah shuffled over until she was directly opposite Lottie, the two of them cross-legged and sloping into each other like the sea and the shoreline. 'If that's really how you feel, and you insist on sacrificing yourself for everyone over and over . . .' She huffed, her round cheeks gleaming. 'Then what do you want me to do? What do you expect me to say?'

Lottie had never seen Binah talk to anyone like this, and she supposed it was because Binah wasn't used to people ignoring her advice. It wasn't until her glasses started steaming up that Lottie realized it wasn't just frustration. Binah was upset.

'I keep trying to help you, Lottie. I'm always helping you, and not because it's an exciting mystery, but because we're friends, and I hate seeing people lost. My whole life all I've wanted is to know everything so I can help everyone.' Behind her, one of the fairy lights began to flicker, but she didn't look away, eyes large in her round glasses, holding her gaze like a magnet. 'This is hard for me; I'm not used to getting things wrong.' There was barely a crack in her voice, yet it was there nonetheless, as small yet painful as a pin prick. 'Jamie is my friend too.'

Swallowing her shame, Lottie looked around the room, at the piles of papers and theories, none of it getting them any closer to bringing Jamie back and stopping Claude. It dawned on her that her attempts to take everything on herself and solve these clues at any cost hadn't helped anyone at all. In fact, she was reminding herself of Ellie.

'I'm so sorry.'

The apology hurt her throat, but not because she resented it. It hurt because it was the hardest thing she'd ever had to admit. She'd done this. She was just as responsible for them losing Jamie. She'd been determined to shoulder the burden herself, trying to find a way to solve Claude's riddles so that she could stay with Ellie and the Wolfsons, so that she wouldn't have to be alone, and she'd ended up more alone than ever.

'I feel so stupid, I just –' Lottie choked on the words but persisted, pushing through her discomfort, because this wasn't about her feelings right now. 'I'm just overwhelmed, and it's making me do stupid things that keep hurting people. I'm sorry.'

Binah grabbed Lottie's pink cheeks in her warm hands, forcing her to face her. Even though Binah was no more than five feet tall, in that moment Lottie felt like her head was the whole world, and Binah was a god holding it in her benevolent hands.

'Thank you for the apology, Lottie,' she said. 'But I want you to know that you can and should open up to me. You are your own person, with your own feelings, who exists outside all this and it's selfish to keep your friends locked out. We worry about you too.' She waited for Lottie to acknowledge she was taking this all in. 'Now tell me what's going on.'

The idea of offloading anything to anyone else felt like a criminal act, and yet here was Binah telling her it was more selfish to keep it bottled up. Binah's eyes weren't pleading or angry; Binah was looking at her with nothing but love.

Lottie relented, the acknowledgement painful and strange. 'It's not just Jamie. I had a fight with Ellie before he went missing. A bad one, and she won't talk about it, or anything. It's like she's hiding something from me. I *know* she's hiding something from me.' She didn't realize she was crying until she felt Binah's thumbs wiping the salt away from her cheeks. It felt like all she was doing was crying recently.

'It's OK,' Binah said. 'It's OK that you're sad about this. You're allowed to be.'

'She said she didn't want me, that I was just her Portman and our relationship would end when she became queen, but since we got back she's pretending it never happened. She asked me . . . she asked me to pretend to be her Portman in the way it used to be, before Leviathan.' Lottie choked on the words; having not even spoken them to herself, they felt fresh and raw like an open wound. 'I know her. I know she was pushing me away on purpose, but I don't understand what she's doing now. Everything feels fake, and I can't stop thinking what if it was always fake? What if this whole time

I've been a complete fool, and the moment I stop being a useful Portman, they'll throw me away?'

Binah absorbed everything, then let out her breath in one steady stream, taking her hands off Lottie's now-dry cheeks. 'That's stupid. Why does it matter if you're her Portman?'

It wasn't the great bang Lottie had been expecting; it was quiet and controlled.

'Because that's all I have,' Lottie confessed, downing a big gulp of air to steady herself. 'Everyone keeps wanting me to figure out what I'm going to do next, to find out who I am. But until I came to Rosewood, until I met Ellie, I didn't have a home. I don't know anything else. Being her Portman is the closest thing I have to a family.'

'I understand,' Binah said, and Lottie knew that she did.

They sat in silence for a moment, Binah resting her head against Lottie's shoulder, letting themselves digest the conversation.

'May I offer some advice?' Binah said at last.

Lottie smiled, and it hurt a little less now. 'Always.'

'You need to remember that Ellie is afraid. She's lost part of her family, and she must feel like the Wolfson name is a bad omen. She wants you by her side, but she doesn't want you to get hurt, especially after what happened to Jamie.' Moving her head from side to side, she continued. 'Maybe right now what this problem needs isn't Lottie Pumpkin the Portman, but Lottie Pumpkin the friend. Do you understand?'

Behind Binah, Lottie caught sight of her tiara, the opal glittering, and there, above it, was Lottie's reflection, as bright as the sun itself, her unstoppable determination.

How could she have been so stupid? It didn't matter if she was Ellie's Portman. It didn't matter how useful she was. They were so much more than that.

'Yes,' she said, smiling back at her own image with a warm welcome. 'I understand.'

34

Mock exam season sent the school into a hive of buzzing study sessions and busy library visits, and it wasn't just cramming that had everyone humming and focused. The Presentation of the Pillars was approaching, and soon Rosewood would come to life with the memories of its namesakes, which would have been exciting, except for the fact Lottie still had nothing to contribute.

With Binah's advice still nestled in her head, Lottie put all her other worries to the side, and set out to finally face what she'd spent so long trying to ignore. It was time to confront herself.

Lottie settled in Room A-2 while Samuel stationed himself outside the door. It was a cosy little room on the top floor of the art department, the very same place she'd first learned of Liliana over a year ago. The white shutters rattled in the cold breeze, the crawling ivy from the outside wall peeping in, curious to see what she was up to. Taking a deep breath, she extracted Jamie's ring from her pocket and put it on her finger, then, as if she were ornamenting herself before a coronation, she placed her family tiara on her head and began.

She was surrounded by art materials, paints, pastels, brushes and an array of canvases. It felt like years since she'd really painted anything this personal, and the thought made her fingers twitch in anticipation, like being reunited with an old friend. Away from the messy art supplies, spread on the tables around her were all the books she could find on Liliana and her alter ego William Tufty. Exactly forty-four books lay open, like a flurry of seagulls in flight, and, out of all the books, only three of them mentioned Liliana, and, out of those, there was only one painting of her. It was the image she'd already seen: Lili – her tiara atop a cascade of tangled curls, a fierce look in her eyes, as she held a sword before her. The very sword Lottie had hidden under her bed now. Only Lottie and her friends knew that this was not the last image of her to survive, that her study was filled with self-portraits and adoring renderings of the people she loved.

It was all there, hidden in William Tufty's rhyme, 'The Vixen and the Delicate Mouse'. Little did anyone know that they were both the same person: Liliana was the vixen and Tufty the mouse. Two sides of one coin.

As Lottie delved deeper into the books, remapping all her discoveries about Liliana Mayfutt the wayward princess, her adventures in Japan, meeting her ancestor Henry, becoming William Tufty, the founder of Rosewood, and locking away that wild part of herself, something rekindled inside her. It felt like a light had been switched on deep in her body, one that had always been there, dimmed, but was now growing, as if every word she ate up was feeding the fire.

How could I have been afraid of this?

She remembered what Ellie had said before their fight, pleading with her to think about what else she could be beyond her Portman role. *Don't you ever wonder what that means? What else you could be?*

As soon as she heard the words in her head, everything shifted. It was as if her vision had been clouded since Jamie had left and it was finally clear.

They had to find out who they were, all of them – and that meant Jamie too.

It hurt to admit it, but it was a sweet ache, a peacefulness settling over her now that she finally understood why Jamie had left.

'I hope you find what you're looking for,' she said to his ring, 'and when you're ready, come back to us.'

His ring winked at her in response as it passed through a stream of sunlight from the window, the stars erupting into thousands of tiny lights. It reminded her of her tiara with the opal moon. Now she had the whole night sky.

With a start she realized that's what they were, the three of them together: Jamie, Ellie and herself. They were a whole universe they'd built themselves and she had faith that one day they'd orbit back to each other.

The thought felt like déjà vu, a happy memory before Leviathan, Claude and the unknowable future. She was dancing in a dress with threads of gold and fabric woven from sunshine. She was twirled between a boy who was a knight, in a suit as dark and wondrous as midnight, and a girl who was a prince, drenched in a dress sewn out of the moon and stars, the three of them spinning together in an endless sunrise.

Jamie had said he'd gone to his family, but he was wrong; they were their own family. He belonged with Ellie and Lottie the way sun and stars belonged to the sky, but she also understood that he had to find that out for himself, just as she had.

Before Lottie could even register what she was doing, her hands were moving over the canvas beside her, graphite lines linking her abstract thoughts to the page.

Soon the empty white was filled with an image of two people dancing, free and happy in each other's arms, just as Lottie had been with Ellie two years ago at the ball. Only this was not her and her princess. This was the two sides of William Tufty, soft as summer like Lottie and intense as a storm like Ellie. It was so obvious now what she'd been missing. Whenever she looked at her reflection and struggled to see which one she was more like now, it was because she was becoming both.

She'd been so afraid of what she'd be without Ellie, pushing away any thought of a future where they might not always be together. But that wasn't right. They would always be with each other. They had been bonded into something strange and new and that would never go away.

She breathed her name into the canvas, colour springing to life where she made her marks, confident bold strokes to tell the world her story. 'Ellie, I don't know what you're hiding from me, or how you plan to save Jamie, but, no matter what, we're meant to be together.'

She knew now that what she needed to do first was to make Ellie see that they were better people because of their differences – and that they were each perfect just as they were. The Wolfsons had lost Jamie because they'd been so afraid of him leaving them. They dreaded that he'd turn into something they couldn't cling to any more, that they couldn't control, and it was exactly that which had driven him away. But Lottie could see it now, so plain and simple, that it didn't matter that they all had their own separate paths and journeys; no matter how they grew and changed into new versions of themselves, they'd always be connected.

She had to speak to Ellie.

Dropping her brush and slipping Jamie's ring back into her pocket, she ran from the room, overalls covered in primaries and pastels fluttering around her like butterflies. 'Sorry, Samuel,' she called behind her, racing down the steps. 'I'm heading back to the dorm.' She was only briefly aware of Samuel giving chase, too focused was she on finding her princess.

When she arrived at Room 221, her breath was ragged with nerves. Without hesitation, she pulled the door open, and there she was, sitting in the centre of their room, right where both their worlds collided into magical chaos. A circle of frosty sunshine from the balcony encased her in a spotlight.

'Ellie, I'm so glad you're here. I wanted to tell you something.' The words tumbled out of her as fast as a downpour, but she had to get them out before she could think about it too much. 'I'm going to apply to art college, to do a foundation. And I'm going to look into my family's history. I want Liliana's legacy to be remembered. I want to be part of it.'

Ellie's mouth parted, and she blinked away the shock of both Lottie's abrupt entrance and the sudden onslaught of information. She looked tired, as usual, purple and blue under the eyes. And there was something else now. Her hair had grown a little too long, the sharp edges of her cheekbones sank a little too deep, and her skin was a little too pale. 'When did –'

'I know this is out of the blue,' Lottie explained, and she felt the telltale heat on her cheeks that let her know they were turning pink, 'but I've been thinking about everything you said, and about us, and I want you to know you don't have to be afraid.' Ellie's eyes willed Lottie to go on. 'Us knowing each other is a good thing, Ellie. It's made us both better people, and I need to trust that I can take everything I've learned from being your friend out into the rest of the world.'

As if they'd become a mirror image of one another, they both sagged, as if a weight had been lifted. The last time Lottie had tried to speak to Ellie she'd been so afraid that she'd said all the wrong things. Now Lottie knew exactly how she felt and exactly what to say.

Ellie slowly stood up. 'Lottie, I . . . What's brought this on so suddenly?'

Lottie couldn't help smiling when she spoke, so relieved to be talking to Ellie again, having her listen, and she could see in the way Ellie leaned forward, just slightly, that the bridge was mending. 'All this time I've been trying to hide away from the fact that one day I won't be your Portman by focusing on Leviathan and Claude and anything that made me feel connected to my job. I felt that if I could stay in this role, then you and I would always be linked.' The more she spoke, the more Ellie's eyebrows crawled up her face, the twitch of a smile playing in the corner of her mouth. 'But I was wrong,'

Lottie admitted, feeling the power in her confession. 'No matter where we go or what we do, no matter whether I'm your Portman or not, we'll always have each other. We're better as a team.'

She grabbed Ellie's hand, holding it dearly to her chest. 'I know it's true, and even if we have to go our separate ways after we graduate we still have one more year to be us. And to become the best versions of ourselves.' She squeezed Ellie's hand tightly and looked her dead in the eyes. 'We're unstoppable, and I don't want you being afraid of that any more. You don't have to push me away. We can survive with each other and apart. I know that now . . . but let's face this together.'

Ellie stood totally still for a long moment, the only sound their ragged breathing mingling. Her painted lips parted once more, and again she seemed about to say something, but she swallowed whatever it was down hard and instead gifted Lottie with her little half-smile.

There was still something Ellie wasn't telling her. She just had to hope she'd trust her soon. She needed to if they were going to rescue Jamie.

'I knew you'd come round,' Ellie said, and with a great sigh she leaned forward, forehead resting in the crook of Lottie's neck, her warm breath tickling her skin. 'I'm sorry.'

The shape of Ellie's words against her neck felt like a kiss, and it took all Lottie's self-control not to fall into it.

'Yes, well, one of us had to –' Lottie was about to make a joke, when she glanced down at where Ellie had been sitting. 'What's all that?'

Ellie turned to the mess and boxes. 'Oh, I was just starting packing, you know.' She shrugged, uncomfortable with the change in conversation. 'I want to get to Maradova as soon as I'm able to for reading week, what with the circumstances.'

'Right, of course. I didn't realize we'd be going back for half term.' Lottie felt silly for not considering such a thing in light of Leviathan having new information on them. 'It's going to be OK, you know?' she added. 'We'll bring Jamie back.'

'Yeah, it's going to be OK,' Ellie agreed, and the look on her face let Lottie know that she really believed it. 'I've made sure of that.'

Lottie tilted her head to the side, not sure if she'd heard her right. 'What do you mean?'

Ellie waved off the question, stepping back to lie on her bed, sizing Lottie up with a mischievous smirk. 'The only thing you should be worried about is the huge smear of paint you have across your forehead.'

'What?' Lottie rushed over to the mirror and, sure enough, there was a massive streak of rose-pink paint that ran from her brows and across down to her ear, the same colour as her cheeks, making her look like a grinning peach. 'Well, it finally happened. The blush has taken over my whole face.'

She turned round, grinning at her princess. It was so easy the two of them falling back into their comfortable teasing, laughing at each other as if nothing had happened at all. But, even though Lottie wanted to let herself go, there was still something that Ellie was holding back.

Whatever it was, Lottie was sure they'd recover from it. As long as they were together.

35

When they awoke on the morning of the Presentation of the Pillars, the Ivy common room had been transformed. Poems written in curly script hung on string and nestled in the petals of pretend flowers, quotes from diverse feminist literature were chalked on to the walls, and statues of deer made from words frolicked in the courtyard.

And that was only the beginning. The whole of Rosewood lay covered in bright streamers and bunting, fragrant petals and scented candles, all purple, yellow and red to represent the three houses. The school and grounds displayed whimsical and painstaking tributes to the namesakes of Rosewood's houses and each piece had the name of the student who'd created it proudly at its side.

Lottie didn't have much time to explore the other works with Samuel accompanying her. She popped in briefly to Stratus Side and Conch House to see everyone's tributes. Someone had organized flowers that hung on trellises on either side of the Stratus tower, each symbolic of Shray and Sana's work. Less tastefully a student at Conch House had fashioned a decapitated wolf's head and placed it on a spike by the bronze statue of Saxon the bear, an ode to Balthazar who'd supposedly taken on a wolf in the woods to save a fellow student. Despite knowing that the wolf was the villain in the tale, she felt a little sorry for it.

Its snarling face reminded Lottie of the knocker on the doors of the palace and it made her think of Jamie and Ellie. They didn't growl because they were angry or mean; they did it because they were scared. Lottie reached up to the growling head and stroked its nose.

'It's going to be OK,' she promised. Satisfied, Lottie headed off, ready to present her piece.

At eleven in the morning, students from Lottie's year made their way into Rosewood's main hall, the whole room smelling of pastries and candied fruits from an array of edible tributes, including an uncanny recreation of Elwin, Ryley and Saxon in miniature. Lottie was not surprised to find Lola's and Micky's names next to them.

Her own tribute was up on the platform, hidden under a cover, with each house mother standing like a guard round it. Even Professor Croak had made an appearance, sniffing curiously round the confectionary table, spindly fingers fidgeting with the effort of not reaching out to pinch a piece.

Lottie saw Ellie and her friends huddled together with Samuel poised nearby as she went to stand beside Professor Devine, anticipation spreading over the room.

Professor Devine turned to her, her silk cloak sweeping a wave of expensive perfume in Lottie's direction. 'Lottie, this is excellent. If you're ready, we'd be delighted for you to present your William Tufty tribute.'

'Yes, I'm ready but –' Lottie looked out over the crowd of students gathered, singling out Ellie instantly like the moon in a clear sky – 'I have something I'd like to say about it, if I may.'

This seemed to please the professor, whose lips twitched into what could almost be described as a smile.

Beneath the platform a slow wave of hush spread over the students. All the students had one thing in common: Rosewood, a world built by her ancestor, and now, standing on the podium, Lottie felt an obligation to continue the work that Liliana had started.

'Before I present the tribute to our school's founder, I have a few words I want to share.' Waiting until everyone was listening, she twirled the ends of her hair.

'William Tufty believed deeply in the importance of humanity bringing out the best in each other. This is why they established the three pillars that each house is built upon. Righteous, resolute and resourceful. Each has its own merit, but when you combine the three, amazing, magical things can be achieved.'

Lottie saw Binah nodding along.

'Tufty also believed in duality, in the power of shouting about your beliefs, and staying quiet to allow others to come forward.' She stopped, pulling the dust sheet away to reveal her piece.

A great gasp, like a firework whizzing up into the air, flew across the hall as students and teachers looked at Lottie's work. Slowly the sound was replaced with murmurs of wonder and delighted chirping.

Held in a gilded frame that shone the colour of the stars, the work was painted in a pre-Raphaelite style to pay homage to William's hidden identity and the many secrets he'd scattered among the school. The colours were rich marigolds and gothic golds that moved together in a Catherine wheel of colour. Two figures blended into one another – the masculine figure of William Tufty and the feminine figure by its side, its face obscured by beautiful shades of gold.

Once the whispers died down, Lottie continued. 'This duality is what I wanted to show in the painting. The two sides of our founder in harmony. They are wild and measured, passionate and tranquil, loud and soft. You might say they are a vixen and a delicate mouse, one of my favourite rhymes growing up.'

Looking over the crowd, her eyes locked on to Ellie's because she wanted her to know that the next words were for her. 'I hope with this painting that I can encourage people to not only strive to bring out the best in each other, but to explore how others can change them, and how we can all grow into better people for us having known them. I think that's what William Tufty would have wanted for us, and that's what I want to share with you all in this piece. Thank you. And I think you're allowed to eat the cakes now.'

Lottie didn't bask in the applause. She ran down the steps straight to Ellie. She flung herself into her arms, the two of them embracing like their bodies were thirsty for each other. 'What did you think?' she asked, still clinging on.

Ellie pulled away first, holding Lottie by her shoulders at a distance, looking her up and down. 'I'm so proud of you,

Lottie,' she said with complete sincerity. 'You're going to do such amazing things in this world.' Lottie felt like she had become the painting, that Ellie was taking note of every detail, wanting to burn it into her memory. 'I'm really glad we got to have this time together.'

Something had sneaked its way into Ellie's voice, a small crack that Lottie couldn't pin down. But then Ellie tilted her head to the side, inky-black hair dusting her pale cheekbones. 'It reminds me of us,' she announced. 'You know, at the ball. The first time we danced together.' She let out a sigh that made Lottie's chest ache where the wolf lay over it. 'That was one of the best times of my life.'

It was the most perfect thing that Ellie could have ever said.

'I feel the same way,' she replied.

But then the moment disappeared and Ellie put back on her mask.

'God, I can't believe I have to do that again next year for their stupid Golden Flower Festival 2019 edition,' she said.

Lottie froze, watching Ellie laughing. It wasn't the joke that caught her off guard; it was the date.

'What did you just say?'

'Next year, the Golden Flower Festival,' Ellie said. 'Remember? They're still going ahead with it.'

Lottie felt the warmth drain out of her. There was something in what Ellie had said and she needed to figure it out right now.

'Ellie, I'm just going to excuse myself for a second.' Ellie's hand curled round hers. 'I promise I'll be back soon.' And she meant it. 'And then I'll tell you everything. I think . . .' She paused, not sure how to phrase this in a way that wouldn't put Ellie on high alert again. 'I think I've found something that could help your family find Jamie,' she said instead, knowing that they wanted to keep her out of it.

Ellie's fingers tightened, the two of them melting like clay into one another where their skin met. 'Don't worry about it. We have to do what we have to do, right?'

There was still that something in the way Ellie held on to her, the way she stared at her.

'Yes . . .' Lottie trailed off, lost in the way Ellie's eyes bored into her.

And, just like that, Ellie let go and a gap came between them like a rift in the earth as her Partizan disappeared into the crowd.

Deep in her own thoughts, Lottie failed to notice that Samuel didn't follow her.

36

The library was almost empty now, with everyone off enjoying the PoP festivities. Only a few students lingered, giving Lottie free rein to untangle her thoughts in the sunlit space.

Her first stop was the history section. She flicked through what felt like hundreds of titles until she found what she was looking for. It was a recent title called *Reign and Conquer: A Brief History of the World's Most Impactful Shifts in Power*. Her history professor was always singing the author's praises.

Grabbing it, she marched over to a table by the closed library cafe and spread out her tiny collection of clues: the numbers, the book and Oscar's diary, turning to the page about the banquet. Licking her lips, she read the start of the passage, drinking it all up.

There have been times in which being a Portman has allowed me insight into rather scandalous affairs. Last year, for example, I had to remain tight-lipped when an older countess from Genovia divulged during Alexis Wolfson's commemorative banquet that she wondered if I would like to add myself to the list of Maravish royalty who have disgraced themselves on her behalf. I politely

declined, but now remain forever curious about which
members of this household she was speaking upon.

Despite the allure of the scandalous tale, this was not the information she was looking for. This entry had been dated 1860, meaning the year before had been 1859. Turning back to the numbers in her notebook, she scrutinized the four lines and with a great gasp realized her mistake.

$$2 \quad 2 \quad 1$$
$$0 \quad 0 \quad 9$$
$$1 \quad 0 \quad 9$$
$$9 \quad 9 \quad 9$$

It wasn't four lines of numbers; it was three lines, written downwards from right to left. 1999, 2009, 2019. It had been right there the whole time, Arabic numerals written from right to left just as the rest of the diary had been.

With shaking hands, she grabbed the history book, flicking through to find the passage she needed.

Sometimes revolution can occur within the nation itself.
This is rather common. What is not common is for
unanimous provision in said overthrowing, as in the case
of Alexis Wolfson of Maradova, who on 12 August 1589
overthrew the current ruler and was met with unbridled
support, even from within the palace. Rumour went so far
as to declare that when he seized the throne, flowers
bloomed and the sun shined in Maradova for the first time
in ten years.

Lottie felt dizzy. Everything plummeted into place.

The numbers weren't codes or combinations or anything to do with her dorm room. It was so much simpler. They were dates, and not just any dates – they corresponded to the Maravish Golden Flower Festival, held every ten years to celebrate the day Alexis Wolfson had seized the throne.

Lottie didn't know what the plan was and she didn't know how they intended to execute it, but she knew with gut-wrenching certainty that whatever terrible thing Claude had in store for them would happen during the ball this summer.

Moving with desperate speed, as if her life depended on it, Lottie raced out of the library. It was the fastest she'd run since she'd been chased by Ingrid in the Rose Wood, her feet flying over the cobbled path as if she was light itself – because she had to get to Ellie. She had to warn her.

Reaching Ivy Wood, she bolted up the steps, aching from the effort of sprinting so hard, and she pushed the door open with so much force it banged against the wall.

'Ellie, I figured it out. Claude –' But Lottie stopped short, the words drying up in her mouth while her breathing continued ragged and confused, sure her mind was playing tricks on her.

Ellie wasn't there. And nor were any of her belongings.

Where her and Ellie's stuff usually blended together like a Rorschach print, there was nothing. Everything that wasn't Lottie's was gone. The only thing to show that Ellie had ever been there at all was the sun-bleached paint around where her posters had hung and a stain on the wooden floor where she'd once spilled ink. Other than the shadows of her presence,

Ellie was gone. All her angry teenage rebellion and passionate pop-culture references had vanished, leaving the room cold and empty. Lottie's things looked lifeless without Ellie's, only taking up a small amount of the space in the wide half-empty room.

Lottie started backing out, still not understanding.

Samuel? she thought. *Where's Samuel?* When had he stopped being at her side?

It was right after she saw Ellie in the hall. He hadn't followed her to the library, so he must have gone with Ellie. She had to find them.

'Congratulations on your painting, Lottie.' Nana Lai, an Ivy girl from Lottie's art class, appeared at her bedroom door, umber hair in a bun, her face full of genuine pride. 'It's really amazing. I'm thinking of applying to art school next year. Maybe we'll cross paths in the future.'

Trying to absorb the compliment, Lottie told herself to respond.

'Thank you, maybe.' Lottie felt the words in her mouth like someone else was talking for her. 'Have you seen Ellie anywhere? I can't think where she's gone.'

Nana shrugged, shoulders rising and falling. 'I thought she left a little while ago.'

'What?'

'Yeah, she had a bunch of suitcases.'

Lottie couldn't make sense of it. It was like the whole world was spinning too fast, everything blurring out of focus. 'Oh . . . OK.' It was all Lottie could manage, and her feet heavily carried her down the steps while Nana stared on in confusion.

Suddenly Lottie thought of Ellie's look when their hands had parted, as if it were the last time she'd ever see her.

Lottie nearly bumped right into Professor Devine on the path towards the main hall, her purple cloak twirling behind her in a big wave when she stopped abruptly. 'Lottie, excellent! We're hoping, with your permission, to display your painting permanently in the grand hall.' The professor gazed down at her from beneath her crop of red hair. 'Lottie, are you all right?'

But all Lottie could do was stare back vacantly. She needed to find Ellie; that's all she knew. Everything else was a jumble.

'I'm looking for Ellie,' she said, because it was the only thing that she could understand right then.

The professor's eyes narrowed. 'Eleanor has gone home early. Did she not inform you?' There was a pointed tone. 'She left no more than half an hour ago. Surely she told you, Lottie?'

Lottie felt her mouth open and close a few times, but no sound came out, like all the air had gone from inside her.

'Yes, of course,' she managed eventually, shuffling past the professor and out of the door.

Lottie's mind went round and round in delirious circles.

Ellie was gone.

Ellie had left, and she was gone. She'd left not long ago.

It had to be a mistake. The look in her eye. The ache in her smile.

I'm really glad we got to have this time together.

It wasn't until Lottie was approaching the edge of the Rosewood grounds that she even realized what she was doing. Vaguely aware of the black-clad security calling for her to stop, Lottie pushed past them and flung herself at full pelt down the hill, feet crunching on the stone path, down, down, past the rows of flowers and the trees, through the cast-iron gates, past the drop-off zone with the wooden canopy, and down, down further along the road.

Then the town was in view, and she could see the station shining like a beacon. Part of her was searching endlessly for a blacked-out car, for Ellie.

Her mind hurtled her back to the first time she had seen Ellie. Leather jacket, dark eyes hidden behind sunglasses, a storm clinging to her, the electric smell of wet earth. If she just thought about it hard enough, she'd be with her again.

She was on her own in the town, the purple tartan pinafore making her completely conspicuous.

People stared as she ran. Children filtered out of shops, pointing. The exposure made her afraid in a way she hadn't felt in years, since long before she came to Rosewood Hall.

Ducking out of view, she bolted down a grey-stone alley, hoping to stick to the shadows on the way to the train station. She only had a vague idea of what she was doing. Make it to the train station, call Ellie on the public phone, wait for them to pick her up.

She reached out to steady herself and was shocked to find her hand shaking. If Ellie was really gone, if her worst nightmare was real, then she was entirely alone.

This wasn't right. She'd made her peace with Ellie; she'd proven they could be together even when she wasn't her Portman. So why had she gone? Why was everyone gone and she was left behind again?

Legs crumbling, she slid down the stone. This wasn't how it was supposed to go. She was supposed to have one more year with her; they were going to face this together. They were going to find Jamie. And now she was completely alone, sitting in a dirty dark alley, no Jamie, no Ellie – and without them she couldn't find herself; she didn't know who she was.

'Ellie, Jamie, where are you?' she croaked.

The loneliness was nauseating and swirled up inside her. She was faced with a version of herself she thought she'd never see again. The sad little girl hidden away in the attic, no family, only drawings and fairy tales for company, dreaming of Rosewood and who she'd become there. Now it was all being ripped away. She was sure she was about to be sick.

'What's that?' A voice from the end of the alley drifted over.

Lottie peered through her hands to see three indistinct figures in the chink of sunlight.

'Looks like someone's lost.'

37

The figures at the end of the alley stepped into the half-light. They were not people she recognized. They were teenagers, not much older than herself, but the way they skulked towards her made her recoil like a trapped mouse.

'Look, she's one of those Rosewood students.' The tallest one pointed at her, nose twitching like he'd caught a scent. 'You must have a big brain, huh? Why don't you let us pick at it over dinner?'

The question took a moment to register with Lottie. His tone was eloquent but not quite friendly, his smiling expression charming but not quite kind.

Now the second stepped forward, shorter and wearing an oversized coat in a decidedly peacocky way. 'How old are you?' he asked, nudging his friend in the ribs, and they all laughed again at whatever joke they were sharing.

Lottie knew what she should do. And she knew exactly what Ellie would do if she were there. She'd grab the tallest man by the scruff of his collar and tell him where to shove his dinner. But Lottie wasn't Ellie, and she didn't have her or Jamie to help her, so instead she backed away.

'Please, I just want to go home, I –'

'We'll walk you home.' The man in the middle grabbed her arm, pulling her up, his hands clammy, the feeling like slime on her bare skin.

On instinct she jerked out of his grip, trying to think of all the escape techniques Jamie had taught her, only she could think of nothing. Without him or Ellie to back her up, there was nothing. She couldn't face the world without them.

'Whoa, no need to cry,' the tall one weighed in, his voice mocking like a jackdaw. 'We're just trying to be friendly.'

'Did your boyfriend break up with you?' the middle one asked. Hoots of laughter ensued, the sound grating.

Lottie couldn't move. There was nothing kind, brave or unstoppable about her. She was just a little girl, who didn't know who she was or what she was doing any more.

'Come on – give us a smile,' the shorter man said, pulling up the sides of his mouth like a clown. 'What problems could a nice young lady like you have?'

Everything faded out of focus except him. He inched closer, his maniacal grin growing wider. She was sure she was about to collapse.

Suddenly the man's smile shattered and his eyes grew wide as he was pulled backwards and flipped, spinning into the air and down hard on to his front where he lay gasping. A tall girl with a mane of golden hair and athletic build pulled his arm behind his back, every tug making the man squeak.

'How's this for "nice young lady", you creep?' Saskia growled at her captive, yanking on his arm again until he let out a pathetic yelp. '*Come on – give us a smile. What are you crying about?*'

Then another small figure came up beside Lottie – curly hair softly brushing her shoulder. Binah looked up at her, glasses magnifying her eyes that were warm brown and as comforting and reassuring as melted chocolate.

She beamed, taking Lottie's arm. 'We've been looking for you.'

How did they find me? Lottie thought, blinking in confusion.

Before she could make sense of what was going on, the other men shouted a list of expletives, marching towards Saskia, furious at being humiliated.

'Come here, you little –'

'Excuse me.' From behind Saskia, Anastacia stepped into the light, sweeping her hair behind her. 'I must be mistaken. Are you threatening the French ambassador's daughter?' she asked, walking up to the tall man without an inch of fear. He looked like he'd just realized he was trapped. 'Because if you were, I would have no choice but to alert Security at Rosewood, who would have you put away for the rest of your sad little lives.' Her eyes narrowed into slits, leaning forward in a way that made her appear to tower over the two remaining men. 'I would make sure of that, *comprenez-vous?*'

Saskia released the man underneath her. The three men gulped and shook as they retreated down the alley, but Saskia kept at their back, cracking her knuckles, itching for one of them to make a wrong move.

'Lottie, do you have anything to say to these men?' Binah asked, nudging her forward. 'Remember you're your own person, and we're your friends no matter what,' she whispered into her ear, her breath tickling her neck. 'What would *Lottie the friend* do?'

Face to face with the three men cowering at her and the rest of her gang, she couldn't believe how blinkered she'd been. She wasn't alone. She wasn't nothing without Jamie and Ellie. She had everything she'd learned from Rosewood and her friends all thumping in her every heartbeat. She was Lottie Pumpkin, built from every experience, good and bad, kind, brave and unstoppable, and she wasn't going to let anyone push her around.

Taking a confident step forward, she brushed off her pinafore, and flicked her hair as she'd seen Anastacia do, coming right up to face the three sweating pigs in front of her.

Cocking her head to the side, refusing to smile, she asked, imitating their earlier tone, '*Want us to walk you home?*'

'N-no thank you,' they stammered, squeezing together.

Smiling now, Lottie leaned forward. 'Then kindly get the hell away from me.'

Saskia moved aside and the three of them bolted off down the alley with all the frantic energy of a balloon rapidly deflating.

The moment they were out of sight, the four girls burst into laughter. It only lasted a few seconds, until Lottie felt the laughter catch in her throat and twist into a sobbing fit, tears rolling down her cheeks.

'How did you guys find me?' she asked through her tears. But she wasn't sad. She was simply overwhelmed and relieved, not able to comprehend everything she was feeling.

'Binah saw you heading to the gates,' Anastacia said. 'She came to get us.'

Shrugging as if it were no big deal, Binah leaned into Lottie, holding her close. 'We'll always be here for you, remember.'

Lottie nodded, not able to speak, knowing she'd start crying again.

'What the hell happened?' Saskia asked bluntly, wrapping round the other side of Lottie as they all began walking back into the light. 'Why are you all the way in town, and how are you so fast?'

Lottie laughed weakly, but she knew she had to tell them.

Together they stepped into the light and she paused, not able to keep going. Something on her face must have caved in, because their expressions softened, turning patient and thoughtful.

'I think –' Lottie began, struggling to find the words, because she hadn't quite admitted it to herself yet. Reaching inside herself, feeling the ache where the wolf lay across her chest, hollow and empty, she knew what had happened, and she had to say it out loud.

'Ellie's left me behind,' she said, voice catching. 'She's gone.'

38

They stayed in town until the sky turned pink and the clouds turned lavender. Lottie explained the situation to them over hot tea that Anastacia treated them to. She told them about the dates, and about the Flower Festival, and Ellie leaving, and her friends listened intently, comforting her when she cried, waiting patiently for her to find the words.

When they arrived back at Rosewood, Dame Bolter was furious, saying she had been about to call the police, but as soon as she saw their faces, as well as the concerned look from Professor Devine, she let them off with a warning.

Grabbing a pillow and Mr Truffles, Binah walked with Lottie to Stratus Side, deciding it would be best for her to stay with her that night, so she wouldn't be alone.

Humming to herself, Binah prepared some loose-leaf tea in her copper dining set, Lottie finding the stirring sound of the spoon against the metal strangely mesmerizing.

Wandering around, Lottie stroked the leaves on the plants in Binah's private garden that she called a room, tracing long hanging vines with her fingers and breathing in the sweet lilies and herbs on the windowsill. On her large bookshelf was an array of crystals. One in particular caught Lottie's eye, a cracked amethyst geode, the light bouncing off its jagged lilac edges, beautiful and pointed, sharp and wonderful, like a storm in summer. It reminded her of Ellie.

Where are you? she thought, and swallowed down another ache in her throat.

'You can stay with me and my parents in London over Easter and the summer,' Binah said suddenly, placing a teacup in front of her, steam wafting into the air from the amber liquid.

'Thank you. I'm sure it won't come to that,' Lottie replied, but her voice wavered, unsure, so she took a sip of tea to try to hide it.

'Either way,' Binah said, not hiding her lack of confidence, 'you're welcome.'

The next morning was exceptionally cold, a wind coursing through the school that whipped at everyone's uniforms, and blew their hair around in great bellows, obscuring faces and making the school appear filled with flickers, haunted and ghoulish.

Trudging through the gale, Binah and Lottie went to meet Anastacia and Saskia in the Conch common room.

'Feels like we're at the beach,' Lottie said, shaking off the last of the wind as she hung up her jacket.

'Or heading into a storm,' Binah countered, but Lottie didn't want to think about storms right then.

Anastacia had commandeered a spot at the bay window, reclining against the plush sofa, wrapped up in Saskia's arms, the two of them looking like the deadliest couple in the whole world. For the first time ever seeing them together made Lottie's heart ache in a way she wasn't used to, her brain flashing up images of Ellie and Jamie in her head without her permission.

'Any news?' Anastacia asked, when Lottie came to sit beside them.

'No,' Lottie said, defeated. 'No messages left for the school, and I asked permission to check my phone – nothing, no note, no letters.'

'What will you do when school closes?' Saskia reminded her unhelpfully.

'She can stay with me,' Binah said so Lottie didn't have to reply.

'The most important thing right now is that we get this information to them about when Leviathan will execute their plan regarding Ellie and her family,' Lottie announced, ignoring how her voice cracked. 'We have to warn them.'

Nodding in agreement, Anastacia pulled out a notebook. 'I've jotted down a few possibilities that –'

'Hey, Princess,' a Conch student called across the room, cutting Anastacia off and gesturing to the large television mounted on the wall. 'Your parents are on TV.'

Lottie felt her skin go hot, like the start of a fever. 'Excuse me?'

'Turn it up,' Saskia called, while Anastacia gave anyone making noise a death glare that quickly had them shutting up.

'*We are now live with the king and queen of Maradova who have relayed that there will be an official announcement,*' the news anchor declared, and, sure enough, the image on the screen showed King Alexander and Queen Matilde stepping

319

on to a podium, both dressed in the regal attire and sashes that Lottie knew were used for important addresses.

'No.' The word escaped Lottie's mouth in a squeak, throat closing like she was drowning, because behind the king and queen was a girl in matching attire, a sash draped over her shoulders. 'Ellie.' The name sent a dizzy jolt of pain through her head.

Lottie could barely concentrate on the king's speech, her brain only snapping back into focus when Ellie stepped up to the podium.

'*The king has now passed the podium over to a young woman,*' the news anchor announced, trying to hide her confusion. '*I believe we will hear her speak next.*'

Her breathing ragged, Lottie stared up at Ellie, who was dressed in a long indigo sarafan dress embroidered with stars that matched the gold sash. The outfit was mesmerizing, flowing with Ellie where she swayed. Her hair was clipped up elegantly with a moon ornament, showing off her delicate neck and porcelain skin. She was so beautiful it made her heart ache – a perfect princess. But it was all wrong. Her dark eyes looked down in defeat, because this wasn't what she wanted and this was never how she'd choose to present herself. Lottie desperately longed to free her.

'Isn't that . . .?' another Conch boy began, but Anastacia scowled at him, practically baring her teeth.

And then Ellie began to speak.

Looking out at the crowd, eyelids half closed in a scowl, making her appear ferocious yet beautiful, Ellie opened her dark lips, her voice coming out as clear and dark as rumbling thunder.

'After nearly eighteen years of being hidden away behind the palace walls, and under the cover of a pretence, I have come to address the world and my people with the hope of fostering a strong and honest relationship moving forward.'

Lottie felt the world crumbling again, the little ledge she'd found for herself falling away beneath her feet. Binah grabbed her hand and squeezed.

'The reasons for our decision to keep my identity hidden were complicated, but we believed this was the best choice in allowing me both the most preparatory upbringing and the chance to learn and grow until I was ready to take responsibility.'

Another hand grabbed Lottie, and Anastacia's pulse thumped against her skin, and Saskia put a hand on her shoulder, steadying her – all of them waiting for the inevitable impact, refusing to let it knock her down. They would not let her fall.

Together they looked up at their friend: a storm and a princess trapped in the tower.

On screen Ellie's lips twitched, her nose crinkling, and Lottie saw that she was afraid – and all Lottie wanted to do was save her. Ellie looked over the crowd once more, taking a deep breath before she spoke the words that would change everything.

'I am the real princess of Maradova.'

Author's Note

From the very start the Rosewood series was designed to be a magical escape from the real world, a fairy-tale place where strange and wonderful things seem just out of reach and good always triumphs over evil. This is what I wanted to share with my readers, a story where the horrors of our world are put away, where anyone, no matter who they are or how they love, can feel safe.

When designing the series, my publisher found me an artist, Qing Han, a young woman with a sharp sense of humour and impossibly positive attitude, whose incredible detailed work had inspired millions of people from every corner of the globe. She weaved her unfortunate and unfair medical circumstances into inspiring messages of hope through her art, some of which consisted of young women painting stars into the air or crying galaxies, which is exactly what she did. She took hold of her situation and painted magic into our world. What Qing provided for the Rosewood series is immeasurable and it would not be what it is without her. She gave the books that feel of escape and wonder the moment you touched a copy, and with the cover art she provided for the series she brought it to life and made it real.

I cannot thank her enough for what she did for my books, and I know she, more than anyone, would take what we all feel about her passing and turn it into something beautiful. Rosewood will not be the same without her, but I hope we can all strive in her name to bring a little magic into the world.

❧ About the Author ❧

Connie Glynn has always loved writing and wrote her first story when she was six, with her mum at a typewriter acting as her scribe. She had a love for performing stories from a young age and attended Guildhall drama classes as a teenager. This passion for stories has never left her, and Connie recently finished a degree in film theory.

It was at university that Connie started her hugely successful YouTube channel *Noodlerella* (named after her favourite food and favourite Disney princess). After five years of publicly documenting her life and hobbies to an audience of 900,000 subscribers on YouTube, Connie closed the book on the Noodlerella project in a bid for more privacy and to pursue her original passions in the performing arts. Connie now writes music and fiction full-time.

Follow Connie on YouTube, Twitter, Instagram and Tumblr
@ConnieGlynn
#RosewoodChronicles

The ROSEWOOD HOUSES

Righteous, resolute, resourceful

There are three Rosewood houses:
IVY, CONCH and STRATUS.
Which one do you belong to?
Read the house descriptions and pick
the one that suits you most.

House Colour: Purple

Ivy is home to the **righteous**.
Named after Florence Ivy, famed
humanitarian and first woman to attend
Rosewood Hall, it is the house of
pioneers, poets and philanthropists.
An Ivy student is not afraid to stand out
or stand up for what they believe in.

House Colour: Red

Conch is the home of the **resolute**.
Fierce and forthright, a Conch student's
greatest strength is their strength of will.
Named in honour of Balthazar Conch
who fought off a wolf to save a
fellow student, Conch is considered
the loyalist house.

House Colour: Yellow

Stratus is home to the **resourceful**,
the creatives, the puzzle-solvers. Founded by
twin artists Shray and Sana Stratus, who said:
'Our heads might seem as though they
are in the clouds but that is only because
we are observing everything.'